MW01491547

# The Path of Progress

a 509 Crime Story

by Colin Conway

The Path of Progress



Cover Design by Rob Williams

ISBN: 978-1-961030-14-5

Original Ink Press, an imprint of High Speed Creative, LLC
1521 N. Argonne Road, #C-205
Spokane Valley, WA 99212



Visit the author's website at colinconway.com

# What is the 509?

Separated by the Cascade Range, Washington State is divided into two distinctly different climates and cultures.

The western side of the Cascades is home to Seattle, its 34 inches of annual rainfall, and the incredibly weird and smelly Gum Wall. Most of the state's wealth and political power are concentrated in and around this enormous city. The residents of this area know the prosperity that has come from being the home of Microsoft, Amazon, Boeing, and Starbucks.

To the east of the Cascade Mountains lies nearly two-thirds of the entire state, a lot of which is used for agriculture. Washington State leads the nation in producing apples, it is the second-largest potato grower, and it's the fourth for providing wheat.

This eastern part of the state can enjoy more than 170 days of sunshine each year, which is important when there are more than 200 lakes nearby. However, the beautiful summers are offset by harsh winters, with average snowfall reaching 47 inches and the average high hovering around 37°.

While five telephone area codes provide service to the westside, only 509 covers everything east of the Cascades, a staggering twenty-one counties.

Of these, Spokane County is the largest with an estimated population of 506,000.

Psalms 41:1

*Blessed is he that considereth the poor:*
*the Lord will deliver him in time of trouble.*

# The Path of Progress

# PART I

## Chapter 1

"They entered through a rear window?" Spokane Police Detective Leya Navarro asked.

Evan Barkuloo nodded. "That's right." He angrily slapped his filthy hands together, then pointed at the case file she held. "Them animals ripped off the sheet metal that covered it and everything."

A couple of teeth were missing from the front left side of Barkuloo's mouth. Leya tried not to stare at the gaping hole while the man spoke, but Barkuloo pulled his lips back and he furiously clicked his front teeth together before speaking. He resembled an excited gopher in a Pixar movie. "They made a real mess of it," he said. "Here. Lemme show you."

The owner of East Sprague Small Engine Repair limped off and waved for her to follow. His arms swung wide with each step. Leya had additional questions, but they could wait. Even though the case file she carried already contained photos of the burglars' entry point, she wanted to see the physical damage for herself.

Barkuloo led her around the sales counter and into a dingy shop that smelled of old oil and unwashed men.

Various grungy lawn mowers and snowblowers sat clustered together. Two halogen lights bent at severe angles to illuminate a disassembled engine that lay upon a soiled workbench. A box of gleaming wrenches lay open next to several shiny screwdrivers.

Leya carefully avoided the dirty surfaces. It had been six months since she left patrol. Back then, she rarely worried about what happened to her dark blue uniform. Stains and smudges were barely noticeable on it. That didn't hold true with the slacks and sports coats she now wore. She never dressed as nicely as Major Crimes detectives but walking around with a blot of oil on her shirt all day would still look unprofessional.

"It's not like I'm a bank or nothing," Barkuloo said. "They might've gotten eighty bucks out of the till if they were lucky. Everybody and their credit cards, you know?"

He was a balding white man in his mid-seventies who stood about Leya's height. Barkuloo was likely taller in his youth, but a severe stoop brought him down several inches. Grease and other filth covered the apron he wore over his plaid shirt and brown slacks.

At the rear of the building, Barkuloo yanked a bolt to the side, twisted a knob, and shoved a door open. Sunlight flooded the shop. He patted a piece of plywood that measured roughly two feet by four feet on the nearby wall.

"This is it," he said.

"The window is behind that?"

"It ain't a window no more." He stepped into the alley. "Another piece is out here."

Leya stepped over an oil stain and joined him.

Barkuloo continued. "I had to replace the sheet metal because of them animals. Look."

She followed his gesture. A second strip of plywood

hung on the outside of the building.

"Twenty screws," Barkuloo said as he knocked on the rectangular piece of wood. "Both sides." He clacked his front teeth together and once again drew Leya's attention to the hole in his mouth. "That's where I made my mistake—believing those rotten animals wouldn't be interested in what little I had."

The alley smelled of cat urine and rotting garbage, but it didn't seem to bother Barkuloo. He tapped on the plywood again and leaned forward to study one of the screws.

Tumbleweeds accumulated along the back fence line. Behind the engine repair shop was a cluster of small industrial buildings with residential homes scattered in. The sun was almost at its zenith and the temperature was in the low sixties. It was an unseasonably warm November day—too nice to linger in the alley's stink. The week's remaining forecast was warm—a pleasant break from the cold and rain they'd experienced the previous month.

Leya glanced left and right. About a block to the west, two men were headed in her direction. She could suffer the alley's stench a couple of minutes longer.

She consulted her file. "The break-in occurred two nights ago."

Barkuloo smacked his hands together again. "Sons o' bitches took all my tools. Can you believe it? Hobbled my business in one fell swoop."

"Did you notice anyone suspicious hanging around before that night?"

He laughed without mirth. "It's East Sprague, darling. This whole place is nothing but suspicious." Barkuloo ruefully shook his head. "Years ago, this part of town might have been a little rough, but you could run a business without looking over your shoulder every other minute. It changed with Ronnie Raygun. Businesses moved out, junkies and whores moved in. Trickle-down economics, my ass."

Barkuloo pointed west. "Then the power company came in with that monstrosity of theirs, waving promises of community revitalization, like they were the second coming of Expo or something."

He was talking about the Catalyst Building, a five-story structure that was self-sustaining, since it wouldn't use any fossil fuels and could produce its own green energy. The structure was hard to miss as it stood out like a sore thumb in the East Sprague Corridor. It led to a wave of recent revitalization in the once economically depressed area.

Barkuloo continued. "All that high-minded bullshit brought was developers who think they can clean up this area." His eyes narrowed. "You know what revitalization really does?"

Leya shook her head. She didn't care about Barkuloo's rant. She was waiting for the two men walking toward them to get closer.

"It squeezes the little guy out," Barkuloo said. "First, we get pinched by the criminals. Then the wealthy put their greedy hands in our pockets." His face reddened. "Because of them, we can't afford our property taxes no more. You think them animals are going to steal from the new properties? Not a chance. Those greedy bastards got better security. They got the fancy cameras that work in the clouds." His hand wafted into the air as he made a sound like a plane taking off. "Besides, the cops watch out for the rich because they're the only ones who can afford to donate to the policeman's ball." Barkuloo's expression softened. "No offense."

Leya lifted a conciliatory hand. "We don't have a ball."

“Gala, then. Either way, I’m frustrated.” Barkuloo’s lips vibrated as he blew air through them. “I’ve been fixing engines almost fifty years, but I’ve had about enough. The world has gotten to where I just don’t understand it anymore.” He noticed the approaching men and put his hands on his hips. “Case in point.”

The two men appeared to be in their late thirties. They had the gaunt and haunted look of those who lived on the streets for too long. Their clothes, while different styles, were covered in the same grime.

“Morning,” Leya said.

The two refused to make eye contact with either her or Evan Barkuloo.

She pulled her sport coat to the side to reveal her badge and gun. “Can I ask you guys a couple questions?”

Their gazes dropped to her waist, but they didn’t stop walking. They didn’t increase their pace either. They simply walked by wordlessly. Dust kicked up in the alley from their shuffling feet.

“You two live around here?” Leya asked.

“Arrogant sons o’ bitches.” Barkuloo banged his front teeth together as he watched the men leave the alley at the end of the block. “They probably live over in that lousy camp.”

She eyed him. “Camp Faith?”

“As far as I’m concerned, the city is responsible for that whole damn mess.”

Barkuloo stepped back into his shop and Leya followed him.

“The city council is nothing but a bunch of bleeding-heart liberals now. They let those animals get away with murder just because they’re homeless.”

He pulled the door shut and slammed the bolt back into place.

“Homeless, my ass. We should call them bums, like

we did when I was a kid. Let's give them a good dose of humiliation instead of coddling them with so many damned handouts and excusing their behavior with sissified words like *displaced.*"

Leya wanted to point out the inconsistencies in his argument. One moment, he spoke against Ronald Reagan and economic revitalization, and the next, he railed against the liberals and the homeless population. Perhaps he was just a cantankerous old man, and nothing would make him happy. She pulled a business card from her coat pocket and handed it to him. "Thank you for your time, Mr. Barkuloo."

He took the card, frowning. "You prolly think I'm a crotchety old bastard—"

She politely smiled.

"But let me tell you something." He flicked the card with his middle finger. "The businesses in this area are suffering from these break-ins, and our customers don't want to come down here because of them bums. Who do you think benefits from that?"

Leya moved toward the door. "I'll let you know if I find anything out."

"Think about what I said, Detective." Barkuloo pointed the business card at her. "Who benefits from what's going on down here?"

***

Leya knocked on the frame of the opened office door.

Sergeant Ryan Yager sat behind his desk but did not look up at the noise. He was hunched over some paperwork with a red felt-tip pen clutched in his right hand. The sergeant didn't correct reports patrol officers submitted since another supervisor had already approved them, so it was likely a report from someone on his team.

Yager leaned in further, as if desperately trying to comprehend whatever he was reading. He grunted something affirmative as the pen hovered over the paper.

"You wanted to see me?" she asked.

Sergeant Yager led the Property Crimes unit. He was one of the department's younger sergeants, just over thirty years old. He was a handsome man—tall and slender with impeccable hair. His dark locks appeared to have been cut by a stylist and not a barber. On the days when his hair looked messy, the disarray appeared purposeful. Many of the women in the department wondered if Ryan Yager led a double life as a model. Once, over dinner with her friends, Leya suggested he might be a struggling actor who picked up roles in local films. That led her unmarried friends down a path of wicked notions, including that he'd been in pornography movies. So far, none of the rumors had panned out to be true, but that didn't stop his name from coming up whenever she and her friends got together for drinks.

Yager circled a word, perhaps a bunch of them, then hastily scrawled a note. He shook his head as he looked up. "How hard is spell check?"

Leya gritted her teeth. Was he reviewing her latest report? "Not hard, sir."

He capped the pen and tossed it onto the desk. "Do you think the others ever use it?"

Maybe this wasn't about her. "Of course. I'm sure."

Yager lifted a sheet of paper to reveal a series of red circles. "Then explain how someone can contact a witless about a stolen vacuum cleaver."

Leya pulled slightly back. The sergeant commenting about another officer's failings surprised her. She didn't know him well enough for that kind of familiarity. Had they been friends while they worked patrol, then she would understand, but they had not been. She carefully asked, “Witless?”

Yager’s face pinched. “As in stupid. That’s right.”

“Vacuum cleaver?”

“Also right.” The sergeant flipped the report back to his desk.

“If they correctly spelled the words, then the checker wouldn’t—”

“A grammar checker, then.” He snatched the paper and studied it once more.

Leya grew uncomfortable and let her gaze drift around Yager’s small office. The desk and two visitor chairs almost filled its entirety. A three-drawer metal cabinet sat behind the sergeant. There didn’t seem to be enough room to open it while he remained seated in his swivel chair. Department awards and certificates were carefully spaced about the walls. The only personal item Yager kept in the open was a photograph of him and a dark-haired woman at some campsite. Their arms were entwined, and they peered dreamily into each other’s eyes.

“You proofread your reports?” the sergeant asked.

Her attention returned to him. “Sir?”

“I don’t catch those types of mistakes on yours.”

“I hope not.” She smiled. “Is this why you wanted to see me?”

Yager furrowed his brow. “Unfortunately, no.” He placed the paper in his outbox. His desk was now clean. “You did some follow-up this morning?”

“On that burglary from a couple nights ago.”

The sergeant closed his eyes and rubbed a knuckle into the left socket. It reminded Leya of the way her girls did it when they were babies. “The East Sprague break-ins are at epidemic levels.”

He wasn’t telling her anything she didn’t know, but she said, “Yes, sir,” anyway.

Yager opened his eyes and blinked several times. “Ease up on the ‘sir’ business. It was nice when you first joined the unit, especially with the lack of respect I get from the others.” He grabbed the marked-up report and shook it. “But the dew is off the lily, as they say.”

She nodded. “Got it.”

“I’m assigning Truscott to help you.”

Leya straightened, and her face immediately warmed. “That’s not necessary.”

“It’s a done deal.”

“I can handle the caseload.”

The paper slid from his fingers back into the outbox. “You do great work, Navarro. No one questions that, least of all me. But you need a second pair of hands on this.”

Her face soured. “Truscott, though?”

“Whatever you’ve heard,” Yager said, “disregard it. The guy’s an experienced Property Crimes investigator.”

What the sergeant didn’t say was Damien Truscott rolled back into the unit a few days ago after failing to make it in the Special Victims Unit—a team dedicated to investigating sex crimes. Leya had never worked with the man before, not even while on patrol, but a cop’s reputation preceded them.

She didn’t know the real reason for Truscott’s getting bounced out of SVU, but rumors abounded. Botched cases, romantic advances toward victims, and a nervous breakdown were some reasons bandied about. The truth lay in there somewhere. Right now, though, no one wanted to work with Truscott because he was tainted goods.

“Besides,” Yager continued, “this doubling up isn’t just because of your caseload, it’s to cover my ass.”

Leya raised her eyebrows at the admission. The sergeant had never been this candid with her before. Had something changed? Is that why he shared the corrections on another officer's report? Had she crossed some invisible threshold and earned the sergeant's trust?

"The pressure on the WSDOT camp is unbelievable." Yager pronounced it Waz-dot like every other administrator. The media and most line level cops called it Camp Faith. He leaned back in his chair and his expression pickled. "Everyone has an ax to grind—the mayor, the media, the business community." He ticked them off on his fingers as he listed them. "Who else? The state and county, too. I'm waiting for the feds to find a reason to jump into this quagmire."

Leya knew all this. She read the local papers and watched the news. She wondered why it mattered so much now. The problem had been growing since last December, almost a year ago.

The sergeant snatched up his felt-tip pen. "Ackerman stopped me in the hall this morning for an update on the burglaries."

"I'm working them as fast as I can," Leya said.

"I know you are." Yager forced a smile. "And that's exactly what I told him. I said all reports along the corridor were still funneled to you, and you had your arms around it."

"And?"

"He stared at me like I failed to deliver a punchline."

Her lips tightened, and she refrained from speaking.

"Relax, Navarro," the sergeant said. "It's not like that." He tossed the pen onto the desk. "The captain appreciates you." He glanced out his office window. "If anyone on this team has his respect, it's you. You earned a lot of juice for what you did with that knockout ring while you were on patrol."

"Then what's the problem?"

"It's me."

Another admission, Leya thought. She softened her expression. "I don't understand."

The sergeant absently waved his hand. "The brass is tied in knots over the burglaries and how it ties into the camp. The game is political hot potato, and the music is winding down."

She nodded. "We're going to get stuck with the potato is what you're saying."

"There was never any doubt." He inhaled deeply. "We're at the bottom of the hill. Everything rolls down until it lands on our heads and by our, I mean, the police department's." Yager chuckled. "I probably need to stick with a single metaphor, huh?"

Leya pointed in the camp's direction. "Those people are trespassing on state land. It's a crime."

That had been the police department's official response. The chief had uttered it many times to the press in the past year. Leya felt confident parroting it.

Yager blew out a stream of air before calmly asking, "And what should we do about it?"

"Kick them off."

"They're trespassing on Department of Transportation land because they have nowhere else to go."

For the third time since she walked into the office, Sergeant Yager surprised her. Leya struggled with her feelings about compassion for the homeless. Her church provided outreach services to that community, but she refused to donate time or money to support the cause. What she saw while working the street didn't jibe with the stories the volunteers told.

Leya said, "The city just leased that warehouse for a homeless shelter. They can go there."

Yager shrugged. "It's more complicated than that."

Maybe it was the sergeant's admission of trouble with the department's leadership, but Leya felt emboldened now. “Did you see how much the city is paying each month for that?”

“It’s expensive,” Yager admitted.

Evan Barkuloo’s final admonition came back to Leya. “Someone is getting rich off the homeless situation.”

“Someone always gets rich off another’s misery.” Sergeant Yager paused as he considered his next words. “The bigger problem is, can we hold folks responsible for trespassing on state land when the overarching issue is a housing crisis?”

She started to speak, but he held his hand higher to interrupt her.

“That’s the sound bite the support agencies will use as a cudgel against us, Navarro. Listen, there are over a half a million homeless in the U.S. The last point-in-time count for Spokane County said there were over seventeen hundred living here. Citizens are frustrated with the problem and the politicians are using it as a bandwagon issue. If we do anything against the political headwinds, the community will judge us as making the situation worse.”

Leya flexed her jaw. “What about the spike in crime?”

“What about it?”

“It correlates directly with the establishment of that camp.” She pointed toward the East Sprague Corridor.

“And?”

Leya’s face warmed, and she wanted to yell. She wanted to shake her fist and ask Yager how he could be so calm.

“Why are you so upset?” he asked.

She swallowed and looked away. She knew exactly why she was agitated.

Leya had worked so long on this problem by herself and now Yager felt the need to assign another detective—a man—to work it with her. To make matters worse, the guy couldn't hack it in the Special Victims Unit and was forced to rotate back to Property Crimes.

She couldn't say that out loud. Instead, she said, "Those businesses are suffering. We need to do something about it."

"What do you want to do about it?" Yager asked. "Not everyone inside that camp is responsible for the uptick in crime."

"How do we know?"

"There are reportedly six hundred people living there. We can't legally or ethically say everyone inside is responsible." He cocked his head. "Can we?"

Her ears felt on fire.

"That's the problem," Yager said. "There is a narrative directed against that camp. The mayor, WSDOT, and the sheriff stoke the issue by claiming the police department is inept in hopes of firing up the citizenry."

The statement infuriated Leya. "The mayor told us to keep our hands off the camp."

Yager patted the air. "Easy, Navarro. This is just you and me here."

She looked down at her shoes. "Yeah."

"No one remembers what the mayor said. Or maybe they do, and they don't give a rat's ass. That's the beauty of politics. They expect her to lie. As for us, we're left with the mess she made with her campaign promises."

"It's wrong."

"Of course it is." Yager tapped on his desk. "The chief serves at the pleasure of the mayor. Therefore, he's her scapegoat. If the mayor can't find an equitable resolution to that camp, all the blame lands on our heads for not breaking it down when it immediately happened."

Leya realized his argument was about the camp itself, not about the burglary epidemic. The tightness in her shoulders relaxed. "What if we discover someone living at the camp is truly responsible for the burglaries?"

"Arrest them," Yager said flatly. "We've dealt with political fall-out before." He spread his hands wide. "But this is why Ackerman thought it was no longer a one-man job."

She smirked. *I knew it.*

"A one-person job," the sergeant immediately corrected. "Nevertheless, it's hard for me to assign the—" Yager looked toward the ceiling. "Person power?" His gaze returned to her. "Personnel. It's hard for me to assign the correct amount of personnel this situation really needs because of our staffing shortage. I'd love to throw all my detectives at the issue, but I can't. So, for now, it's getting two."

"Me and Truscott." She didn't bother to hide her disappointment. "I can't get out of it?"

"You can go back to patrol."

Leya sucked her lips into her mouth to avoid saying something that would get her in trouble. Right now, Sergeant Yager wasn't as handsome as she had previously thought. His liberal beliefs about the homeless camp, combined with the open support of Damien Truscott, confused her. She had considered him to be a good leader, but right now, she only wanted to go back to her desk.

"Ignore the rumor mill," the sergeant said. "Truscott is a talented investigator. He got things done when he was previously in this unit."

She didn't know how Yager could say that since he didn't lead the team back then.

"All right," she said finally, "but just one thing."

"Fire away."

Leya motioned toward his outbox. "Tell me that wasn't one of Truscott's reports."

# Chapter 2

Detective Damien Truscott peeked around the edge of the cubicle. "You busy?"

Leya lifted her hands from the keyboard and leaned back in her chair. She had been updating the Evan Barkuloo file. "What's up?"

Truscott stepped fully into view and casually leaned a shoulder against the cubicle's edge. He was an athletic man with broad shoulders and a trim waist. The sleeves of his shirt were rolled up to his forearms and his blue jeans had been pressed so many times a permanent white crease had developed. His boots and large belt buckle gave him more of a Wyoming deputy look rather than a city detective.

He said, "Yager wants us to team-up on your burglary problem."

*Your burglary problem*. "That's what he said."

"You okay with that?"

Truscott should have been able to read that she wasn't. From what she knew of the man, he had plenty of experience as an investigator. He had started in Property Crimes, worked on the Domestic Violence team for a brief stint before his elevation to the Special Victims Unit.

Leya had met Truscott earlier in her career while he was a DV detective. He had an affable demeanor then, and she believed he was well-liked in the department. After his transfer to SVU, the rumors started about his attitude changing. He lasted less than two years in the unit.

She shrugged in response to his question of teaming up. "Why wouldn't I be okay with it?"

“This is your case,” Truscott said. “I wouldn’t like someone else getting into my mess kit.”

Her brow furrowed.

“It’s what soldiers eat their meals with. At least, they used to.”

“Ah.” She’d forgotten he’d been in the military prior to joining the department. The graying hair at his temples should have reminded her that he had a life before law enforcement. “What you’re saying is you don’t share well with others.” It sounded cattier than she intended.

He smiled, and the edges of his eyes crinkled. “I prefer to ask for help rather than it being thrust upon me.” He waggled his hand. “But it seems neither of us has that luxury in this circumstance.”

Leya didn’t want his help or anyone else’s. Property Crimes detectives didn’t team up like those in Major Crimes—the cases weren’t of the same magnitude. She had hoped the string of burglary cases would highlight her tenacity or her creativity at problem solving. However, that wasn’t going to happen now. The political ramifications deemed she play nice with others.

“I could…” she said carefully, “use the help.”

“How many burglaries have you got?”

She consulted her notepad. “Over the past three months, there have been twelve break-ins along Sprague.”

Truscott pursed his lips. “That’s significant, but not horrible.”

Leya nodded. “Broaden that to a corridor three-blocks wide, from downtown to Freya Street—”

“What’s that? Forty blocks long?”

“Forty-two. And that number jumps to thirty-three burglaries.”

Truscott gnawed on his lower lip as he thought. “Three months is twelve weeks. Thirty-three burglaries works out to about three a week. Doesn't sound like an epidemic to me."

Leya's eyes narrowed. "Might feel like it to those businesses."

"You're probably right about that," he conceded.

She consulted her notes once more. "Broaden that corridor to six-blocks wide and include residential burglaries—" Leya tapped her finger on her notepad. "And the number jumps to fifty-two."

Truscott whistled. "And they've funneled all those cases to you?"

She turned her palms upward. "What can I say?"

"You should have asked for help sooner."

Leya shook her head. "I've got it handled."

"There's no shame in asking for someone to pitch in."

"I'm doing fine." Her words sounded sharp.

Truscott lifted his hands in mock surrender. "I believe you."

"Contrary to popular opinion, I haven't been working this alone." She turned to her computer and clicked the mouse. "Crime Analysis is in my corner."

A heat map popped up on her screen. The area along the East Sprague Corridor was dark red. As it moved out from there, the color lightened to orange and eventually yellow. Various points were plotted to correspond with the break-ins.

Truscott crossed his arms. His movement caught the illumination from the overhead light, and the inlaid jewels on his belt buckle sparkled. There was some script in the middle Leya couldn't discern, but she didn't try too hard. She didn't want to lean in and give him the wrong idea. It was too easy to give anyone in the department a mistaken impression.

"Who put the map together?" Truscott asked.

"Uh." She switched back to her email program. "Hold

on."

"You don't have a relationship with someone in CA?"

She glared at him. "A relationship?"

"A working friendship."

"I know what I'm doing."

"It's just that—"

Leya's lips pinched. "This isn't my first day."

Truscott took a deep breath and held out his hand. "Hi, I'm Damien Truscott. I've been assigned to work with you."

"What're you doing?"

"Starting over."

Leya shook her head. Maybe she had been a little harsh. "Whatever."

Truscott motioned toward the computer. "I read the Hot Sheet every morning, so it's not like I don't know what's going on out there, but damn if this whole problem doesn't sound worse than the numbers show."

"No kidding."

"The brass is just making a stink about it now?"

"That's not my worry."

"It should be."

She cast a sideways glance at him. "What's that supposed to mean?"

"We're not in Kansas anymore, Toto."

Leya frowned. She understood the reference since she'd recently watched *The Wizard of Oz* with her girls, but she didn't understand how it fit into her situation.

Truscott must have sensed her confusion. "Detectives can't hide among the mass of patrol. We're another level closer to the bosses. They know our names. They know our work. Screw up now and they'll come for you."

She wondered if he was speaking from experience. Is that what happened to him in SVU?

Truscott's gaze lowered as he seemed lost in thought.

When his attention returned to her, he said, "This is about the budget."

"Excuse me?"

"The reason they haven't jumped on this sooner." He glanced around the Property Crimes office. "The budget. There's no authorized overtime. No additional manpower."

Leya grimaced at the "manpower," yet Truscott was right. Sergeant Yager had said only a few minutes ago he would throw his entire team at the problem if he didn't have to worry about the staffing shortage.

"You're on an island the brass created," Truscott said.

"And you're supposed to rescue me?"

Truscott spread his arms wide. "Detective Lifeboat, at your service."

"I feel better already."

He covered his heart. "Ouch."

"Sorry."

"I get it. Like I said, I'd rather ask for help than have it thrust upon me."

She crossed her arms. "I guess I'm still getting used to the idea."

Truscott motioned toward her computer monitor. "Have you identified any trends?"

"Besides the affected area and time of break-ins?" She shook her head. "The entry points change each time. So do the methods of access. They have kicked in doors. Broken windows. The one I was on this morning—they pried off a metal covering so they could access a window."

"They're persistent little buggers," Truscott said. "Have you checked the pawnshops?"

She raised an eyebrow.

He again lifted his hands in mock surrender. "It's not your first day."

"I didn't find anything." Leya's head bounced from side to side. "But it's probably a good time to visit them again."

He dipped his chin. "I'm happy to help if you don't mind me tagging along. It's been a while since I've made the rounds."

Leya shrugged a single shoulder.

Truscott snapped his fingers as if he thought about something. "Craigslist and eBay—have you checked them?"

"I have but got nothing."

"Facebook Marketplace?"

Leya hadn't thought to check there. "Would they be so shameless?"

"Look who we're talking about. Besides, how hard is it to create a fake profile?"

"Right," she muttered.

Truscott hooked his thumbs behind his belt buckle. "The gist of this story is you've got no hot leads."

"I wish."

"Why don't we go for a ride and walk through some pawnshops? Let's see if we can scare up some momentum."

Leya eyed her computer. Getting back in the field sounded better than sitting at her desk for another hour. Especially if others would see her working with Truscott.

She stood. "Are you driving?"

He shook his head. "This is your case. You should have the wheel."

***

"Again?" Hugh McBride asked from behind the service counter. "You were just here, like two weeks ago."

McBride frowned and folded his arms over his ample belly. He resembled a fat, hairless cat. His soft, greasy skin bulged in all the wrong places. Even his lips seemed over inflated. His bald head glistened under the store lights and his eyes seemed about to pop out without the anchor of eyebrows. He wore a blue zippered hoodie and brown slacks.

Next to him, a flat screen security monitor flicked to a new image. It appeared to be the back of the building. A car drove down the alley.

"We can come here daily if we want," Leya said. "It's the law."

"But that's harassment." McBride mashed his plump lips together and shifted his gaze to Truscott, who perused a rack of DVDs on the far wall. "Who is that? I know him."

They were at Avenue Pawn, a run-down operation at the corner of Sprague and Cook. The neon sign attached to the front of the building hadn't worked in years, or it never seemed to brighten once darkness fell. Navarro hadn't once seen it illuminated in all the years she worked graveyard.

The store's wooden floors were marred, and grayish carpet peeked out from underneath shelving and counters. It appeared as if someone had simply cut away as much of the old covering as possible while moving none of the heavy furniture.

Power tools and small kitchen appliances lined dusty shelves alongside vintage video game systems and stereo components. Guitars and brass instruments hung from the walls. Bicycles stood side by side in the far corner.

The store smelled musty, and there was a dampness in the air that felt wrong for this time of year. Overhead, a poppy rock song played.

Leya shifted her stance. "What's it going to be?"

"This is some cockamamie bullshit," McBride muttered. He reached underneath the security monitor, which now showed an image of the front of the store. A buzzer sounded at the far end of the counter. It continued to hum until Leya walked over and pulled the security gate open.

"You're a prince," she said.

"You won't find nothing. My paperwork is always in order."

Truscott stepped over to Leya and reached behind her to hold the gate. He motioned for her to enter. "After you," he said.

She followed McBride into the storeroom. Fluorescent lights provided a dingy, yellow glow to the small warehouse.

Large shelving units lined the exterior walls. The only area they didn't cover was where the two doors stood—one back into the lobby and the other into the alley. Items of all varieties lined the shelves, much the same way they did out front. The only difference was each item had a tag attached to it and a sheet of paper tucked underneath it. Larger items like lawn mowers, bicycles, and a dirt bike were clustered together.

A metal desk with a new computer sat in the middle of the room. Paperwork was strewn about its top. McBride pulled the chair back and tapped the keyboard. The monitor brightened. "Let's get this over with."

State law mandated pawnbrokers record every transaction they made. This information was to be shown to a law enforcement officer upon request. Pawnbrokers could be required by a local police department to submit reports for all transactions conducted the preceding day.

The Spokane Police Department administered a tracking program for some time, but it fizzled out because of budgetary constraints. Now, it was up to Property

Crimes detectives to monitor the efficacy of the law. Ethical pawnbrokers knew not to take in stolen property while those who skirted the law were savvy enough not to list hot goods on their records.

Truscott approached a shelving unit and slipped a piece of paper from underneath a video game unit. He perused the document, then examined the bottom of the black box.

Leya turned to the shop owner. "How often do you turn away someone you think has stolen property?"

McBride looked over his shoulder. "People know I don't deal in hot stuff."

"How do they know that?"

"My reputation."

She folded her arms. "I've never heard of that reputation."

McBride spun in his chair so he could face her. She wished he would have stayed in the other direction. He sat with his legs spread wide. His pants tightened around his groin and the legs pulled up to reveal pale, flaking skin around his ankles. "I run a legitimate business, Officer."

Leya frowned. He knew she was a detective. She'd corrected him twice on previous contacts. Either he was forgetful, or he was purposefully messing with her.

McBride motioned toward Truscott. "Why is he here? Who is he?"

"It's me, Hugh," Truscott said.

The pawnbroker leaned forward in his chair and squinted. "Officer Truscott? You're back?"

"Your serial numbers don't match."

McBride furrowed his brow. "That's a bunch of nonsense."

Truscott carefully set down the video game box and shook the piece of paper. "Your numbers—they don't match."

"The hell you say." The pawnbroker sprang from his chair. It was an agile move for someone of his size and age. He stalked over to Truscott and snatched the paper from his hand. McBride squinted at the document before tugging a set of cheap reading glasses from his sweatshirt pocket. He slipped them on and reconsidered the paper. Then he consulted the bottom of the video game box. "One digit off," he muttered. He slammed the box back into place. "Harmless error."

"It's still wrong," Truscott said.

"A three instead of an eight." McBride plucked the glasses from his face and pointed them at Truscott. "You always did this."

"Found your mistakes?"

McBride's face reddened. "Hardly worth the trouble."

"It's still trouble."

The shop owner anxiously waved his hand about the warehouse. "You won't find another error like that in all the store."

"You sure?"

McBride slapped his chest with the hand holding the paper. "I'd bet anything."

Truscott chuckled. "I wouldn't do that. That's the first one I checked. The odds are in my favor."

"Name the wager." McBride frantically waggled the paper. "It won't happen twice."

Truscott pulled a sheet of paper from underneath a stereo component. Leya did not know what it did, but the black box looked fancy and expensive. Truscott consulted the paper, then the serial number underneath the unit. "This one is correct."

"See?" McBride's eyes narrowed and his lips pursed together. "I told you."

"But you're only at fifty-fifty, Hugh. That's a terrible

record."

McBride looked to Leya. "I play by the rules, Officer. You know this. I play fair. Why are you harassing me?"

"Me?"

"Him!"

Truscott smiled innocently. "You're the one with faulty paperwork."

The pawnbroker used both hands to snap the paper several times. "Harmless error, like I said."

"Let me ask you this," Leya said. "Have you ever been broken into?"

The pawnbroker seemed momentarily confused by the question. He poked his tongue out to lick his lower lip. "No," he said. "Never once."

"Aren't you worried?"

"Why would I be?"

Leya thumbed over her shoulder. "Someone is burglarizing the businesses along the corridor."

"It's that camp," McBride said. "They're responsible for it. Not me, not my business, not my customers."

"But you're not worried. Why not?"

"I got my reputation for being smart and being careful." McBride returned to the desk and dropped into his chair. He clicked the mouse and the monitor filled with multiple camera feeds. For as outdated as Hugh McBride and his store felt, his security system seemed quite modern.

"I got cameras all around the building." He waved his hand in a circular motion. "And it's automatically saved to the cloud. If anyone comes in here, they can't delete anything from this computer. That can only be done from my home or my phone." McBride tapped his head. "I'm not as old as you think I am. No one is going to rob me and get away with it."

Leya eyed Truscott. "Anything else?"

"You and I never finished our bet, Hugh."

She widened her eyes and mouthed, "What are you doing?"

Truscott ignored her silent question and continued to study the pawnbroker.

McBride spun away from the computer and grabbed the log sheet for the video game unit. "It was a simple mistake—that's all, but I'll bet whatever you want. Name it."

"If I come back in here and find another one—"

"You won't." The pawnbroker snapped the paper with both hands.

"You close for a week."

McBride's expression flattened. "You can't do that."

Truscott shrugged. "So, you're admitting there are more mistakes with your paperwork?"

The pawnbroker's upper lip quivered. "I never said that."

"You're certainly acting like it."

McBride lifted a single finger. "One day—if you find a mistake. I'll shut down for one day. That's more than fair."

"Make it three," Truscott said. He held up as many fingers.

"Two."

Truscott seemed to consider the offer for a moment. "All right, two days."

"And if you find nothing?" McBride asked. "There needs to be something in this bet for me."

Leya shook her head. She didn't like what she was witnessing.

"What do you want?" Truscott asked.

"You leave me alone," McBride said. He flicked the paper with the back of his hand. "You stop all of this harassment and never come back."

"We can't do that." Truscott's eyes drifted toward the ceiling. "But how about we stay away for a month?"

Leya couldn't believe what she was hearing. They were investigating a crime spree involving stolen goods which might someday end up in a pawnshop—maybe even McBride's. They needed the right to search any and every operation. Her new partner—the one thrust upon her less than an hour ago—was gambling it away in a blatant show of testosterone. She balled her fists and looked away.

"A year," Hugh McBride said.

Truscott scoffed. "Twelve months? You gotta be kidding." He held up a couple of fingers. "Two months, at the most. Take it or leave it."

Leya put her hands on her hips and flexed her jaw. She ground her teeth as she bit back her desire to call her new partner an idiot.

"Fine," McBride said with a satisfied nod. "Two months, but it's a gentleman's agreement." His eyes darted around the shop. "If you find something, I close for two days, but you don't report it since that's more punishment than I would likely face. My record stays clean."

Truscott stepped forward. "Like you said, Hugh, a gentleman's agreement. Between you and me. No one else." He stuck out his hand.

The pawnbroker stood and shook it. He quickly eyed Leya. "You witnessed this." He happily pumped Truscott's hand. "We have an unbreakable deal."

Leya turned and left the store.

***

Leya opened her car door, but paused before getting in. "You can't do that," she said.

Truscott had lowered himself into his seat, but he stood again and looked at her over the roof of the Chevy Impala. They had parked the car curbside along Sprague, just down the block from Avenue Pawn. "What can't I do?"

She jerked her head toward the pawnshop. She fought to control the fury in her voice. "Make a deal like that."

"Why not?"

"What if we never find something? Then we can't go back in there for two months. In case you forgot, we're investigating a string of burglaries."

"I know that."

Leya rested her arms along the Impala's roof. "Then why would you do that?"

His face relaxed as a smile formed. "Honestly? I forgot how much fun Property Crimes was. Relax. My agreement isn't enforceable."

"Whether it's enforceable is not the question. It's not professional. We work with these business owners."

Mischief sparkled in Truscott's eyes. "Not professional? Look at you. How long have you been a detective? Six months? And you're telling me how to do the job?"

Leya wanted to bring up his recent demotion, but she held her tongue. She looked away so as not to say something she would regret.

Truscott waved at the pawnshop. "Did it seem like Hugh enjoyed our haggling?"

She pursed her lips, but still refused to look at him.

"Well?"

"What's that got to do with anything?"

"It's called community relations."

Leya looked at him now. "You can't negotiate away our ability to search his records." She repeatedly pointed at the pawnshop for emphasis. "Maybe he's going through his paperwork right now to make sure everything is perfect just so he can win that bet."

Truscott's expression flattened. "And why exactly is that bad?"

"Because—" Leya's brow furrowed. "If we don't find anything, we can't go back in there for two months."

He barked a single laugh. "We?"

"That's right."

"It's nice of you to include yourself in my deal, Detective Navarro, but if you paid attention, we clarified the deal was between him and me."

Her lip curled. "I noticed how you slathered on that gentleman's agreement crap."

"If you insist I keep my word in the interest of professionalism, then I'm the only one who can't go into the store. Hugh gets his win, we ensure his records are clean, and you still get to inspect his operation. How did the citizens of Spokane lose anything?"

Leya reluctantly shook her head.

"Well?"

"You're lucky it worked out that way."

"I've done this job for a few years longer than you." Truscott dropped from sight.

She lowered herself into the driver's seat and closed her door. Leya put her hands on the steering wheel and took a deep breath. "I apologize for misreading the situation."

"It's all right." Truscott pulled the seatbelt around his body. "You've probably heard the rumors I'm a fuck-up."

Leya eyed him but remained silent.

"Don't worry about it." He tapped the inside of the door with his knuckles. "I'll try not to prove it's true. Where to next?"

# Chapter 3

"I gotta hand it to this place," Truscott said. "They do it right." He inhaled deeply. "I forgot how it always smelled so clean."

Leya couldn't argue with that assessment. Right now, an aroma of cinnamon floated through the store. As far as hock shops went, Lucky's Pawn was on the opposite end of the spectrum from Hugh McBride's operation.

The interior walls were two-tone—an Irish green made up the lower portion while a bright gray band ran the upper length. On the east and west walls—the longest—autographed concert memorabilia hung between the likes of guitars and brass instruments.

Commercial-grade carpet covered the floor. There were no wear patterns or stains. Glass cases were interspersed about the store and contained the likes of video game systems, cell phones, computer tablets, and jewelry.

Handguns were kept in a glass booth that acted as the customer service counter. A rack of long guns hung on the back wall.

Overhead, Taylor Swift's latest hit played. Leya had streamed it several times over the past weekend. It was angsty with over-the-top imagery, but Leya loved it. She sang it to herself and bobbed her head in time with Taylor's words.

Leya and Truscott waited behind a line of four customers—each held something to purchase. Five others shopped inside Lucky's Pawn. Everyone seemed to enjoy the store's musical choice, since most bobbed their heads along with the song, too.

Truscott ran a finger along a shelf of nearby DVDs.

"Lucky's always had the best selection." Racks of DVDs were placed near the checkout line. Truscott continued to search the titles as the line moved forward. His finger tapped a title. "This is a good one," he muttered. "Haven't seen it in years."

She didn't bother looking at him.

Two men in green bowling shirts stood behind the counter. The younger looked to be in his late twenties, with shoulder-length brown hair and a five o'clock shadow. The other was Grady "Lucky" Fitzgerald, the owner of the business. Leya had met him twice before.

"I come in peace," Truscott said to her. He lowered his voice when he added, "And you go in pieces."

Leya rolled her eyes.

Fitzgerald was in his late-forties and looked like an aging fullback. He had a thick neck and chest, but his stomach bulged as if he drank too much beer without the counterbalance of an exercise program. Fitzgerald's mane of wavy, dark hair framed a round, pleasant face. He looked up, made eye contact with Leya, and smiled.

She tapped Truscott on the arm. "Give it a rest, Fandango. We're up."

Fitzgerald waved them forward as he moved to the far end of the counter.

A large cardboard advertisement for Security Solutions of Spokane guarded the entry gate. The ad featured a muscled man with his hands on his hips and heavy iron chains crisscrossing his bare torso. The tag line read *Protect What's Yours!* A phone number with a 509 area code was underneath with the ominous warning *Call before it's too late!* It was tacky at best, Navarro thought, and schlocky at worst.

Affixed to the upper left corner of the cardboard cutout was an orange star made from construction paper. A handwritten message inside the star read, *Get the Lucky discount!*

Fitzgerald opened the security gate. "You never have to wait, Detectives."

"We didn't want to interrupt your business," Leya said.

He dismissed their intrusion with a wave of his hand. "You have a job to do. I totally understand."

Most of the customers watched their interaction. It didn't seem that any of them appreciated the detectives' interruption. The guy behind the cash register cast a furtive glance in their direction.

Fitzgerald lifted his chin in Truscott's direction. "Detective Truscott, been some time. Good to see you again. Still a movie buff?"

Truscott looked back into the store. "Business is hopping."

The pawnbroker shrugged. "Could be better."

Leya said, "There've been more burglaries along the corridor."

"All business, all the time." Fitzgerald looked to Truscott but gestured toward Leya. "Never any chitter-chatter with this one. Takes all the fun out of it."

Truscott pointed at the cardboard advertisement. "What's with that?"

"I got a deal on a new security system." Fitzgerald shrugged. "My old one took a dump, and I couldn't be without one. Not in my business." He hugged the cardboard caricature. "These guys cut me a break if I allowed them to put an advertisement inside my business. I figured, what the hell? A deal's a deal. They'll cut an extra ten percent off for anyone who says they heard about them through my store. You need a home security system?"

Truscott shook his head. "I'm good."

Fitzgerald patted his hip. "I'd imagine you guys carry

your security systems with you."

Both detectives stared at him.

Grady smiled. "So, what can I do for you?"

Truscott glanced at Leya before asking, "Mind if we look at your storeroom?"

"Not at all." Fitzgerald motioned for them to pass through the security gate. "Whatever you need, help yourself." He turned to the clerk at the register. "Trevor, I'm going back with the detectives."

The clerk acknowledged Fitzgerald with a lift of his hand but kept his focus on his customer.

Racks of pawned items lined the warehouse. Two computers sat side-by-side on a waist-high table. Leya and Truscott spent a few minutes perusing the various items and their associated tickets. It didn't take long to surmise everything seemed in order.

Leya wouldn't have expected anything different from this pawnshop. The two times she'd visited, she found nothing out of order. She asked, "Have you turned anyone away recently that you believed was trying to pawn stolen items?"

Lucky nodded. "Oh, sure."

"What did they look like?"

He shrugged. "Meth addicts, I guess."

She suspected he would have described them as being homeless. Or at least pointed her toward Camp Faith. Almost everyone did lately. That seemed the scapegoat du jour.

"You know the type," the pawnbroker said. "All twitchy like." His hands jerked and his head dipped. "They got those little marks on their faces. Can't keep eye contact."

"Did you get their info?" Truscott asked. "Maybe a photo from the security cameras?"

Fitzgerald shook his head. "We're too busy for me to

always focus on that. They come in all the time, and we turn them away so we can move to the next customer. Maybe try one of the slower shops for a picture." His smile was playful. "I'm just kidding. I'll try to remember to grab their info and a picture the next time someone like that comes around."

Truscott nodded. "Sure."

"What can I say?" Fitzgerald spread his arms wide. "It's the curse of a prosperous business. Everything happens so fast." He snapped his fingers repeatedly. "Always on the go. It's hard to keep up with the paperwork you guys want."

"The state requires it," Truscott said. "Not us."

Fitzgerald flippantly waved his hand. "You know what I mean. The state, the city. It's all one big government in our minds."

Truscott's eyes narrowed. "You'll get us their info next time?"

"Of course, Detective Truscott." Fitzgerald held his hand over his heart. "And their pictures, too. I promise."

"Well, if you promise." Truscott headed for the warehouse door.

Leya's gaze bounced between Fitzgerald and her exiting partner. "Thank you for your time."

"Did I offend him?"

She didn't bother to answer. Instead, Leya left the warehouse. "Truscott," she called.

He held up a hand as he walked through the lobby. She hurried to catch up.

From behind them, Fitzgerald hollered, "Take care, Detectives."

Outside, Leya trotted up to Truscott and grabbed his arm. "Hey! What's wrong?"

He stopped and studied the outside of the building. "He can see us now."

She eyed the building. Two cameras were visible from where she stood. One above the entry and one near the end of the building that faced into the parking lot. “Yeah, so?”

“That’s why I’m not getting angry,” Truscott said, “but that son of a bitch promised me the same bullshit when I was in the unit the first time.”

Leya turned her back to the store. “He failed to deliver on a promise? So what? He’s a pawnbroker. They’re skeevy.”

“You don’t understand.”

“I understand enough. It was years ago, so why get mad about it now? Besides, Avenue Pawn didn’t have any info for us either.”

He rolled his eyes. “But Hugh McBride said no one tried to sell anything illegal to him for whatever reason.”

“Look at his store.”

Truscott shook his head. “Fitzgerald knows better is my point.”

“I still don’t understand why you’re getting angry.”

“His not getting pictures is lazy, and it pisses me off. The corridor is getting pounded by thieves and he doesn’t care because he’s making money.”

Leya looked at the amount of cars in the parking lot. Another pulled in at that moment. “Probably a lot, too.”

“That’s what I’m saying. Here’s the point—” He gestured toward the building. “If I cut a guy some slack, I want something in return.”

“When did you cut him a break?”

“It doesn’t matter.” Truscott angrily started toward their car but stopped. He turned back toward her. “That guy kept shitty paperwork. Like a bad joke, it was so shitty. If I wanted to, I could have cited him six ways to Sunday. Maybe even put him out of business.”

“Why didn’t you?”

"Because I thought it would be better in the long run to have a guy like him on our side. Someone who appreciated that the department worked with him instead of against him." Truscott kicked a pebble. "That's how stupid I was. Instead of writing him up, I gave him leeway, helped him get his ducks in a row. Maybe no one before cared enough to work with him, but I wanted him to succeed within the system. I didn't want to cite the guy for failing to report. Maybe I should have just hung some paperwork on him and not worried about it."

Truscott walked toward the car and Leya followed. When they got there, he continued his rant.

"I thought he'd be one of the good guys because of the help. That he would remember the department when the chips were down. Instead, he's only worried about himself."

Leya still didn't understand why he was so upset. "So your problem is he's shining you on when he ought to owe you some gratitude?"

"When you put it that way—" Truscott scrunched his nose. "It makes me sound like an asshole."

"Or naïve."

"Great," he said. "Just fucking great." Truscott patted the top of the car as he looked down Sprague Avenue.

"What do you want to do about it?"

He shrugged and slowly turned his attention back to her. "Not much we can do."

Leya thumbed over her shoulder toward the pawnshop. "Let's go in there and check out everything. We'll do it with a fine-tooth comb."

"Nah."

"Why not? Let's give him a good kick in the balls so he'll remember us in the future."

Truscott smirked. "That's how I sound?"

She lifted her eyebrows.

"Oh, this keeps getting better." He once again patted the roof of the car. "Listen. I apologize. I shouldn't get ramped over this. Nobody's hurt. Nobody's been assaulted."

"All better?"

He forced a smile. "My attitude has been adjusted. Thank you. Where to next?"

Leya looked to the south. "Let's swing by the camp and see what's what."

***

"It's like a Mad Max movie," Truscott said.

Leya shifted in the driver's seat. "Is that the one with Charlize Theron? I never saw it."

"Count yourself lucky."

They parked in a vacant lot at Second Avenue and Ray Street. Across the way stood the WSDOT camp. Grungy RVs, rusted pickups, and dented hatchbacks huddled on a double city block. Tents, tarps, and scrap pieces of wood filled in almost every available space of the jerry-built community. The residents deemed it Camp Faith, and it had grown from a lack-of-shelter protest.

Three banners fluttered from a makeshift pole standing in the middle of the camp—an upside-down United States flag, a black Prisoner of War emblem, and a yellow *Don't Tread on Me* streamer.

At the corner, under the intersection's Stop sign, rested a crumbling piece of plywood with a spray-painted plea, *Honk if you love Jesus*. No one had honked since the detectives arrived.

"You remember when this started?" Leya asked.

Truscott grunted. "Seems like forever."

During the coldest snap of the previous December, dozens of homeless men and women had bivouacked on city hall's sidewalk for two weeks. The shoddy encampment of blue tarps and large cardboard boxes was a black eye for the municipality. It could be argued the black eye was well deserved as the mayor and city council were slow to react to the city's homeless problem since neither of them wanted to deal with the steadily increasing population.

Leya gripped the steering wheel and shifted her position. "Who do you blame for this?"

"Plenty of blame to go around."

She eyed Truscott. It was a noncommittal answer. Leya thought about pushing him but decided to leave it alone. Her thoughts returned to the camp's origins.

Initially, no one wanted to enforce an existing anti-camping ordinance and open the city up to massive litigation as the specter of a recent decision by the 9th Circuit Court of Appeals loomed over their heads. That ruling stated cities cannot enforce anti-camping ordinances if there are not enough homeless shelter beds available for its itinerant population.

Eventually, the City of Spokane's attorney found enough footing within the law to issue notices for eviction. The police department was called to clear the sidewalks. The homeless moved to the Second Avenue land owned by the State of Washington's Department of Transportation.

"You remember all the homes that were along here?" Truscott asked. He looked over his shoulder.

Leya nodded. "I had my first DV arrest down along this row."

"Saw my first motorcycle versus tree down here." He thumbed down Second Avenue. "The tree remained for years. It's gone now."

For several years, the Department of Transportation purchased homes in this area—a thirty-block stretch along Interstate 90—so it could eventually connect what was colloquially known as the "North Spokane Freeway" but officially coined the North Spokane Corridor (NSC).

Spokane was Washington State's second largest city but currently had only one freeway—an east-west route that provided ease of traffic to and from Seattle. The NSC was originally conceived in 1970. Residents in the initially proposed right-of-way banded together and blocked the freeway's construction. Spokane gave lip service to the path of progress so long as it wouldn't change the status quo.

Truscott set his hands on the dashboard. "What do you want to bet the freeway never gets built?"

"It'll get built," Leya said.

"They've been trying for decades. As long as the politicians in Seattle control the purse strings, we're screwed."

She wanted to argue with him but this wasn't an issue she'd win.

Seattle, Spokane's wealthier sister to the west, welcomed progress. In those years from 1970, it built freeways, diverted them, and resurfaced when needed. State funds for roadways came and went. It took until 1997 before Spokane's proposed NSC reached a critical point where the state and locals reached an agreement for its construction. The project's expected completion date was set for 2030, almost sixty years after the idea was originally conceived.

Truscott motioned toward the camp. "*Fury Road* was the worst of the bunch."

Leya's lip curled. "What?"

"Mad Max movie."

"There were more?"

He turned to her with a look of dismay. "There were four. How do you not know this?"

She shrugged. “I don’t like fantasy movies.”

“They’re not fantasy.”

“Whatever.”

“They’re post-apocalyptic science fiction.”

Leya eyed Truscott.

He pulled back. “What?”

“Do you go to comic conventions?”

“No.”

“You sound like you do.”

“Because I like movies?” Truscott shook his head. “There’s nothing weird about that.”

“I noticed you checking out the DVDs at the shops.”

“And?”

“People stream movies now.”

“Whatever.” He returned his attention to the camp and muttered, “Fantasy.”

Dozens of people moved about Camp Faith. All appeared dirty and most traveled with a companion. A couple walked along Ray Street and held hands. They dressed like twins—black sweatshirts, desert camouflage pants, and untied combat boots. The only difference was their hair styles—his was short while hers was long and stringy. They appeared headed for a cluster of porta-potties at the end of the block.

“What’s that they’re wearing?” Truscott asked. “Are those ID cards?”

Red lanyards hung around their necks and small white cards dangled from the ends of them.

“Looks like it,” Leya said.

He grunted. “They’re giving entry badges to this pit now?”

“That’s harsh.”

“In the original Mad Max trilogy—”

Leya’s shoulders slumped. “We’re back to this?”

“Mel Gibson played Max—”

She clicked her tongue against the back of her teeth. "I don't like him."

"And he goes up against these bad guys—"

Leya pointed at the camp. "The homeless are bad guys?" She felt like Sergeant Yager by asking that question. She didn't enjoy being put in that position.

He held up a hand. "Let me finish. These bad guys are marauders—"

"Marauders," Leya said under her breath.

"Who roam the wasteland—"

"There's a wasteland?" she asked, not hiding her sarcasm. "This keeps getting better."

"And they've got these vehicles cobbled together by some demonic imagination."

Leya rolled her eyes. "You didn't just say that."

"Say what?"

"Write that down. You should be a poet."

Truscott cast her a sideways glance. "Does your husband appreciate this side of you?"

"I'm actively listening. They taught us that at the academy."

"Uh-huh." Truscott shook his head. "What I'm saying is these marauders attack these makeshift villages and take what they want."

Leya pointed at the camp again. "Are these the villagers?"

"Maybe."

She cocked her head. "This is important because?"

"That's the way this camp looks." He leaned forward again. "I imagine it was like Bartertown before Thunderdome was established."

"None of what you say makes any sense."

"It would if you had seen the movies."

Leya studied him. "Did you hit your head somewhere, and I missed it?"

"No."

"Your point is?"

"There's no way I would want to live in there."

"You had to tell me all that Mad Max stuff to get to that?"

He shrugged. "I thought it was appropriate."

"It wasn't."

"Would you want to live here?"

Her face pinched. "I already said I didn't, but I wouldn't want to be homeless either. Living here is probably better than that."

"I don't know," Truscott said. "If I was homeless, I wouldn't want to be here."

"Don't you think these folks are just trying to get by?"

"You sound like a counselor."

They fell silent for several moments. Leya grew overwhelmed watching the camp. She did not know how anyone could apply the term "faith" to this encampment. The emotions she experienced while observing it were despair and humiliation.

A shabbily dressed woman walked along Ray Street. She dragged a blue recycling bin behind her. Clothes and other items were piled to the top.

"Do you think," Leya asked, "her whole life is inside that can?"

Truscott motioned toward the woman. "I think she stole that bin."

Leya scoffed. "That's what you take from this moment?"

"It's city property."

"Can't you empathize with them at all?" Sitting with Damien Truscott was pushing her to act more like Sergeant Yager. She definitely didn't appreciate the feeling. Her flip-flopping emotions on the homeless issue bothered her.

Truscott fell back in his seat. "Sure I can empathize, but we need to be realistic about what's going on here."

A flatbed truck with chain-link fencing stacked on its back turned onto Ray Street. It pulled to the curb. Two pickups followed the larger vehicle to the side of the roadway. Men hopped out of the various vehicles and moved toward the rear of the flatbed.

"What now?" Truscott asked.

"I heard about this on the news," Leya said. "They're putting a fence around the camp."

Truscott turned to her. "You gotta be kidding."

The men unhooked the tie down straps and tossed them curbside. They yanked the first section of fencing from the flatbed.

Two women in blue security jackets approached the fence workers.

"The camp has security, too?" Truscott asked.

Leya nodded. "They're volunteers."

Truscott's expression darkened. "This is ridiculous. We're coddling them."

"The city is penning them in like livestock. That's hardly coddling."

"Look at it this way," Truscott said. He twisted in his seat to face her. "These people are trespassing on state property. The city feeds them and protects them." He pointed down the street toward the porta-potties. "We're even providing them shitters."

"Volunteers feed them," Leya corrected, "not the city." She glanced down the road. "A porta-potty is for sanitary reasons and basic human dignity. Wouldn't you want that? The city isn't protecting them with the fencing. They're trying to reduce crime in the area. You should appreciate that. I know I do."

Truscott's face pinched as a group of Camp Faith residents gathered to watch the erection of the fence. All wore red lanyards with white ID cards. Leya expected Truscott to say something awful about them, but he refrained.

To her surprise, she had enjoyed some of the time with Truscott this afternoon, yet the change in his demeanor while sitting across from the camp was troubling. He had a definite dislike for the homeless. As far as she was concerned, that was all right if he could compartmentalize it. Cops didn't have to like the citizens they swore to protect; they only had to do their jobs.

Until this afternoon, she probably thought she was more in line with his thinking than with Sergeant Yager's. However, being around someone like Damien Truscott showed her where her humanity really lay. She might need to reconsider volunteering at the church.

Truscott checked his watch. "Let's call it a day. We can get back to this tomorrow."

She nodded and started the engine.

They drove back to the department without another word.

***

"How was work?" Leya asked.

They were on the back patio, standing next to the barbecue. The girls—Rose and Violet—chased each other through the yard. Their playful screams excited Benny, a Jack Russell terrier, who barked as part of the frivolity.

The evening sun hung low on the horizon. The summer months were gone, but the couple still tried to do as much outside as they could. Ernie held a long, silver spatula in one hand and a bottle of Tecate in the other. He wore a zippered sweatshirt and a pair of Gonzaga basketball shorts. His feet were bare. The outfit was in sharp contrast to the suits he wore at work.

"We're looking to purchase a new bus fleet," Ernie said.

He flipped a burger, and the fire sizzled as grease dripped below. His gaze stayed on the grill as he moved to the next burger. On the platform next to the barbecue sat a paper plate with multiple slices of cheddar cheese.

Ernie continued. "So there's a lot of infighting between the bean counters and the operations folks. Why should we buy this brand over that brand? Why should we buy this year instead of next? Wah wah wah." He lifted his beer and took a healthy swig. "It's the same old story—I can lead them to water, but I can't make them pull their heads out of their butts."

Ernie was the Chief Planning and Development Officer for the Spokane Transit Authority. He'd risen to the position through the years and was good at it. That didn't mean he loved his work. Being a member of a public transit authority's executive team wasn't Ernie's dream job, but he did it for their family. Ernie had frequently told Leya he would run a food truck if he could do anything in the world. The idea of selling burgers and sides at sporting events excited him far more than buses.

He loved cooking on the grill. Unfortunately, their menu was often simpler fare—like the burgers tonight—because two little girls fought against more complicated food. Whenever the kids stayed with Leya's parents, Ernie went crazy with meal preparation. He'd rather cook something imaginative on the grill than go out to dinner.

Plates and silverware were already on the table inside the house. A platter filled with traditional burger fixings sat in the middle—lettuce, tomatoes, and pickles. Every weekday, Ernie picked up the girls from daycare after he left work, then immediately prepped dinner.

Music played from a wireless speaker attached to the house. Ernie was streaming something nice, something she'd never heard before. He was good at finding new artists. It had a '70s disco vibe but sounded fresh.

Ernie grunted. "I don't want to talk about my stuff anymore, and you probably don't want to hear about it."

"I'm happy to listen."

He dismissively waved the spatula.

"Whatever happens," she said, "you'll figure it out."

"Tell me about your day." He pushed one burger into a better position over the fire. "Your stories are always better."

"Not anymore."

He chuckled. "Whatever. They're still more interesting than buses."

She shrugged. "I'm working on the same problem."

Ernie shot her a sideways glance. "The break-ins along Sprague? Any movement?"

"None."

"You'll figure it out," he said, parroting her words from a moment ago.

She smiled, then sipped her beer. After she swallowed, she said, "They assigned me a partner."

He faced her now. "Is that normal?"

"In Property Crimes?" She scoffed. "No."

"Why did they do it?"

"Because the burglaries are out of hand, and it's become a political issue."

Ernie absently spun the spatula. "How's that make you feel?"

"Playing doctor now?"

"I always wanna play doctor." He lifted his eyebrows several times. "Show me where it hurts."

The girls screamed playfully as they continued to chase each other through the backyard's shadows. Benny barked and hopped between them.

Leya sipped her beer again. “His name is Damien Truscott.”

“Truscott,” Ernie repeated. “You’ve never mentioned him.”

“First time we’ve worked together. He rotated back to the unit late last week.”

Ernie poked a burger with the spatula. “Where had he been?”

“SVU.”

His brow furrowed. “Sex crimes?”

“You pay attention.”

He absently toasted her with his beer. “From what I’ve been told, paying attention is the best way to score points with a pretty lady.”

She rolled her eyes. “You’re stupid.”

Ernie poked another burger. “Is that normal? Rotating back like that?”

“No. People start in Property Crimes, then they move up and out. No one ever wants to come back.”

“What’s this guy’s story?”

“He’s an asshole.”

Ernie stared at her.

She knew why; she never swore at home. In fact, she rarely swore at all. Sometimes while on the job and occasionally while drinking with her friends. It was her upbringing in the church that governed her tongue. Ernie didn’t swear much either. She liked that about him. They had built a nice, wholesome life in their home. It was radically different from the lives she witnessed while at work.

Leya shrugged. “Maybe he’s not that way all the time, but Truscott sure came off as such today.”

“What set him off?”

“The homeless.”

Ernie frowned. "Seems a strange thing to get upset by."

"Then there are the rumors."

"Is he running around on his wife or something?"

She shook her head. "It's got to do with why he came back to Property Crimes. I'd already heard some of them." She waggled her beer. "Like the one about him liking it too much."

Ernie's nose scrunched. "Ew."

"Tell me about it. There's this other rumor where he got into it with a victim about false reporting."

"What do you believe?"

"I don't know. He probably hated it for all I know."

Ernie closed the lid on the grill. "What are you going to do about it?"

"What can I do? I'm going to work with the guy. According to Yager, he's a decent investigator. I guess I'll find out."

Ernie nodded several times, then looked over his shoulder. "Girls! Let's go! Dinner!"

A collective moan came from the backyard.

"Do we have to?" Violet hollered.

"Yeah," Rose said, "do we have to?"

Even Benny barked his displeasure at the interruption of their game.

Leya toasted her husband with her beer. "It's nice when they appreciate your hard work."

# Chapter 4

Leya sipped her cup of coffee as the email program opened. She leaned in as new messages flooded the inbox. "Crud."

Most of them were nonsense. The city was notorious for creating digital garbage. Human Resources was the biggest offender. Their newsletter this morning was titled—*5 Ways to Improve Your Metal Health.* Someone had misspelled mental. Leya deleted the email without opening it, deciding fewer messages from HR would be number one on her list.

The police department ran a close second for clogging her inbox. The chaplain sent an email titled *Staying Spiritually Safe in Moments of Strife.* Leya wondered if the new chaplain purposefully wrote in an alliterative manner, or if it had just worked out that way. Regardless, she deleted that email, too. Leya and Ernie attended church every Sunday—she didn't need a police chaplain's input on her salvation.

She deleted emails from administrators about updating personnel files, staff changes, and policy reminders. The same babble seemed to dribble out routinely over a ninety-day rotation. It only took a couple of minutes, but Leya was ready to face the reports assigned to her. Usually, these trickled in through the day, but right now three new reports sat waiting for her.

How long had Sergeant Yager been in the office this morning? She arrived a few minutes before eight and immediately fired up her computer. Yager assigned her two burglaries and a Field Interview as her responsibility. The department's reporting software generated automatic emails after the sergeant assigned reports.

Leya double-clicked the first email, which was simply labeled Burglary with an accompanying East Riverside address. It opened and revealed Damien Truscott was copied on it. She clicked the link inside and was taken to the department's report writing program. She quickly scanned the report. Someone had gained access to a vacant house by breaking a window. A contractor was renovating the property and had wisely secured his tools every night in his truck. No materials were stolen. The reporting officer noted the illegal entry and interviewed the business owner. Since nothing was stolen, there wasn't much Leya could do with it. She printed the report and added it to her case file.

She opened the second email, which was also labeled *Burglary*, but this one had an address on South Altamont. Once again, Truscott was included on the assignment. The victim business seemed to be a car lot. The rear door had been kicked in, but nothing of value was taken. An alarm alerted a security company and likely scared away the intruders. Beyond the broken door, there was nothing of evidentiary value. She printed this report, although it was unlikely she could do much with it.

Even though two burglaries had occurred in the Sprague Corridor, there were likely more that had not been reported. That was the problem with this type of crime. Sometimes citizens did not immediately realize they had been victimized. This could occur because entry happened at a point that wasn't often checked—a basement window, an unconnected garage—or the citizen simply failed to lock their doors and windows.

Then there were those citizens who distrusted the police because of previous contacts, or they simply had a belief that crime reporting never resulted in successful resolutions. Whatever it was, those citizens simply moved on with their lives as silent victims of burglary.

There were some national reports that suggested up to sixty percent of property crimes went unreported each year. Leya found that hard to believe but begrudgingly accepted it.

The final report sent to her that morning was a Field Interview. An FI was a brief document officers completed after contacting individuals that didn't result in arrest. Its intent was purely one of criminal intelligence. A simple Field Interview helped to catch a serial killer over twenty years ago. That story was drummed into cadets during every academy since to relay the importance of completing those documents.

Leya read that morning's FI. According to Officer Josh Hernandez, he contacted Clifford Upchurch at 03:13 a.m. while the man lurked in an alleyway behind Ironsides, a bar in the East Sprague Corridor. Upchurch carried a plastic bag filled with various items of clothing. He stated he lived at Camp Faith but couldn't return since he missed curfew.

When Hernandez asked about the rash of burglaries, Upchurch reportedly said, "I seen them. They're pretending to be us, but they ain't us." The officer pressed the man for further details, but all Upchurch would do was continue to deny he was lurking. Hernandez cut off the contact because of an Officer in Distress call in the county.

Leya printed the report. After collecting it, she went to Damien Truscott's cubicle. His feet were up on his desk, and he was reading a document.

She waved the paper she held. "Did you see the Field Interview that came in?"

Truscott turned the paper he was reading. "Checking it out now."

"What do you think?"

"'They ain't us.'" Truscott wriggled his fingers.

"Kinda sounds like *The X-Files*. What do you think, Scully?"

Leya cocked her head.

"You're Scully." He pointed to himself. "I'm Mulder."

She rolled her eyes. "Let's go find this guy."

He dropped his feet to the ground.

"Before we go—" She motioned in the general direction of Camp Faith. "If you're going to have a problem with them, I can handle it on my own."

Truscott tossed the paper he held to his desk. "I'm okay."

"But your attitude yesterday—"

"Was out of line." He held up an apologetic hand. "I have a lot going on in my life at the moment."

Leya tried to appear confused by what he was talking about, but she was sure she failed miserably. He had to be talking about SVU.

"None of it concerns you, though. All I'm saying is life gets messy sometimes, and it throws us off whack. Understand?"

She shrugged. "Sure."

"Anyway, I'm sorry. I shouldn't have acted that way. Do I support that camp? Not a chance, but I didn't need to act like my father on Thanksgiving, either."

Leya smiled. "No, you didn't."

***

Chain link fencing now surrounded the entire block. Black fabric was attached to each panel and stopped anyone from peering inside. Camp Faith no longer resembled a ramshackle city, it looked like a cheap prison. Two guards in blue security shirts patrolling the perimeter didn't lessen that image.

Leya and Truscott left her car along Ralph Street and

approached the access gate.

A heavy-set woman stood next to a portable wooden podium. She wore a bright blue security shirt and faded black jeans that seemed uncomfortably tight. She piled most of her dark hair high, but several stray wisps fell in front of her forehead. An ID badge hung from a red lanyard around her neck. Her eyes narrowed when the detectives approached.

"Morning," Leya said.

The guard smirked. "That it is."

The access gate stood open, and camp residents occasionally moved by it. Nearby conversations could be heard, but those involved couldn't be seen because of the black fabric on the fencing.

Traffic zoomed along Second Avenue. A car honked its horn and several folks yelled, "Amen" from inside the camp.

Leya pulled her sport coat to the side and revealed her badge and gun. "Detective Navarro. This is Detective Truscott."

The guard's gaze shifted between the two.

"And you are?" Leya asked.

"I don't have to give my name."

Truscott leaned in and read the badge that dangled from the lanyard. "Caprice Ozbat."

The guard slapped a hand over her ID card and her face pinched. "You can't do that."

Leya said, "We're here to talk with Clifford Upchurch."

Ozbat scowled. "We don't reveal who our residents are, especially to the cops."

"Why's that?"

"Because," Ozbat said as her head bobbled with righteous indignation, "the sheriff is openly hostile to what's going on here—"

“Illegal camping?” Truscott asked.

“That!” Ozbat’s eyes widened. “That’s my point. Right there. You cops are all the same.”

Leya lifted a hand. “We aren’t here to cause trouble.”

“Yes, you are.” Ozbat tapped the portable podium with a finger. “You totally are. The sheriff flew his helicopters over the camp last night and used his spotlights. I bet you cops were part of that, too. Your type hasn’t done one good thing for these people.”

“These people,” Truscott said, “sounds sort of racist.”

She inhaled sharply. “It’s not!”

“You’re right. I misspoke. It’s classist.”

Leya glared at Truscott, but he wasn’t paying attention to her.

“How dare you?” Ozbat said. She angrily pointed into the camp. “These people—”

“There you go again,” Truscott interrupted. “Don’t you hear the classist overtones?”

Ozbat’s face reddened. “They just want to be left alone.”

“We understand,” Truscott said. “That’s what every criminal wants.”

The guard inhaled sharply. “They are not criminals.”

“They’re trespassing,” Truscott said. “That’s a crime.”

“These people—” Ozbat flinched. “They’re doing their best to get by.”

Truscott nodded. “On land that doesn’t belong to them.”

“We’re getting off track,” Leya said with barely contained frustration. She faced Ozbat. “We need to find Clifford Upchurch.”

The woman glared at Truscott. “*He* is not welcome here.”

Truscott turned his palms upward. “Why is that?”

“Because you called them criminals.”

"You mean I judged them unfairly?"

"That's right." She nodded emphatically.

"Sort of like how you judged us?"

Ozbat barred her teeth. "I never."

"'You cops are all the same.' That's what you said."

The guard's lip curled. "That's true."

"So was my statement—trespassing is criminal behavior."

Leya caught Truscott's eye.

"What?" he asked.

Her eyes widened.

"Fine." He walked toward her car.

Ozbat turned to Leya. "He's an asshole."

"He's also right."

The guard's jaw flexed.

"Send Upchurch out or we'll be back with additional officers to walk through the camp. You won't like what happens after that."

Ozbat's lip curled. "You need a warrant to come inside."

"No, we don't."

"We have the right to be here." The guard pointed at the ground. "WSDOT gave us permission."

Leya's eyes narrowed. "You know that's not true."

"Maybe not direct permission but they haven't kicked us off. What's that say to you?"

"Force me to get a warrant and I will." Leya motioned toward the camp. "Do us both a favor and send Upchurch out."

Leya headed toward the car.

***

The two of them sat on the hood of the Chevy Impala.

"I wish I smoked," Truscott said.

Leya scoffed. “That’s stupid.”

He waved flippantly. “In the movies, this is when the hero lights up and says something important, maybe even poignant.”

“You’re the hero in this movie?”

Truscott looked sideways at her. “Everyone is the hero in their own story. I think mine would be a redemptive character study and yours would be—” He paused and faked smoking a cigarette. “You got me. What’s your story?”

“A working married woman with two kids.”

“That’s not a story. It’s a sentence.”

She frowned. “I don’t consider it a sentence.”

He puffed his cheeks. “A sentence fragment. Don’t be so touchy.”

“I don’t want you dogging on my marriage.”

“I wouldn’t do that.” Truscott inhaled on his imaginary cigarette. “I like being married.”

Her eyes flicked to his left hand. He didn’t wear a ring. Not that it meant anything. Plenty of cops didn’t wear the wedding band. “Kids?” she asked.

“Two boys. You?”

“Two girls.”

“Look at that,” Truscott said. “Common ground.”

The patrolling guards had returned to the gate. They huddled with Caprice Ozbat and cast furtive glances toward the detectives.

Leya shook her head. “That guard was right, you know?”

“When?”

“When she called you an asshole.”

Truscott frowned. “I must have missed that.”

“Why did you argue with her?”

He shrugged. “Because I’m tired of being called the bad guy.”

"You personally, or cops in general?"

"Us in general." He inhaled once more on his pretend cigarette, then mimed angrily throwing it away. "There are hundreds of people living in there, flaunting how they're breaking the law, and all these agencies rally around them. When did society become so weak we can't do what's right?"

Leya cocked her head. "I thought we were past this."

"Past what?"

"You hating the homeless."

He pshawed. "This isn't about the homeless. I don't hate them. I hate that we don't call things for what they are." Truscott slid off the hood. "Trespassing is a crime, but we ignored it until the problem festered into something nasty. Now we don't know how to deal with it except by throwing money and platitudes at it."

Leya wasn't sure what to make of Damien Truscott.

He pointed toward the gate. "I think our boy just stepped out."

A dirty white male with shaky head movements stood with Caprice Ozbat. They both looked toward the detectives. After a moment, the man shuffled in their direction. He walked slowly, as if taking great care with each step. His head bounced in a slow, gentle rhythm. He wore a soiled Army jacket, gray sweatpants, and filthy running shoes. One of the shoes was untied and the frayed strings whipped about as he trundled forward.

Leya hopped off the car. "You ever wonder how these folks end up this way?"

Truscott grunted. "Not really."

The man stopped in front of them and crossed his arms. "Uh," he said softly, "I hear you might be looking for me."

"Clifford Upchurch?" Leya asked.

"Cliff."

His head stopped moving long enough for him to nod twice, but then it returned to its mellow, wandering path. His eyes never seemed to focus on either detective. The rest of his body didn't jerk or spasm, though. Leya doubted his condition was drug related. Rather, she assumed it was a physical or mental impairment.

She pointed to herself. "I'm Detective Navarro. This is Detective Truscott."

Truscott studied Upchurch the way a doctor observes a patient.

Leya continued. "You talked with an officer a couple of nights ago. Do you remember that?"

Upchurch's face pinched. "He said I was lurking."

Leya shook her head. "You're not in trouble."

"That cop made it sound like I was. Lurking sounds bad. It's not nice to say about a person."

"I understand," Leya said.

"I know what it means."

"You're not in trouble with us, Cliff."

He looked over his shoulder. The three guards remained near the camp's entrance and watched the detectives with intense scrutiny. When Upchurch turned back, he cleared his throat. "They said I don't have to talk with you."

Truscott glared at the security guards, which seemed to make them extremely happy.

"No, you don't," Leya said. "This is a voluntary contact." She further softened her expression. "Although, I'm hoping you will speak with us because we need your help."

Upchurch cocked his head, which caused the bobble to go off on a new trajectory. "My help?"

"When you chatted with that officer, you said—" Leya forgot the exact words and pulled her notebook from the pocket of her sport coat. She'd written Upchurch's statement down before leaving the station.

"'I seen them,'" Truscott said. "That's what you said. 'They're pretending to be us, but they ain't us.' Do you remember saying that?"

Leya found the page in her notebook. Truscott's recollection of the Field Interview report was exactly correct.

Upchurch nodded. "That's what I said, yeah."

"What did you see?" Truscott asked.

"Some men wearing these—" He tugged on his Camp Faith ID badge. "But it wasn't these."

"What were they?"

"Make believe."

"You mean fake?" Truscott asked.

Upchurch nodded. "They wouldn't get in here with them." He glanced over his shoulder again. "Those guards could tell they're fake. They're pretty strict about who comes and goes."

Truscott eyed Leya. "We found that out."

"They check our badges every time against the list."

"And you have a curfew?" Truscott asked. "That's why you were out so late that night."

"I didn't make it back in time," Upchurch said, "so I spent all night walking." He shook his head. "But I wasn't lurking. I don't care what that officer said."

Leya leaned closer to Upchurch. "Back to those men you saw—the ones with the fake ID badges. Were they like you?"

"What do you mean?"

She couldn't find a nicer way to say it, so she just said, "Homeless."

Upchurch shrugged. "I never seen them before, but they sort of looked it."

"Could you point them out if you saw them again?"

He shrugged a single shoulder. "Maybe. It was dark,

but I think I got a good enough look at them."

"Where did you see these men?" Leya asked.

Upchurch pointed toward Sprague Avenue. "Behind the pawnshop on Sprague."

"Which one?"

"The big green one."

Truscott cocked his head. "Lucky's?"

"That's the one. Though I never have much luck pawning stuff there because the owner is a jerk. He doesn't like my type."

"What time did you see these guys?" Truscott asked.

Upchurch shrugged. "A little before the officer stopped me."

"He stopped you at one in the morning," Leya said. "So this had to be about midnight?"

"I guess so." Upchurch's head bobbled. "I don't have a watch. I'm not so good with time."

Truscott leaned in. "Did you see the owner of Lucky's with these men? The guy who was a jerk to you?"

Upchurch's face pinched. "No, but the back door was open. Someone was in there. It might have been him. I don't know."

"Could these men have broken into the store?" Truscott asked.

"It didn't look that way. They were just standing there, talking. They weren't taking nothing out."

"Did you see anybody else from the store?" Leya asked.

"Not that I know of, but I'm not in there a lot. Like I said, the owner is a jerk."

"How did you see the badges?" Truscott asked.

"One guy in the back handed them out." Upchurch tugged on his lanyard. "But it wasn't exactly like this."

"You said that." Truscott pointed at the ID hanging from Upchurch's lanyard. "You could see that from where you were?"

"Not at first, but when they walked by where I was at, I saw them."

Leya and Truscott exchanged looks before she asked, "What were you doing in the alley when you saw these men?"

A sheepish smile formed on Upchurch's face. "If I had to put a name to it, I guess you could probably say I was lurking then, but that wasn't what I was doing when that cop found me."

***

Leya and Truscott headed toward the front gate of the camp while Cliff Upchurch walked toward Sprague. "It's better if I'm not seen conspiring with the enemy," he had said before wandering away.

Along Second Avenue a group of protesters assembled. They appeared well-dressed, especially for this neighborhood. Some held colorful placards attached to wooden sticks. Others carried bright banners. The words were too hard to read from this distance, but the message was easy to discern.

"The NIMBY crowd has arrived," Leya said.

Truscott waved a hand. "Can't say as I blame them."

Officers dealt with nuisance complaints daily and most of them had an element of the "not in my backyard" attitude. Noisy neighbors, barking dogs, property line disputes, trashy yards, and junky cars on the street were all part of that NIMBY mix. Most of the complaints were civil, though, and beyond a patrol officer's duty.

It only rose to the level of law enforcement involvement when tempers flared and an assault occurred, or a citizen broke someone else's property, or a neighbor trespassed. But it usually started as a civil issue.

Security guard Caprice Ozbat stood at her portable podium and watched the action along the arterial with open disgust. Her eyes slid to the detectives as they approached. "Something else?"

"A question," Leya asked.

Ozbat's eyes narrowed. "About?"

"Cliff said he saw some men with ID badges that looked like the camp's."

The guard absently covered hers with a hand. "Only residents and volunteers get a pass."

"We understand. How can someone counterfeit one?"

Ozbat moved her hand and looked down at her badge. "I guess it wouldn't be that hard. They're made with a color printer."

Leya leaned in. The pass had the bearer's picture and name. At the top of the badge were the words *Camp Faith*.

"But the pass is just half the equation," Ozbat said.

"Explain it to us."

Ozbat pulled her lanyard taut. "We make sure the pictures match their faces." She lifted a stapled document that appeared severely wrinkled. "Then we check their names against this list. It gets updated every day."

"What's the list?" Leya asked.

A horn honked along Second Avenue

Both Truscott and Ozbat muttered, "Amen."

Leya eyed them.

Truscott shrugged as an embarrassed smile formed on the guard's face. It vanished as cheers erupted from the protesters along Second Avenue.

"Greedy assholes," Ozbat said. "Those people want to do away with what little these folks have."

"The list?" Leya prompted.

Ozbat reluctantly returned her attention to the document she held. "This is who's allowed to be here. It was hard to keep a lid on everyone before the fence. I can't tell you what a difference this has made in just a day."

"Are there rules?" Truscott asked.

"Sure. No drugs. No assaults. No stealing. Basically, they have to follow the Golden Rule."

Leya half-expected Truscott to bring up trespassing, but he asked, "Do they have to sign anything?"

Ozbat shook her head. "It's the honor system."

Truscott lifted an eyebrow.

"Call it something else if you want," the guard said, "but if they break the agreement, they gotta leave. They don't call attorneys to argue for them. They don't ask for arbitration. They pack their shit and go. Even when they screw up, they stand by their word. So, you tell me, whose system is better. Yours or theirs?"

More cars honked now, but neither Truscott nor Ozbat said an affirmation to the Lord.

"Great," the guard said. "Here he comes. Why can't he let these people be?"

A group of roughly thirty protesters marched northbound on Ralph Street. Most of them waved signs above their heads. At the head of the procession, a white male carried a bullhorn and spoke with a female reporter. A cameraman walked backward to film the whole spectacle.

"Who's out front?" Leya asked Ozbat.

"Fred Zimmer. He owns the tire shop over there." The guard motioned across the freeway.

"Him?" Leya said. Zimmer had been on the news almost daily, complaining about Camp Faith and its effects on neighborhood crime. "He's leading protests now?"

"Business must be slow," Ozbat said.

Leya turned to Truscott, then jerked her head toward

their car.

"And have them film us running away?" Truscott shook his head. "No, thanks."

The protesters angrily chanted, "Hell, no! Make them go!" For such a small crowd, it was loud and forceful. The men's faces reddened, and the women in the group seemed almost in hysterics with their shouting. Some shook their fists while others waved their signs.

Leya had seen historical images of frenzied gatherings like this before, but they were usually for things like book burnings or record breakings. It was odd to see people so worked up over homeless people, especially with winter right around the corner.

Fred Zimmer animatedly talked with the reporter, who smiled and nodded in return. When the group reached the camp's entry, Zimmer lifted his bullhorn. "Camp Faith is a beacon of crime."

The crowd shouted back, "Hell, no! Make them go!" Protest signs fluttered high in the air.

Caprice Ozbat rolled her eyes. "Fuck me. Here we go."

"The city provides security and accommodations," Zimmer said into the bullhorn. He pointed like a circus ringmaster at Leya and Truscott.

The cameraman spun around to film them, but both detectives stared impassively back.

"Hell, no! Make them go!"

"To an epidemic plaguing our neighborhood."

"Hell, no! Make them go!"

"When will the governor," Zimmer said, "do something about this blight?"

"Hell, no! Make them go!"

The reporter tapped the cameraman's shoulder, and he turned around to once more film Zimmer.

Ozbat leaned toward the detectives. "See what we deal

with?"

The tire shop owner continued. "It is time we, the residents and business owners of this neighborhood, tell our elected officials this is a bridge too far."

"Hell, no! Make them go!"

"And… cut," the reporter said with a pat on the cameraman's shoulder. She smiled at Zimmer. "Great. Just great. Thanks, Fred." The reporter turned to the detectives. "Hi, I'm Crystal—"

"No comment," Leya said.

Truscott motioned toward Leya. "Ditto."

The reporter frowned. "May I ask what you're doing here?"

"We're leaving." Leya headed toward her car. Truscott walked next to her.

A moment later, a man called, "Officers, please wait."

Fred Zimmer hurried toward them. He grinned as he approached. "I hope I didn't interrupt anything back there."

"We were finished," Leya said.

"Good, good." Zimmer nodded.

He looked back at the group of protesters. Their enthusiasm had waned because of the loss of their leader or the disappearance of the news crew. Zimmer faced them once more. "I own Lug Nutz, the tire shop on Freya."

Leya knew the place. The business had been around for years. Until recently, it seemed as if the business had fallen on hard times. The building's paint job had faded, and someone had tagged it with graffiti. Last year, though, the structure was repainted with a bright red and black scheme. Zimmer replaced the old awning with a new black metal canopy. From the outside, it appeared as if business might have turned for the better.

"This camp has been terrible for business," Zimmer

said. "Customers don't want to come down here. It's never been a great area, but the amount of riffraff running around is at an all-time high. It's like the zombie apocalypse." He smirked as he faced the camp. "Can't you smell that? It's like a cancer in our neighborhood."

"Did you have a question?" Truscott asked.

"I saw you talking to that security guard. Is there something I need to be aware of?"

Truscott and Leya exchanged glances. They simultaneously said, "No."

"I'm not stupid." Zimmer crossed his arms. "You're detectives, which means you're investigating something."

Leya stepped toward her car. "We have to go."

"Tell me," Zimmer said. "We have a right to know. This is our neighborhood. Do you know who I know?"

"Have a nice day," Truscott said.

"What are your names?" He thrust a finger toward the camp. "These people are ruining our lives and the police are doing nothing!"

The two detectives dropped into their seats and closed their car doors.

Zimmer continued to shout and now pointed at them. Several of the protesters hurried in their direction.

Leya started the car and backed away. "That didn't go well," she said as she checked the rearview mirror.

Truscott shook his head. "We're probably going to hear about this."

# Chapter 5

Sergeant Yager poked his head around the edge of the cubicle. "Where's your partner?"

Leya's fingers slid off her keyboard as she leaned back in her chair. "Watching a building."

She had dropped Truscott off at his car when they returned to the station.

Yager checked his watch. "You guys got a lead on something?"

"Feels like it."

The sergeant glanced over his shoulder. "Is it good?"

"Might be nothing."

His attention returned to her. "It's good enough for him to sit off?" Yager stood on his tiptoes and peered over the top of the cubicles.

"Something going on?"

He dropped back to his regular height. "The captain wants to see us."

"For?"

"Why do you think?"

Leya's brow creased. "When?"

"Right now. Let's go."

She grabbed her notepad and stood. The two headed for the hallway.

This wasn't good, she thought. She rarely spoke directly with Captain Gary Ackerman. The man oversaw the Investigations Division, and she mostly had hallway interactions with him—brief nods or clipped greetings such as "Good morning" or "Afternoon."

While on patrol, she had worked closely with two Major Crimes detectives on a rash of unprovoked assaults loosely known as the knockout game. Ackerman was heavily involved in the department's response to that, and she had gotten to know him then. Yager said she earned some juice from that investigation, but Ackerman always seemed reserved around her. Then again, she was willing to bet he seemed reserved around everyone.

Yager stopped outside the captain's office and knocked on the closed door.

A voice came from inside. "Enter."

The sergeant nodded once at Leya before opening the door. He said, "Good morning, sir," and stepped out of the way to allow her to enter first.

Documents and manila folders cluttered Ackerman's desk. His computer was angled slightly so Leya could see *The Spokesman-Review* banner across the monitor. An article about Camp Faith was displayed.

The captain leaned back in his chair, then scratched his cheek near his right eye. His perfectly combed gray hair appeared recently trimmed. His white shirt was crisp, and his tie was tight around his neck. His suit jacket hung on a wall hook.

Leya tried to recall a time when he might have looked disheveled, but she came up dry. Some of her friends had called Ackerman a silver fox, but she couldn't see him that way. He always looked too much like a politician for her liking.

"The chief is going before the mayor this afternoon," Ackerman said. "He wants an update from Investigations on the WSDOT camp. I need to give him something positive."

Yager turned to Leya.

She turned a palm upward. "We haven't made any connections yet between the camp and the burglaries."

"Patrol has made some arrests related to drug possession and assaults in the area. Maybe there's something there you can work with?"

Leya said, "None of the arrestees had stolen property on them."

"We're missing something, Navarro. If PACT was still operational—" The captain didn't finish his thought and, instead, waved it off.

Putting the Patrol Anti-Crime Team on the problem was no longer an option. The PACT was a ten-officer team built to address emerging crime trends and prolific offenders. Hard-charging, Type-A types filled the unit. Out of the gate, the PACT was extremely effective. As the years went by, rumors emerged about the credibility of some officers and their arrests. Almost ten years after its formation, the chief disbanded the team when a U.S. District Court judge noted discrepancies in arrest reports involving an illegal weapons deal. The officers involved on the team were rotated back into patrol.

For a time, Navarro had wanted to join the team, but now she was thankful she missed the opportunity.

A silent pause hung in the room. Leya glanced at Sergeant Yager, who motioned for her to speak. She ventured an opinion she didn't fully believe or hadn't totally thought through. "Maybe we're looking in the wrong spot."

Ackerman's face pinched. "Explain yourself." His expression made her immediately wish she'd kept her mouth closed.

She shifted her feet. "There's a chance the folks behind the break-ins are, you know—"

"Spit it out, Navarro."

"We're thinking they may not be at the camp."

The captain's face relaxed, and he glanced at Yager. The sergeant shrugged. Ackerman's attention returned to Leya. "The WSDOT camp is a crime magnet. We have the statistics to prove it."

She nodded. "Yes, sir."

Leya's jaw flexed, and she immediately regretted diverting the course of this conversation.

Ackerman rested his forearms along the edge of his desk. "Here's the issue, Navarro. None of those people vote. The business owners in the area do. The homeowners, too. Both groups are pissed and letting their representatives know. Wouldn't you be upset if that camp moved into your backyard?"

"Yes, sir."

"You've given me excuses," Ackerman said. "Now, give me something I can give the chief. The mayor is taking a beating from the sheriff and the governor about the crime epidemic. She's laying it all at the chief's feet."

Leya was hesitant to repeat Cliff Upchurch's assertion that others were attempting to pin the burglaries on residents of Camp Faith. At that moment, it still seemed a fantastical allegation, and Upchurch wasn't a rock-solid witness.

Ackerman frowned at her silence. His gaze slid to Sergeant Yager. "You said you were assigning someone to assist with the case?"

He nodded. "Truscott."

The captain grunted.

"He's fine," Yager said. "Truscott will be a big help."

"Maybe you need a different team altogether."

Leya stiffened.

Ackerman must have noticed the motion because he faced her again. "No offense, but maybe it's time for a new set of eyes."

Yager lifted a hand. "I assigned Truscott yesterday. Let's give them time to work this together."

Leya's face warmed, and she imagined her cheeks reddening. She disliked the way Ackerman openly spoke about replacing her. She had put a lot of time and effort into the corridor burglaries. She didn't feel like it was her fault she hadn't located a suspect yet. Leads hadn't broken her way. If she kept working the cases, a break would come soon enough.

Ackerman eyed the sergeant again. "Who else do you have on the team?" he asked. "Maybe someone else can help?"

"We're already strained as it is," Yager said. "Let's give Navarro and Truscott an opportunity to deliver."

Leya balled her fists but remained silent. She didn't dare look at Yager. Instead, she stared straight ahead.

"Maybe," Ackerman said, "I should ask one of the Major Crimes detectives to come over and review the case files. You know, look over your detectives' shoulders in sort of a mentoring way."

Leya couldn't stand it any longer and she blurted her response. "Men are burglarizing businesses while pretending to be Camp Faith residents." Her voice shook with anger.

Sergeant Yager's eyes widened with surprise.

Ackerman cocked his head. "Say that again, but slower this time."

Leya steadied her voice. "A witness saw a group of men wearing fake Camp Faith IDs. These men gathered at the back of a pawnshop."

Ackerman leaned forward. "And?"

"That's all we've got at this time."

The captain fell back into his chair. "Nothing." He looked at the ceiling. "It's worse than nothing. It's misdirection." His gaze returned to Leya. "The guy who told you, who is he? He's probably part of the burglary ring and he told you that story to send you on a wild goose chase."

"I don't think so, sir."

Ackerman grabbed a file. "So basically I've got to tell the chief that my detectives are nowhere." The captain looked at Yager. “I need a solution, and I need it fast. Find one for me or I’ll find it for you. That’s all.”

Yager exited without further word.

Leya hesitated to follow. She wanted to say she wouldn’t have told Ackerman about Cliff Upchurch’s claim until she verified it. Leya knew the allegation wasn’t credible until she had something to back it up. Just believing Upchurch told the truth wasn’t enough. Leya also wanted to apologize for not having something solid for Ackerman to take to the chief. She felt like a failure.

But she didn’t say any of that, though. Instead, she turned to leave.

“Navarro,” Ackerman said, his voice soft and remorseful.

Leya turned, hopeful he might apologize for the brusque end of the meeting.

“Close the door.”

She pulled it shut after her.

***

Leya approached the Chevy Impala. She opened the passenger door and dropped into the seat.

Truscott set a pair of binoculars on the dashboard. “Look who joined the party.”

“How’s it going?”

He scoffed. “You ever watch grass grow?”

Leya leaned forward and looked past Truscott. They were parked on Riverside Avenue, roughly half a block north of Lucky’s Pawn. Their view to the rear of the store was between two structures. The newer industrial building on the left was the headquarters of a roofing company. The dilapidated house on the right appeared vacant.

“It’s only been a couple of hours,” she said.

"That I'll never get back." Truscott reached for the binoculars but stopped short of picking them up. "How much time do we waste on the word of a hobo?"

Leya studied him.

"What?"

"*Hobo?*"

He grabbed the steering wheel with both hands. "It's a perfectly good word."

"It's offensive."

"Says who?"

"The world." She rolled her eyes. "The world says it's offensive."

"No, the world doesn't." Truscott tapped his thumbs on the steering wheel. "What about vagrant? Can I use that?"

"Are you kidding?"

"Two hours is a lot of time to reconsider the words we use for this segment of society. There seem to be so many better ones—like derelict."

"No." She waved her hand like a scolding mother. "Definitely not."

"Beggar?"

"You're sounding like Evan Barkuloo."

"Who's that?"

"The owner of a small engine repair business." She motioned toward Sprague Avenue.

Truscott nodded. "I'd probably like him."

"You probably would. You're roughly the same age."

He cast a sideways glance. "How old is he?"

Leya motioned toward the pawnshop. "Why don't we just go talk with Lucky?"

Truscott reluctantly followed her gaze. "And tell him what? That a bum—"

"No."

"—accused him of working with a group pretending to

be Camp Faith residents?"

"We don't have to tell him that," she said. "Maybe we ask to look at his cameras."

"How do we convince him to let us do that if he actually is involved with something hinky?"

She frowned. "Right."

"Maybe this is a big ball of nothing. Perhaps Upchurch got his details wrong. It's possible."

"And it's entirely possible," Leya said, "Upchurch got his details right and something shady is going on with the pawnshop. Remember, you were the one who was upset with Lucky that he didn't get the information or photographs of folks he suspected of dealing in suspect property."

Truscott absently tapped his thumbs on the steering wheel but remained quiet. His attention was on the rear of the pawnshop.

Leya glanced around the neighborhood. "You know," she said, "one of us should contact the neighboring businesses to see if they might have video footage of the night in question."

"That's a good idea." He made no move to get out of the car.

She sighed and reached for the door handle. "I'll be back."

Truscott sighed. "Relax, Navarro. I contacted everyone when I first arrived. If anyone finds anything, they'll call."

"You couldn't have said that?"

"I could have, sure." He returned to tapping the steering wheel. "But where's the fun in that?"

She leaned back in her seat. There was no reason for them to be sitting there watching the rear of the pawnshop. Although she was in no hurry to return to the station. She had plenty of cases to work, but Chief Dillon was probably debriefing the mayor right now about the burglary situation. When he returned, who knew what hot potato he would bring back? Better to stay gone for a while.

"Let me ask you something," she said.

"*Stakeout*."

"What?"

He glanced at her. "I thought you were going to ask what I was thinking about."

"And you're thinking about being on a stakeout? How original."

"No, I'm thinking about the movie, *Stakeout*."

She stared at him.

"You've never seen it?"

Leya lowered her chin.

"Fantastic film. 1987. Richard Dreyfus. Emilio Estevez. Madeleine Stowe. Directed by Richard Donner. Seriously, it's a classic."

"Never mind."

Maybe she should go back to the office. She reached for the door handle.

"Hold on." Truscott lifted a finger, but his attention swung back to the rear of Lucky's Pawn.

Leya leaned forward and looked past him. She couldn't see anything that might have piqued his interest. "What?" she whispered, as if afraid of spooking whoever Truscott was watching.

"John Badham directed it."

"Whatever." She popped open her door and got out of the car.

"Okay, okay. What is it you want to know?"

Leya settled back into her seat and closed the door. He smiled as he watched her.

"It's actually two things," she said.

Truscott's eyes darkened and his lips pursed. He

turned his attention back to the rear of Lucky's Pawn. "Ask your questions. I'll see if I want to answer."

"Sex crimes—why did you leave?"

"And the other?"

"Why do you hate the homeless?"

He slowly shook his head. "You don't get the meaning of casual banter, do you?"

"I can leave," she said. "I've got paperwork to do." She rested her hand on the door handle. She didn't want to go, but she waited for him to say something.

It was quiet in the car for several moments. Truscott tapped his thumbs on the steering wheel before he looked down the road. "My brother lived on the streets."

Leya's hand slipped from the handle.

"Not here. Los Angeles, Phoenix, Tucson, Albuquerque. So many places I eventually lost track."

"Drugs?"

"Mental issues, too. They were so intertwined that we didn't know where one problem ended and the other started."

"Is that where you're from? California?"

He shook his head. "I'm from here. Grew up in the valley. My brother wanted to be an actor, so he moved to Hollywood."

"That's when he started using?"

Truscott's right hand gripped the steering wheel. He tucked his left hand underneath his leg. "If what he did only affected him, I wouldn't have cared." He paused. "That's not true. I probably would have cared, but I wouldn't have hated him for it. But the hell he put my parents through was unforgivable." He paused as if reflecting on his past, on his brother's past. "My parents provided for him early on during his addiction. They gave him money and food. They let him move in whenever he promised to get clean. Then he would skip out a week or two later and repeat the cycle. Eventually, the writing on the wall was hard to miss. He would never get clean. He didn't want it. My parents had to protect themselves. They had to stop doing for him."

"I'm sorry," Leya said. She would have liked to say more, but now wasn't the time. This wasn't an interview, and she didn't want to interrupt with follow-up questions. Truscott also wasn't a friend. Offering further condolences would sound hollow.

"When my parents stopped sending money," Truscott said, "my brother begged them. When that didn't work, he blamed them for his circumstances. He yelled at them, called them names, threatened to hurt them, threatened to hurt himself. After all that, he called my aunts, my uncles. It was the same story with them all. My brother was an emotional terrorist."

"Did he call you?"

"Until I stopped answering." Truscott lightly banged the bottom of his fist on the steering wheel. "He sent me a letter once—it was eight pages of psychotic scrawl. Where he got the paper and pen, I'll never know. Probably the shelter. He blamed me for every problem he ever had. He said it was too hard to live up to the standard I set as his big brother." The banging on the steering wheel became harder. "It's not like I didn't have my own fuck ups, but I didn't go around blaming others for them."

"Were you two close?"

The banging stopped. "We were twenty months apart in age. We were close until high school. That's probably when our personalities set in. He had his friends, and I had mine. But still, he was my brother, you know?"

She nodded.

"When I left for the Navy, we drifted apart. He moved to Los Angeles with some friends and that's basically the last real contact I had with him. The guy who called after that was a stranger. He became more and more unreal as the years passed."

Leya opened her mouth to speak, but Truscott's cell phone buzzed in the cup holder. He grabbed it and swiped a thumb across the screen.

"Detective Truscott." He eyed Leya. "Uh-huh. Yes." He nodded. "Thank you. Can we swing by now? We're parked in front of your business." He chuckled once. "That's right. Okay, we'll be right in." Truscott ended the call.

Leya lifted an eyebrow. "Good news?"

He motioned toward the dilapidated house. "They found something on their camera feed." He reached for the door handle.

"Hey," she said.

"Yeah?"

Leya softened her expression. "I really am sorry about your brother."

"Don't worry about it." Truscott popped open his door. "He's dead."

# Chapter 6

Leya followed Truscott up the crumbling concrete stairs to the dilapidated house. Its pitched roof needed new shingles and tan paint chipped from the clapboard siding. Curtains were drawn behind the windows and cobwebs formed in their sills.

A car with a rattling muffler and a loud stereo raced down Riverside Avenue. The detectives watched it go by.

"How'd you know somebody was here?" Leya asked.

"I didn't, but I figured I better check to be sure."

Truscott pressed the doorbell. A placard above it read, *Yesterday's Dreams*.

"What's the business do?" Leya asked.

"He didn't say."

The door opened to reveal a heavy white male in a dingy *King of the Hill* T-shirt and khaki shorts. White ankle-high socks were on his feet. "Hey, Detective." He smiled at Truscott, then nodded at Leya. His dark hair was messy and unwashed. It appeared he hadn't shaved in days.

"This is Detective Navarro," Truscott said.

The man extended his hand. His smile seemed unpracticed and embarrassed. "Brian Kuhn."

"Nice to meet you," Leya said.

His palm was clammy, and his grip was weak, but Kuhn didn't seem self-conscious of either. He pulled the door further open and stepped back. "I think I found what you were looking for."

Leya surreptitiously wiped her hand against her pant leg and followed Truscott inside.

The house smelled pungent—a combination of body odor, decaying garbage, and wood rot. Leya nonchalantly lifted her left hand to her face and pinched her nose.

Shelving units filled the front room. Computer peripherals and manuals littered each shelf. Leya couldn't decipher what most of the various pieces did, but a layer of dust covered most of the items. It looked like a technology graveyard.

A large black trash bag huddled in the room's corner. Several Big Gulp cups sat prominently on top, and a moldy burger was stuffed into one of them.

Kuhn closed the door, and the room darkened. The only light in the house came from down the hall. "Sorry," Kuhn said. "The bulb burned out a while back. Follow me." He walked backward and trailed his fingers along the wall. "Watch your step. The carpet is loose in some spots."

He led the detectives down a narrow hallway, past a bathroom, and into a bedroom. The curtains were drawn over the small windows, and only a corner lamp provided illumination. It pointed toward the ceiling.

Leya briefly wondered if Brian Kuhn was a vampire. He certainly smelled like the undead. She had briefly let go of her nose, caught a whiff of the man, and quickly clamped down once more.

A workstation sat along the room's far wall. Three very large monitors clustered together on the desk while a computer tower was on the hardwood floor.

"It's over here." Kuhn looked back and smiled awkwardly at Leya.

She smiled behind the hand holding her nose and did her best to make it look like a natural action. Leya tugged on her nose, wiggling it back and forth, as if it might have an itch.

Kuhn's gaze shifted to Truscott, and his silly grin faded. "Right," he said. He passed through a maze of opened boxes. Several had old film canisters sticking out of them. Another large trash bag sat near the desk. More empty Big Gulp cups spilled out of the opening. The business owner didn't seem bothered by the mess.

Truscott followed him through the cardboard maze and took a position over his left shoulder.

Leya paused long enough to consider the various posters pinned to the wall. They held no thematic thread—*Monty Python's Holy Grail, Sailor Moon*, and *World of WarCraft*. There was one of an older, dark-haired woman in a skimpy blue bikini that barely contained her large breasts. She autographed it *Love Large, Lisa Ann*. The woman was attractive with smoldering eyes. She must have been an actress in some TV series Kuhn watched—probably campy science fiction.

Kuhn dropped into his chair—a high-back swivel affair with speakers near his head—and spun toward the desk. He craned his neck to look at Leya. "Sorry for the mess."

Leya moved forward to stand over Kuhn's right shoulder. Unthinkingly, she released the hold on her nose and caught a hint of the man sitting near her. She couldn't remember the last time she was around someone who smelled so badly. She took a half-step back and shook her head once to expel the odor from her nostrils.

Truscott glanced at her, but she pinched her nose once more and stepped closer to the workstation.

Two monitors showed the same image—an anime drawing of a nude woman holding an overly large fiery sword. The other screen had some video software with a paused image of several men gathered at the back of Lucky's Pawn.

"Oh, geez," Kuhn said with an embarrassed laugh. He clicked the mouse twice and two programs flickered to life. The nude drawings vanished. Kuhn looked over his shoulder at Leya. "My friend drew that."

Leya released her nostrils so her voice wouldn't be affected. "Uh-huh." She quickly pinched them again. She hoped Kuhn hadn't noticed her movements.

His grin widened. "She's from a movie."

Leya nodded.

"Can we get to the video?" Truscott asked.

Kuhn's smile faltered, and he sheepishly turned away. "This is what I found."

The video started and was slightly grainy. That might have to do with the hardware's quality and could have been because of the time of night. The rear of Lucky's was well lit. Unfortunately, the line of sight from Yesterday's Dreams to the pawnshop was not great. The back door to Lucky's was sliced in half by the edge of the screen.

"Why is your camera pointed in that direction?" Truscott asked.

Leya leaned back to study her partner. Why wasn't the other detective affected by Kuhn's stench? Maybe she'd gotten soft in the six months off patrol, but Truscott had been a detective for years. She didn't like the idea he was tougher than she was. She let go of her nose. It took only one inhale to regret that decision. She pinched her nostrils again. Maybe it was a guy trait, and they couldn't smell another man's funk.

"I've got two cameras pointed in opposite directions," Kuhn said. He turned to look at Leya. "The crime around here is crazy."

She lifted her eyebrows. Leya tried to look as natural as she could while squeezing her nose. She crossed her arms and tucked her right hand under her left elbow. She hoped it gave her a contemplative look.

"Has anyone broken into your building?" Truscott asked.

Brian turned to him. "No, but I can't be too careful."

On the monitor, a man stepped out of the back of the pawnshop. All three men wore tattered clothing. The one who had just stepped out from the store handed something to the others.

"What is he handing out?" Truscott asked.

Leya leaned closer. "I can't see." Her voice squeaked because of the pinched nose.

Kuhn looked over his shoulder at her.

She straightened but didn't release her nose.

On the screen, the three men now slipped something around their necks.

Truscott and Leya said, "Lanyards," simultaneously.

On the monitor, the pawnshop's back door closed, and the three men headed west in the alley.

Kuhn paused the video and looked at Leya. "What do you think they were doing?"

Truscott pointed at the screen. "We never saw who was inside the store."

"Could be Lucky," Leya said into her hand.

"Could be anyone," her partner said. "Any of those guys look familiar?"

She shook her head.

"Let's get a copy of this to Crime Analysis." Truscott tapped Kuhn on the shoulder to get his attention. The business owner shifted in his seat to look at him. "Can you email me a copy of this?"

"Sure, but it'll be pretty big. I can upload it to my Google Drive and send you a link." He shifted in his seat to look at Leya again. "Will that work for you?"

Truscott spread his arms wide and bowed slightly. "Does that work for you, Madam Detective?"

She released her nose. "Works great."

"All I need is your email address," Kuhn said. "I can have it to you in like five minutes."

Truscott rolled his eyes. "Send it to me." He pulled a business card from his pocket and held it in front of Kuhn's face.

The man reluctantly accepted the card and held it with both hands. He briefly considered it, then looked back to Leya. "It was nice to meet you."

She released her nose long enough to say, "You, too."

"Yeah," Truscott said. "You were a big help."

Kuhn nodded twice, then spun toward his computer. He put his hands on the keyboard but didn't move for several seconds. Then his fingers jumped across the keyboard and a new program popped up on the screen.

"Hey," Leya said after releasing her nose. "What is it you do here?"

He turned. "Video transfers. Eight millimeter, VHS, that sort of thing. If you ever need anything done, I'd be happy to do it for you." He beamed. "Free of charge, of course."

She nodded.

"Okay," Truscott said. "We'll see ourselves out."

Kuhn waved goodbye to Leya. "Have a nice day."

***

Debbie Wallette leaned back from her computer when Leya and Truscott walked in. A half-eaten macaroon was stuck between her teeth. A box of the colorful delights sat next to her elbow.

"Mmpph?" she grunted. Her eyebrows rose, and she smiled the best she could.

"Late lunch?" Truscott asked.

She sucked the rest of the small cookie into her mouth and chewed quickly. "Treats from Dallas," she said.

Nash, Leya thought. She hadn't done much work with the Major Crimes detective. Her eyes flicked back to the box of colorful cookies. Was it customary to bring items like this to the Crime Analysis team or was something going on between Debbie and Dallas?

Her gaze flitted to the others in the office. Each had an item that could be considered a gift—a box of chocolates, a container of shiny candies, and a tin of popcorn were the treats Leya could see from where she stood. Was that how work got done in this section? Were the wheels of analytics greased by snacks?

Debbie Wallette led the Crime Analysis team. Along with four others, they correlated the data officers input in the system, interpreted its meaning, and then identified trends. Leya didn't know the others on the team. Debbie had stopped by the Property Crimes office and welcomed Leya after her promotion.

Truscott helped himself to a macaroon.

"They're so good," Debbie said. Her attention shifted to Leya. "You should try one."

She smiled but felt slightly embarrassed she'd come empty-handed. She also sent her requests via email. It was Truscott's suggestion they stop by to talk with Debbie.

"What can I help you with?" Debbie asked.

Truscott motioned toward the computer. "I sent you an email a few minutes ago."

"The video link." Debbie turned to her computer and clicked her mouse twice. "I downloaded it and ran a scan." The video they'd watched with Brian started. "What am I looking at?"

"Can you identify any of these men?" Truscott asked.

He reached for another macaroon, but Debbie smacked his hand. "They're not cookies. They're expensive." Her eyes shifted to Leya. "Are you sure you won't try one?"

Leya shook her head.

"Why can't I have hers?" Truscott asked.

Debbie rolled her eyes and Truscott grabbed a second macaroon. He pointed at the screen with it. "If you can identify any of those men, that would be great, but especially the one in the middle."

Debbie leaned in and studied the monitor. After a moment, she shook her head. "Nope." She lifted a few inches out of her chair. "Listen up." She whistled and the other analysts looked her way. "Check this out."

Three men and a woman moved toward her. Leya and Truscott stepped back so the analysts could get a closer look at the monitor. "Any of these guys look familiar?" Debbie asked.

There was some mumbling amongst the team, but the consensus was that none did.

"All right," Debbie said. "Thanks."

The team returned to their individual desks.

"It'll take some time," Debbie said. "The facial recognition software we've got isn't like the movies. The photos need to be aligned almost perfectly. I know there's better stuff out there but we're on a municipality's budget. We'll pull a photo of each guy, blow it up, and send it around."

"That would be great," Truscott said.

"Do you want us to send it to the PIO?"

The Public Information Officer could get photographs on the local news and the department's social media sites. Truscott eyed Leya. "Not yet."

Leya cocked her head. "How come?"

"Because we don't know what this is." He motioned to the frozen picture. "We don't have any evidence of a crime."

"But it's suspicious behavior."

Truscott lifted an eyebrow. "Being suspicious isn't criminal."

Debbie reached for a macaroon and bit into it. Her eyes bounced between Leya and Truscott.

Leya didn't like it. She would have released the video for a Persons of Interest find.

"If you want," Truscott said, "we'll run it by the sergeant and get his take on it. If he says to notify the PIO, then we will. Fair enough?"

Leya reluctantly nodded.

Truscott pointed toward the computer again. "Let us know what you find. Thank you for the treats."

"Mmph," Debbie said. A macaroon was once again stuck between her teeth.

***

"The guy is handing out lanyards with fake ID cards," Leya said.

"And you know they're fake how?" Sergeant Yager asked.

"Cliff Upchurch said so."

"The homeless guy."

"That's right," Leya said with a nod.

Yager looked down and seemed to contemplate the story she'd just told him. He grabbed his pen and banged the end against his other hand. When he finally lifted his head, he looked at Truscott. "You think we shouldn't release the video?"

"I didn't say that."

The sergeant continued to tap the pen. "You didn't have to. If you two agreed, you wouldn't be here. You would have already talked with the Public Information Officer." His gaze returned to Leya. "Am I right?"

She nodded once.

Yager studied Truscott. "Your argument for not releasing is what?"

"I don't want to spook these guys. If they are transient and they get word we're looking for them, they'll pick up and move on."

The sergeant now tapped his pen on the edge of his desk. "Reasonable."

Truscott spread his arms in a questioning manner. "If that happens, what have we got?"

"We've stopped the burglaries," Leya said.

"If they're the right guys."

Yager sighed heavily. "Why haven't you interviewed the owner of Lucky's about this video?"

Truscott shoved his hands into his pockets. "I want to know who those guys are first."

"He's got a history with the owner," Leya said.

"The guy's a bullshitter, Sarge. I want our side locked down before we go in asking questions. That's all."

Leya crossed her arms. Truscott's argument to wait made sense, but she didn't have to like it.

The sergeant set his pen down. "Here's what we're going to do. We'll give Crime Analysis twenty-four hours to work their magic. If they don't have a name for you by tomorrow, we'll ask the PIO to get involved." He eyed both detectives. "How's that sound?"

Leya and Truscott exchanged glances.

"Well?" Yager asked.

Truscott shrugged. "Works for me."

"Yeah," Leya said, "me, too."

Yager picked up his pen and resumed his tapping. "I'm glad I could be of help. Now, go write a report so we can send it up the chain."

***

After getting the girls to bed, Leya reclined on the couch with her head in Ernie's lap. She flipped through

Facebook on her iPad while he watched *SportsCenter* on their flat screen TV.

"So work?" he whispered.

"What about it?"

"We never talked about it over dinner." He sounded distracted.

Leya grunted.

The lights in the room were off and the television was muted. Shadows danced across the room. Leya and Ernie kept their voices low. The girls looked for any reason to crawl out of their beds and scamper into the living room. If Leya and Ernie were in their own bed, the girls would crawl in with them. They established this nightly routine as a way for the kids to learn to sleep alone. Leya wanted to be in bed right now, but they had to ensure the girls were asleep first.

She stopped scrolling on a high school friend's update. The woman had recently remarried and was on a family vacation in San Diego with her new husband. She was thirty-seven with two kids. He was twenty-eight with six-pack abs. It would never last, Leya thought. Either the abs would go, or the marriage would. She flipped upward.

"How's the new partner?" Ernie asked absently.

"He's not my partner," Leya muttered.

"I thought he was."

She rolled back on her head so she could look up at him. His attention remained on *SportsCenter*. "We don't have partners," she said.

Ernie shifted so they could more easily look at each other. "We had those detectives over for dinner. They were partners."

"They were Major Crimes," Leya said.

He turned back to the television. "We should invite them over again."

"That'd be weird." She dropped her head to where it was previously.

"Why?"

"Because they're not a couple."

She felt Ernie tilt his head, but she didn't bother looking at him.

"Why would that be weird?" he asked. "Were they a couple, then?"

"No. We were working something."

"Working something," he said in a mocking tone. "Well, there you go."

Leya scrolled past political memes, baby pictures, and personal diatribes for several moments until she landed on one from her sister. She paused to read the update.

Ernie leaned over her. "What's she up to?"

"New boyfriend."

Her sister had posted a photo of her and her new boyfriend at a Spokane Chiefs hockey game. The guy looked like he fought in UFC matches; he had a crooked nose and cauliflower ears. Maybe he wrestled in college and was one of those jocks who refused to wear ear protection.

Ernie snorted his disapproval.

She flicked upward on her feed and a video post from the local NBC affiliate popped up. The headline read *Camp Faith Draws Ire of Local Community*. She started the video and a news anchor—the blond one with the plump lips and overly large breasts—said, "*Continuing our coverage on Camp Faith*."

Leya hurriedly turned the sound down. The volume had been up from when she had listened to an audio book while washing the dishes. "Sorry," she whispered.

Ernie patted her shoulder as he muted *Sportscenter*.

"You don't have to do that," Leya said.

"It's all right."

The news anchor smiled as she read from the teleprompter. Leya could barely hear the woman speak.

"*Reporter Laynee Lewis was out with a neighborhood group letting their voices be heard.*"

Footage of the Camp Faith protest played while a new woman's voice began. "*Many who live and work near Camp Faith came together today to express their frustrations with rising crime in the area.*"

A woman anxiously waved a yellow *Honk to Send the Bums Home* sign at passing cars. Cars blared their support as they drove by. Leya recalled hardly anyone had honked for Jesus while she was out there.

Fred Zimmer's face filled her tablet's screen. His name was shown in the lower left corner. Under that, it said, 'Local entrepreneur/Lug Nutz owner.'

"*We're out here,*" Zimmer said, "*to bring attention to the crime epidemic Camp Faith has spawned since the city wants to ignore it.*" He pointed at the camp while he continued. "*These people are ruining this neighborhood. They scare our customers and our families, and they're driving property values down. The mayor and city council don't care because they don't live here.*"

The camera angle changed to the reporter, an attractive young woman with dark hair and wide eyes. "*How do you respond to claims these people have nowhere else to go?*"

Zimmer's face pinched. "*How is that our problem?*" He tapped a finger into an open palm. "*I've started businesses, hired employees, and paid my taxes." Once again, he pointed at the camp. "What have those people ever done except leech off society? If I stopped paying my taxes, the city would take away everything I own. Those people don't pay anything and the city keeps handing them more. How is that even remotely fair?*"

Ernie leaned over her. "Fair has nothing to do with

being poor."

Leya paused the video just as it switched to a council member for their comment. "What's that?"

"The guy should go to church."

"He's not entirely wrong."

Ernie pulled back slightly. "How can you say that?"

She sat up and crossed her legs. "Those people aren't trying to improve their condition."

"How do you know?"

Leya shrugged. "I've been there. I've seen it."

Ernie nodded but didn't comment.

Her thoughts tumbled in on themselves. She couldn't decide where she fell on this issue. At certain moments, she wanted to reach out with a helping hand as the church taught. In others, she felt like most cops did—the homeless were not the helpless victims the media and support agencies portrayed them to be. Her feelings weren't consistent on this subject, and it frustrated her.

Leya's finger hovered above the screen, about to restart the video.

"There was an article in yesterday's paper," Ernie said, "about the couple at the camp waiting to get an apartment." He looked at Leya. "The woman works two jobs. Her boyfriend is on disability because of an injury from his construction job. They're trying to improve their condition."

Leya sighed. She had read the article. "I'll give you that one, but you know as well as I do, not all of them living there are because of the housing shortage."

"Some have mental issues."

"Yeah, and there are a lot who are making a choice. They don't want to live by society's rules and expectations."

Ernie shrugged. "All I'm saying—" He motioned toward the iPad. "—is the guy in that video could use some of the gospel."

Leya believed in the Word and had attended church since she was a child. However, she also believed people got out of life what they put into it. "How's the church going to help Fred Zimmer?"

"Humble his heart, maybe. What does it say in Psalms?"

She chuckled. "What doesn't it say?"

"Blessed is the one who considers the poor."

"Oh, that's just great." Leya tossed the tablet to the furthest couch cushion. "What's Fred supposed to do with that while crime is spiking in his neighborhood?"

"I don't know," Ernie said. "Maybe he'll lighten up on his rhetoric."

"Why should he do that?" She motioned toward the tablet. "The guy's a first-class jerk, but he's got a point. I wouldn't want those people in our neighborhood. Would you?"

"No," Ernie said, "I wouldn't, but a guy spouting off like that is likely to get punched in the mouth."

Leya considered her tablet. "I really don't think Fred Zimmer gives a good damn what others think of him."

# Chapter 7

"You're not going to school that way," Leya said.

"Yes, I am." Violet scowled at her mother. It was the same look Ernie gave when he didn't get his way.

Leya was in her daughters' shared bedroom. The scene that played out this morning was a regular occurrence. Each child had her eccentricity. Rose took extra items with her—last week it was a box of stuffed animals she couldn't survive a day without. Violet's quirks were about her wardrobe.

"We've had this conversation before," Leya said calmly. "You can't go looking like that."

Violet wore a Thor helmet, butterfly wings, sweatpants, and knockoff UGG boots. On her right arm, she carried Captain America's shield. "Why?"

"Because you look stupid," Rose said. She gleefully hopped on her bed, twisting and throwing her hands in the air.

"You're not helping," Leya said. "Get off the bed."

"Aw," Rose whined and flopped to her butt. "You're no fun."

Leya turned back to Violet. "And you."

"Call me Revenger." Violet thrust her fist into the air. "The next Avenger!"

"No." Leya snapped her fingers. "Take that stuff off."

"It's my costume."

"Fine. You're on dish duty with me for the week."

"Heroes don't do dishes."

Leya wanted to argue with her, but she said, "You'll be the first. It'll be your superpower."

Violet snatched the Thor helmet from her head. "You're no fun."

"Your sister already said that."

Ernie stuck his head into the room. "You should probably see this."

Leya turned. "See what?"

"That guy from last night."

"The one with the tire store?"

Ernie nodded. "His building is on fire."

"Shit."

"Mom!" the girls cried out together.

Leya looked at them both. "Get ready. Now."

She followed Ernie back to their bedroom. The small TV on their dresser played the Channel 4 news. The sound was indistinct, but the video showed flames shooting out of the Lug Nutz business. Fire crews sprayed water into the building. This must have happened at night or in the early hours, since the sky was dark.

Ernie watched her. "Does this have something to do with your Camp Faith problem?"

"I don't know." Leya shrugged. "Maybe." She grabbed her jacket. "Listen, I gotta go. Can you—"

He nodded. "I'll get the girls ready. Good luck."

Leya kissed him, then hurried out of the house.

***

Leya first stopped by Lug Nutz, but she didn't get out of her car. She wasn't a fire investigator, so there wasn't much she could do at this moment. She just wanted to drive by the scene since she knew this was going to be a hot-button issue today.

The commercial building was mostly destroyed. The exterior walls remained, but the roof had collapsed, and the windows had exploded. The tires inside must have accelerated the fire. Black inky smoke rose from the interior.

SPD patrol cars blocked the nearest lane of traffic and a single fire engine remained. From the video on the news channel, several trucks had originally responded. Several firefighters with pickaxes moved about the interior of the building. They were likely dealing with the remaining hot spots.

A group of citizens stood nearby on the sidewalk and watched the activity. Fred Zimmer was in the group. Councilwoman Marjorie Hembree patted his shoulder in a conciliatory gesture. Also standing nearby were the mayor, the chief of police, and the county sheriff.

This was definitely going to be a hot-button issue.

Leya watched the scene for a few minutes, then dropped the gearshift into Drive and headed south.

***

A line of protesters blocked Ralph Street, so Leya continued along Second Avenue. They waved homemade signs and yelled at the residents of Camp Faith. Leya was amazed so many people had mobilized this quickly in the wake of the Lug Nutz fire. It was barely eight in the morning, and there were already three times as many protestors today as there were yesterday. Anger was an effective motivator.

Faces twisted with hatred. Signs carried messages like, "Send Them to Seattle!" and "Support Retroactive Abortion!" The man holding the latter sign wore a *White Lives Matter* T-shirt.

The dark fabric attached to the fencing around the camp stopped anyone from seeing inside. It also limited folks from looking out. Leya thought the residents had to know what was occurring. Why would any of them dare step outside now?

She turned on Ray Street. A patrol car sat a block

away at the corner of Pacific Avenue. Leya pulled alongside. Officer Pauleen Sherman rolled down her window and Leya did the same.

"What's up, Princess?" Pauleen loved teasing Leya about her name. It was usually lighthearted while at work, but it could get ruthless while they were drinking. "How's working so closely with the dreaded empire?"

"Still good."

"And Han Solo?" That was her nickname for Sergeant Yager.

"He's fine."

"Yes, he is." She smiled. "Is he still seeing that counselor?"

Leya shrugged. "No idea, but her picture is still on his desk."

Pauleen frowned. "She's got a boy's body. He might as well do it with a stick."

Leya jerked her head toward the camp. "Waiting for something to jump off?"

"Work, work, work." Her friend languidly turned in the direction Leya was looking. "I thought something might happen, but mostly the protesters seem content to bitch and moan."

"Why not wait around the corner where they can see you?"

She smirked. "If I get too close, they'll complain to me. I can do without that."

"Can't we all?"

Pauleen raised an eyebrow. "You'd tell me if a rumor was true, right?"

"Of course."

"Is there something going on with you and Truscott?"

"What are you talking about?"

Pauleen made a circle with her thumb and forefinger and poked another finger through it.

Leya's face warmed. "The shit?"

"Oh, my." Pauleen laughed. "You're going to have to confess that this week." She mimed the sign of the cross. "Oh Father, how art you in heaven?"

"Whatever you've heard," Leya said, "it's not true."

"I didn't think so." She smirked. "Not from you."

"I hope you stopped that rumor wherever you heard it."

"I did, but I still had to ask in case it was true."

Leya shifted in her seat. "Who said that about me?"

She rolled her eyes. "You know how this place is. People talk."

"Truscott and I have worked together for two days. That's it."

Pauleen's eyes narrowed. "Truscott? It's Truscott now?"

"It's his name. I call you Pauleen. That doesn't mean we're doing it."

"Point taken." She shrugged. "Whatever. You be careful around him."

"Why? What have you heard?"

It was then Leya realized she never got an answer from Truscott yesterday about why he left the Special Victims Unit.

Pauleen glanced around as if searching for eavesdroppers. Leya self-consciously did the same. It was stupid since they were parked side-by-side. No one would sneak up on them.

"The rumor I heard," Pauleen said, "is he got turned on while handling a rape case."

"How would they even know?"

"They caught him with a boner."

"Gimme a break."

Pauleen nodded. "Real sicko."

"I don't believe it."

"Believe what you want. He's your partner." Pauleen straightened, then lifted her chin in the camp's direction. "You get any leads on those burglaries?"

"Some. Maybe."

"If you need help, you let me know. I'd love to bust this place up. I can't believe the mayor let these animals do this." Her lips twisted. "I wouldn't let my dog shit in a place like this."

"I hope that's not the most poetic thing I hear today."

"You wish you could talk like me."

Leya dropped her car into gear. "If I did, I'd be in confession every day."

"Fucking-A right, you would be."

Pauleen whooped as Leya drove away.

# Chapter 8

Leya found Truscott at his cubicle. He held a cup of coffee near his mouth and didn't notice her approaching. He seemed to be intently concentrating on his computer screen.

"Did you hear?" she whispered.

He turned and looked up. "About?"

"Lug Nutz." Leya glanced over her shoulder before continuing. Déjà vu flashed through her. Pauleen and she had just gone through a similar act, but it didn't feel so stupid now. "Fred Zimmer's business burned down last night."

Truscott shrugged. "I heard." His attention returned to the screen.

"It'll blow back on us."

He raised an eyebrow and grunted, but Truscott didn't bother looking in her direction.

She tried to keep her voice low, but she was frustrated by Truscott's apparent lack of worry. "You know it will."

"People always look for someone else to blame. It's not like we can stop them."

Leya knew that, but she at least wanted him to show some concern. One of Camp Faith's most vocal opponents had his business torched. The department was going to get filleted by the press today, which meant she and Truscott were, too. "What're you looking at?"

"Crime Analysis got a hit on one of our guys—Quaid Webb."

Leya stiffened. "Which one?"

"The mope passing out the lanyards." Truscott pointed at the monitor. "I'm reading his history now."

"When did this come through?" Leya's brow

furrowed. “I didn’t know.”

“Five minutes ago. They copied you on it.”

The notification must have come in while she parked, but she hadn’t checked her email since before leaving the house. The fire at Lug Nutz had consumed her thoughts. “Can I look?” she asked.

“Help yourself.”

She stepped behind Truscott to look over his shoulder at his monitor. Quaid Webb was thirty-two, white, with a history of misdemeanor crimes—theft, malicious mischief, trespassing, public intoxication, and defacing a state monument—but no burglaries.

“Let’s contact radio,” she said, “and put out an ATL.”

“Already done.”

She hadn’t heard it while driving in, so a dispatcher likely sent an Attempt to Locate on Quaid Webb electronically. Only the officers and supervisors on patrol had computers in their cars. Detectives and those in specialty units wouldn’t have seen the alert. Had it been a higher priority request—such as a murder suspect or missing child—a radio operator would have verbally broadcast it as well. However, Leya believed the electronic way was often the best. Most officers continually checked their computers. They would refer to the ATL broadcast throughout their shifts. Some would also take the electronic broadcast as a challenge and immediately search for a subject like Webb.

“Navarro, Truscott,” Sergeant Yager said.

They both turned toward him.

“Let’s go.”

“Where to?” Leya asked.

“Pow wow.”

***

The department's conference room was an intimidating place. Leya had been in there before, but that didn't decrease the awe she felt now. The administration regularly met around the long table to decide the department's direction. The press often assembled in the room to receive updates on major cases. Employee promotions and award ceremonies weren't conducted there, though. They usually handled those in the second-floor roll-call room. Even detectives climbed the stairs to get handed a certificate.

Framed photographs of the city were displayed around the room. The national and state flags stood proudly in the corner. A flat-screen television hung on the east wall and ran a morning newscast.

Chief Liam Dillon sat at the head of the table. To his left was Captain Gary Ackerman. Neither man acknowledged the entrance of the Property Crimes team.

The chief leaned back in his chair and folded his arms over his chest. Even seated, he was a commanding presence in his dark blue uniform. The fluorescent lights shimmered off his bald head.

Ackerman rested his right arm along the conference table. His silver hair was perfectly combed, and his tailored suit looked new. Leya thought he looked like a well-dressed businessman. Since he'd promoted to captain, she could count on her hand the number of times he'd worn the department's uniform.

A laptop sat near the captain's hand; cords connected to its back ran through a hole in the conference room table and somehow connected it to the TV.

On the television screen, the news report flashed to Fred Zimmer.

The Chief's lip curled in response. "Pause it."

Ackerman tapped the computer's space bar, and the image froze.

The chief pointed at the flat screen. "Either of you had contact with this guy?"

Sergeant Yager stepped to the side as both Leya and Truscott nodded.

"When?" the chief asked.

"Yesterday," Leya said. "At Camp Faith."

Ackerman glanced at the chief.

Dillon knocked his knuckles against the table. "That explains it."

The captain said, "We got a call from Councilwoman Hembree yesterday about a couple of officers harassing Fred Zimmer."

"We didn't harass him," Leya said. "We were following up on some leads and he was there, leading a protest. He came over to talk."

"About what?" Dillon asked.

"He wanted to know what we were doing there. We didn't feel it wise to share with a citizen what we were working on."

Sergeant Yager nodded his support of Leya's statement.

Chief Dillon said, "We received another call this morning from the councilwoman. She's upset someone from the camp targeted Zimmer."

"How does she know that?" Truscott asked.

The chief cocked his head.

"How does she know it was someone from the camp?" Truscott spread his arms wide. "Does he have security equipment? Cameras around the building?"

"From the early feedback," Ackerman said, "the fire destroyed his security system."

The chief leaned forward and rested his forearms on the table's edge. "The media is saying it's arson."

Leya glanced at Truscott before saying, "But the fire isn't even out yet."

Chief Dillon shrugged. “It’s likely arson. Can we agree on that? The politicians are going to jump on this.” Leya was sure the chief included the sheriff in that bunch. “The WSDOT camp is a lightning rod.”

“Why would someone go after Zimmer?” Truscott asked.

“Because it was Zimmer.” The chief flicked his hand toward the television. “The guy is on the news almost daily.”

“In the newspaper, too,” Ackerman added.

Dillon nodded. “If I lived in the camp, I’d be offended by the things Zimmer says. It’s easy to imagine someone exacting some revenge on the guy.”

“But we’ve got to consider other suspects beyond the camp, right?” Truscott asked.

“You go where the evidence takes you,” Captain Ackerman said.

Truscott pointed at the TV. “Then why are we letting politicians dictate our actions?”

Chief Dillon jammed his finger into the table. “Councilwoman Hembree isn’t dictating this investigation. She’s calling with concerns about a constituent. Fred Zimmer owns businesses and real estate. The people at the top listen to people like him because he contributes to their campaigns.” Dillon pointed at the frozen image of Fred Zimmer on the television. “Now, someone has burned down his principal business. If you don’t think someone from the camp did it, who else might have it out for the man?”

Leya and Truscott fell silent.

“Just so you know,” the chief said, “SIU and CTF are now looking into the camp. Maybe they’ll come up with a suspect.”

Leya frowned. If the Special Investigation Unit and the Criminal Task Force were poking their noses into the

Camp Faith problem, there was a chance the entire case was going to be taken away from her.

"SIU?" Truscott asked. "Is there a gang problem inside the camp?"

"No," the chief said, "but drug sales have increased in the area. The county's gang units are watching that activity, too."

Truscott glanced at Leya before continuing. "A guard at the camp said the sheriff buzzed them with a helicopter."

Chief Dillon clicked his tongue. "We got word he's taking infrared photographs of the camp. Getting the layout of where people are shacking up."

"All agencies are prepared if something goes down inside," Ackerman said. "SWAT flew a drone over the camp a week ago in case they ever needed to make entry. The TAC team has practiced scenarios."

The chief set a hand on the table and tapped his index finger. "Where are you with that burglary lead?"

It took ten minutes for Leya and Truscott to explain what they'd discovered, including the recent lead on Quaid Webb. When they finished, the chief asked, "How sure are you of this?"

Truscott shrugged. "It makes more sense that it's a coordinated effort. With an epidemic of random thefts, someone was bound to be caught either at the crime scene or trying to pawn an item. Yet we haven't caught them at either activity. What are they doing with the goods they've stolen?"

Leya watched Truscott. She now understood why Yager said he was an experienced investigator. He not only understood how to put together a case, but he also knew how to present it to the administration. He confidently maintained eye contact with the chief, with only an occasional glance to Ackerman.

The chief faced Ackerman. “If this spree isn’t because of the WSDOT Camp, there’s going to be some crow to eat.” The edge of his mouth hinted at a smile. “I’d love to stuff a helping of it into the sheriff’s mouth, the sanctimonious bastard.”

“That means the mayor’s going to eat crow, too,” Ackerman said. “Some of the council as well.”

Dillon’s smile faded. “That’s a problem.”

Silence descended over the room again. The chief bowed his head and studied his hands.

“Sir?” Ackerman said, but the chief lifted a finger for him to wait.

In a moment, Chief Dillon slowly looked up. “Here’s what we’re going to do.” He focused on Leya and Truscott. “You two, continue on. Find this Webb character and bring him in. But no talking to the press about him.”

Leya and Truscott nodded.

“We don’t announce anything,” the chief said. “Nothing about the burglaries until you’re sure of what you got. Understand?”

Sergeant Yager said, “They’ve got it, sir.”

Chief Dillon knocked on the table. “The politics around this are sticky enough. Let’s focus on getting it done right. If we zap the sheriff in the process, that’ll be a bonus.”

# Chapter 9

Leya parked on Bernard Street, just north of Main Avenue. Two patrol cars were already in the alley. Truscott hopped out of the passenger seat before she turned off the engine. He stood by the front of the car and waited for her to exit.

She grabbed the manila folder from the dashboard before climbing out.

A white male leaned against the back of a brick building. Officers Pauleen Sherman and Bartolo Silva talked with him. Pauleen noticed the detectives and moved toward them.

"Look who we found," she said with a proud smile.

"You're turning into a regular bloodhound," Leya said.

"I'm building a reputation."

Leya laughed. "Girl, you've already got a reputation."

Pauleen's smile withered as she eyed Truscott. "How's it going?"

"Good." His attention remained on Quaid Webb.

"What was he doing when you found him?" Leya asked.

"Leaving his apartment." She pointed toward a nearby building. "He lives above The Onion."

The Onion was a celebrated local restaurant, known for its hamburgers and beer selection. Leya had eaten there several times with Ernie and had gone there with her sister for drinks before a show. An early Field Training Officer of hers told her a movie had been filmed there, but she couldn't remember what it was. She briefly wondered if Truscott might know, since he was a movie fan.

"How'd you know where he lived?" Leya asked.

Pauleen spread her arms. "It's Quaid. He's not exactly a do-gooder poster child, now is he?"

Truscott eyed her now. "Crime Analysis didn't know him."

"Data crunchers are fine and dandy," she said loud enough for Bartolo to hear, "but it's patrol that makes the world go round."

Bartolo hollered back, "Preach on!"

Leya rolled her eyes. "He say anything?"

"Only that we're violating his constitutional rights." She shrugged. "He must have learned that in law school."

"Let's go talk with him."

Pauleen led the way.

As they approached, Webb quit talking with Bartolo and leaned his shoulders against the building. His T-shirt was tucked into his jeans and his Converse shoes appeared to have been recently purchased.

Officer Silva lifted his chin to the detectives. They nodded in return.

"I know my constitutional rights," Webb said.

"So we've heard," Pauleen said.

"I'm gonna have your badge, lady." Webb jerked his head toward Officer Silva. "His, too."

Pauleen smirked. "Why don't you tell these detectives which constitutional rights we violated?"

He sneered. "They already know."

"Of course, they do." She motioned toward Leya. "This is Detective Navarro. She has some questions for you."

Leya glanced at Truscott, but his attention stayed on Quaid Webb. He didn't let Pauleen's slight bother him.

"Fuck their questions," Webb's gaze flicked to the folder Leya held. "I don't have to answer nothing."

"Right now," Leya said, "you're detained for

questioning. We can have this conversation here, or we can have it down at the station."

"But I got shit to do."

"Our interview will go faster if we do it here," Leya said, "but it's your choice."

"What kind of questions?" Webb motioned toward the file Leya held. "Because I don't know shit."

"We want to know about a string of burglaries up and down the Sprague Corridor."

Webb's eyes narrowed. "Hey now, don't put that shit on me, lady. I didn't have nothing to do with that." He slapped his chest with both hands. "I don't break into buildings."

"You're a thief. You take things without asking. It's only a hop, skip, and jump to a burglar."

He glanced at Truscott. "I didn't do whatever she thinks I did. I'll swear on my mother's eyes."

"Is that so?" Leya asked.

"Yeah, lady." His head bounced from side to side. "Can I go?"

"No."

"This is bullshit. I'm gonna be late for my job." Webb threw his head back and banged it against the building. "Ow!" His face contorted, and he covered the back of his head with both hands. Webb bent over and muttered, "Jesus."

Leya tapped the folder into an open palm. "Where do you work?"

"Huh?" he groaned.

"Your job?"

Webb looked up. "Can't you see I'm hurting?"

She stared at him.

He slowly straightened but held onto the back of his head. "Why do you want to know?"

"Where is it?" Leya motioned toward Truscott. "My

partner would be happy to call your employer and let them know you're helping us solve a case."

Webb rubbed his head. "I ain't doing that."

"Why not? He'll put in a good word with them." She turned to Truscott. "Won't you?"

Truscott nodded. "Maybe they'll even see you as a hero."

Webb's lip curled. "More like a rat. No, thanks."

"All right," Leya said. "It's settled." She opened the manila folder and removed a photo. "Tell us about this."

Webb's gaze flicked to the picture, and his eyes briefly narrowed. When recognition set in, his hands slipped from the back of his head. He didn't say anything, though.

"Well?" Leya asked.

"What about it?"

"What were you doing there?"

"Hanging out with some friends."

Leya turned the photo and considered it. "Friends?"

Webb nodded. "That's right."

"Okay, then." She spun the photo for Webb to see again. "Who are they?"

"What?"

"Tell me who the others are."

"Why should I do that?"

"Because I'm curious who hangs out with you in the middle of the night behind a pawnshop."

"I don't have to tell you nothing." Webb dropped his shoulders against the building. He was careful not to touch his head against the bricks. He shoved his hands into his pockets.

Truscott moved next to Leya. "You might want to rethink that."

Webb chuckled. "You going to be bad cop now?"

"With all these witnesses around?" Truscott glanced

around the neighborhood. The Onion hadn't opened yet, but there were plenty of cars driving by and pedestrians walked on the sidewalks. "No," he said. "You're safe."

Webb cocked his head. "Then I'm not rethinking shit."

"Let me help you understand the situation," Truscott said. "That picture came from a video of you and your friends."

"A video?"

"That's right, and we've also got a witness."

Leya watched Webb for a reaction. Cliff Upchurch hadn't seen any of the men break into a building. He only saw them gather behind Lucky's Pawn, then walk by him with what he believed were counterfeit Camp Faith passes. However, her partner could legally lie, within reason, to coax a confession.

"My ass." Quaid hawked a loogie on the ground between his new Converse shoes. "You got dick is what you got."

Truscott tapped the photograph that Leya held. "The witness saw you hand out counterfeit lanyards, so you and your friends looked like residents at Camp Faith."

"Putting the blame on them," Leya added.

Webb's laugh was unconvincing. "You're barking up the wrong tree."

"Then what were the lanyards for?" Truscott asked.

"I don't know what you're talking about."

"You're wearing them in the picture."

"Whatever."

Leya asked, "Did you pass them out every night? Or was this the first night you wore them?"

Webb looked around. "I don't have to answer your questions."

Truscott tapped Leya's photograph again. "Sooner or later, we're going to find your friends. You know that, right? Everyone thinks they can keep a secret, but the truth always leaks out."

"The only way to keep a secret is to not have them," Leya said.

Truscott smiled. "Or make sure everyone else who knows the secret is dead."

Webb rested the back of his head against the building and winced. He quickly straightened. "I don't have to listen to any of this."

"Here's something else you didn't consider," Truscott said. "You probably could have kept doing this for years." He glanced at Leya.

She didn't know where he was going with this, but she nodded and said, "Yeah, probably."

Webb looked down his nose at them. "Whatever."

"You guys were mostly breaking into commercial buildings." Truscott shrugged. "Nobody gives a damn about businesses. They're making money hand over fist, anyway. Big deal."

Leya mimicked his shrug and repeated, "Big deal."

Pauleen and Bartolo watched them with confused expressions.

"Here's the thing—" Truscott dismissively waved his hand. "Cops don't give a shit about burglaries. Stolen stuff is a low priority, and you know that."

That wasn't true, Leya thought. Property crime was a major issue for the citizens of any town, and it was especially so for Spokane. The Lilac City boasted one of the highest rates of property crimes in the nation. Citizens were far more likely to be a victim of a car prowling or a garage burglary than murder or rape. However, the police response always skewed toward those crimes affecting life. There were only so many resources to go around. The resulting perception was the city administration, and the police department were soft on property crimes.

Webb shrugged a single shoulder. "That ain't no

secret."

Truscott continued. "But one of your crew got stupid and burned that building."

"What?"

"Arson's no joke, Quaid. It's a felony."

"Felony?" Webb stepped forward. "We didn't have no part of that."

Truscott lifted his hand. "Stay where you are."

"Don't be accusing us of starting no fire!" He glanced at Leya. "That ain't right."

Leya struggled not to smile. Burglary was a felony, too, but Truscott had somehow convinced Quaid Webb that arson was a worse crime. Perhaps it was the visual impact of a burning building. "All right," she said calmly. "If you and your friends didn't do it, tell us who did."

Webb rubbed his face. For a moment, he looked like a scared animal. He took a deep breath and exhaled slowly. His eyes returned to the photograph Leya held.

She tapped it. "Tell us this—was Lucky Fitzgerald involved?"

"I probably should talk to that lawyer now."

"Maybe we should move this downtown," Leah said, "so we can continue our conversation."

Webb shrugged. "So long as I get that phone call."

"You can call," Truscott said, "when you get to the station." He waved Pauleen over.

"All right." Pauleen grabbed Webb by the elbow. "Let's go."

***

Sergeant Yager approached Leya's desk. "Who's Truscott got in the interview room?"

"Quaid Webb."

"You found him?" He glanced over his shoulder at the

closed room. “He admit to anything?”

Leya stood. “Not yet. He clammed up when we asked if Lucky Fitzgerald was involved.”

Yager’s brow furrowed. “Why aren’t you in there?”

“He wanted to talk with his lawyer. Truscott’s babysitting him until the counselor arrives.”

“Who’d he call?”

“Bryce Harmon.”

“That fat bastard?” The sergeant shook his head. “Business must be slow if Harmon is slumming with some two-bit burglar.”

Leya’s desk phone buzzed.

“Excuse me,” she said to Yager and picked up the phone’s receiver. “Detective Navarro.”

“Hi, this is Carl.” She couldn’t remember Carl’s last name, but he was one of the senior volunteers who occasionally staffed the front desk. “Mr. Bryce Harmon is here to see his client.”

“I’ll be right out.” She hung up.

Yager said, “I’ll brief the captain that there’s been a recent development.”

“Don’t get his hopes up.” Leya grabbed her notepad and a pen. “I’ve got a bad feeling about this.”

“Understood, but keep us updated.”

Yager headed toward Ackerman’s office while Leya went toward the front of the Public Safety Building. She took an alternate route, so she didn’t have to walk with the sergeant and go past the captain’s office.

When she pushed through the double doors to enter the PSB’s lobby, she immediately saw Bryce Harmon waiting with a leather satchel in his left hand. She’d never met the man before but had seen him in news reports and on bus bench advertisements. The guy had a physical presence that was hard to forget.

Harmon stood a couple inches over six feet and might

have been as big around. He leaned backward to support the weight of his belly. He wore a black suit and a white shirt. His jacket hung open and exposed red suspenders. His tie stopped two-thirds of the way down his torso and looked like a bright red arrow pointing over a cliff.

Leya approached him. "Mr. Harmon? I'm Detective Navarro."

He walked forward; his heels scuffed the ground with each step. "Where's Mr. Webb?"

"In interview room one. He's waiting with Detective Truscott."

Harmon's eyes widened. "Damien Truscott?"

"That's right."

The attorney pointed at the double doors. "Take me there—now."

"Is everything all right?"

His face pinched, and he bellowed, "Now!"

Leya glanced around the lobby. Several people stopped what they were doing to turn in their direction.

Harmon's face reddened. "What are you waiting for?"

She didn't like being bullied by an attorney, but she wasn't going to make a scene. Harmon was doing a good enough job by himself. She pulled a wallet from her jacket and pressed it against the security reader. It read a chip inside her ID card and unlocked the double doors. Leya yanked one open.

"I'm sure everything is fine," she said.

Harmon leaned his bulk forward and barreled through the opening. "If he's interrogating my client—"

"I'm sure he's not." Leya hurried to catch up to Harmon.

The attorney's face purpled from the effort of movement. "You don't know… what he's capable of." Even though he'd only started hurrying, Harmon's words sounded jagged.

"As I said—" Leya left the rest of her thought unspoken because she didn't know what Damien Truscott was capable of. Perhaps he was in the interview room violating Quaid Webb's rights and forcing the man to incriminate himself.

They turned the corner and passed the captain's office. The door was open. Yager stood in front of Ackerman. Neither man looked into the hallway.

Harmon's briefcase swung wildly as he huffed and puffed. His eyes bulged and never blinked. Navarro feared the man might have a heart attack because of the sudden exertion.

"We should slow down," she suggested.

"I don't…" he rasped, "trust him."

The heels of Harmon's loafers scuffed the floors as they hurried along the hallway. Fluorescent lights glimmered off the recently waxed linoleum floors. Voices came from nearby offices.

When they arrived at the interview rooms, Harmon briefly stopped to check the room number.

Leya said, "They're in—"

But Harmon didn't allow her to finish. Instead, he burst into interview room 1. Leya followed him in.

Truscott reclined in his chair with one ankle crossed over another. An arm rested on the interview table. He was laughing.

On the other side of the small table, Quaid Webb also laughed. The man wasn't handcuffed and held a can of Coca-Cola in his lap.

They looked up at the sudden entrance of Bryce Harmon and Leya. Their laugh stopped for a moment then continued, but louder this time.

"What's going on in here?" the attorney demanded. Venom dripped from his voice.

"I told you everything was fine," Leya said.

"Mr. Webb," Harmon said, "what have you been talking about?"

Webb coughed twice to regain his composure before saying, "Dodgeball."

The attorney's lip curled.

Truscott held up a hand as his laughing calmed. "I told him about that time you—"

Harmon pointed at the open door. "Out."

"Aw, don't be that way, Bryce," Truscott said.

"I would like… a minute with… my client."

"It's a funny story."

The attorney's arm dropped, and he angrily clutched the leather satchel with both hands. "You had…," he muttered, "no right."

"We were kids," Truscott said. "Things happen."

"It's all right," Webb said. He gleefully slurped his soda. "I peed my pants, too." He shrugged. "I was usually drunk when it happened."

Harmon's face darkened as he inhaled. "I'm filing a complaint about this."

Truscott stood. "We'll give you a minute with your client."

He passed Leya, and she pulled the door shut behind her. She followed Truscott back to his desk.

"What's this about pee?"

"He had an accident in second grade. Happened in front of the entire class."

"How long did you go to school with Harmon?" she asked.

"Kindergarten through high school." Truscott dropped into his chair. "Bryce was likable back then. A bit of a goober, but nice."

"Then why throw him under the bus with his client?"

"Your question shows you haven't been in a trial with him. Once you are, you'll understand. He changed after law school."

She looked toward the interview room. "You worried about the complaint?"

He shrugged. "I didn't question Bryce's integrity or impugn his character. I told a story about when we were kids. If he wants to make it even, I'll go in and tell a story about when I peed my pants."

Leya grimaced. "I think we could do without that."

"Just saying."

She motioned toward the interview room. "Before the reunion, did Quaid give you anything we could use?"

"One. He said he was proud for memorizing Bryce's phone number."

She leaned against the edge of Truscott's cubicle. "How did he come by it?"

"He didn't say, but I feel they didn't know each other."

Leya said, "What do you want to bet Lucky told him to memorize it just in case something bad happened?"

"I don't know. I'm still hung up on the idea of Fitzgerald running a crime ring. The guy bothers me, but…" He let the thought run off.

"Do we have enough to book Quaid?"

Truscott crossed his arms. "Our probable cause is weak. What have we got? A photo of him and some guys behind an open door at Lucky's Pawn? It didn't look like they stole anything from there and Fitzgerald never filed a report."

"Quaid didn't admit to anything, let alone the burglaries. All he said was he didn't set the fire at Lug Nutz."

"He was adamant about that." Truscott shook his head. "It feels like he's our guy, but we don't have enough to tie him to anything yet. We should get a search warrant for his apartment."

"What about Lucky?" Leya asked. "Should we check the store again? We checked it once, but maybe we missed something?"

Truscott shrugged. "Let's say Fitzgerald hired those guys to burglarize the neighborhood. Why did he do it? And where did he hide the goods? His house? A storage unit?"

"When do you want to interview him?"

"After we're done with Webb."

***

Leya sat across from Quaid Webb in the interview room. They brought in an additional chair for Bryce Harmon. Truscott leaned against the wall in the far corner.

"As a reminder," Leya said, "this interview is being recorded." Her eyes flicked to the red light on the wall above them. Webb's gaze followed hers, but Harmon's attention remained locked ahead.

She continued. "And we've already advised you of your rights."

"Read them again," Bryce said.

Leya cocked her head.

"I wasn't here earlier. I'd like you to advise my client of his rights."

Truscott grunted and shifted his stance.

Leya had expected further animosity between the two men and insisted she lead this part of the interview. She didn't see the harm in jumping through a hoop to make the attorney happy. She opened the file, removed a Miranda Warning card, and read the listed rights.

After she finished, Leya asked, "Do you understand each of these rights I have explained to you?"

Quaid Webb nodded.

Bryce leaned over. "Say it loudly for the camera."

"Yes." Webb looked up at the red light. "Yes, I do."

Leya read the last question on the Miranda Warning card. "Having these rights in mind, do you wish to talk to us now?"

Bryce Harmon turned to his client. He shook his head in a sagely, reassuring way.

Webb sat up straighter and pulled his shoulders back. "No."

Leya glanced at Truscott. "No?"

Harmon collected his briefcase from the floor. "My client does not agree to speak with you."

"But he said—"

"He'll say nothing more."

Truscott pushed off the wall. "Webb, don't let this hack—"

"That'll be enough." Harmon stood. "Either charge my client, or we're leaving."

Leya closed the file. She tried to make eye contact with Webb, but the man looked down at his hands. She faced Harmon. "We can talk with the prosecuting attorney about making a deal."

Harmon said, "Either charge my client or we're leaving."

She looked at Truscott. His jaw flexed before he shook his head.

A picture of Quaid Webb with some men behind Lucky's Pawn wasn't enough to tie him to a string of burglaries. The closest he got to admitting involvement in the burglaries was a denial they set a fire.

Leya reluctantly motioned toward the door. "You're free to go."

Webb's chair scraped across the floor as he abruptly stood.

"We can find our way out," Harmon said.

The two men left the interview room.

Leya and Truscott stared at each other.

"What now?" she asked.

"We get to Fitzgerald before Webb talks with him."

Truscott hurried from the room.

***

If the parking lot was an indicator of activity inside Lucky's Pawn, the store was doing brisk business. Leya pulled near the curb and stopped the car.

"If he's always this busy," she asked, "why would Lucky get involved with burglary?"

"Maybe he's not," Truscott said, and he popped open his door.

His anger clearly hadn't subsided since they left the station. Truscott slipped out of his seat and slammed the car door behind him.

Leya hopped out of the car as a Spokane Transit Authority bus lumbered by. A line of cars followed it.

Truscott waited patiently at the front of the store. "You're lead," he said when she approached. He yanked opened the door, and she stepped inside.

Overhead, some eighties song played. Leya had heard it before and figured the song was called "Wild Boys" since that chorus repeated so often. She didn't know who sang it, but it was sort of catchy.

A long line of customers waited for help. Only a single employee stood behind the counter—the young one from a couple of days ago.

Leya and Truscott approached the front. They weren't going to wait their turn today.

"Hey," a woman near the back of the line whined, "no fair."

"It's the cops," someone whispered.

"I didn't do it," another said, which elicited a giggling, "Me neither."

The lone employee behind the counter wore the business's green bowling shirt. His name tag proudly announced his name as *Trevor!* His brown hair appeared mussed and the five o'clock shadow he had was filling into an actual beard. The clerk's attention snapped to Truscott's gun and badge. "Officers?"

"Where's Lucky?" Leya asked.

"In the back." The employee jerked his head toward the warehouse doors while he reached under the counter.

The security lock buzzed, and Truscott grabbed the small gate at the end of the counter. He pushed it open, stepped through, and held it for Leya. The two detectives entered the warehouse.

Grady 'Lucky' Fitzgerald sat next to a computer and spoke into a cell phone. He glanced in their direction. "Right," he said, "okay. Listen, I gotta go. Some folks just showed up. I'll call you back in a few minutes." He ended the call and stood. His smile was forced—a salesperson on the make. "Detectives, back again so soon? To what do I owe this honor?"

Leya said, "Tell us about Quaid Webb."

Truscott stepped away from her, giving them a tactical advantage if Fitzgerald fought. Leya didn't expect the man to do so but appreciated her partner's situational awareness.

Fitzgerald frowned and glanced at Truscott. "I don't know anyone by that name."

"He knows you," Leya said.

The pawnbroker's attention returned to her. "Detective, people come into my store every day. Some I do transactions with. Some of them work with my employees. They see my name on the building, my name on the sign, and they think they know me. That doesn't mean I know them."

"Who were you just talking to?" Truscott asked.

"My sister," Fitzgerald said. "Not that it's any of your business. What's going on?"

Leya pulled a folded photo from inside her suit jacket. It was the still of the men gathered behind the pawnshop. She tapped above Quaid Webb's head. "What about now? Does this jog your memory?"

Fitzgerald leaned in. "I don't know who that guy is." His eyes jumped over the paper. "Or any of them, for that matter."

"But they're outside your store, correct?"

"Yeah," he said, but dragged the word out exaggeratedly. He glanced over his shoulder at the back of the building. Perhaps he was trying to figure out just where the men were standing, but Leya imagined him trying to determine where the camera was that had taken the picture.

The pawnshop owner studied the photograph more closely. He looked up at Truscott. "When was this taken?"

Truscott motioned toward Leya.

"Four nights ago," she said.

Fitzgerald flicked the edge of the photograph with the back of his fingers. "I'm never here at night. There's never a reason for me to come back to the store after we close."

Leya pointed at the picture. "You're telling me you've never met this guy?"

"Never seen him."

Truscott crossed his arms. His scowl showed he fought hard against saying something he would regret.

"Could one of your guys know them?" Leya asked.

"You mean my employees?" Fitzgerald shook his head. "I doubt it."

She pointed at the picture. "These men were behind your store with an open door. We have video of this man—" Leya tapped Quaid Webb's face. "—entering and exiting the building. You never filed a police report, so obviously no crime took place here."

Fitzgerald frowned as he considered the photograph.

A bad feeling crept into Leya's gut. Either Grady Fitzgerald was an exceptional actor, or the man really didn't know Quaid Webb. If that were true, how did they end up in this situation? Were they trying to push a square peg into a round hole?

"Quaid Webb," Truscott said, motioning to the photograph, "said your name when we popped him an hour ago." It was a lie, but Leya kept her face expressionless. "He said you're behind the Sprague Corridor burglaries."

"I'm what?" Fitzgerald seemed genuinely confused. His gaze bounced between the two detectives. "Someone said I was part of the burglaries?"

"That's right," Truscott said.

"Why would I? I've got a business to run." He pointed toward the front of the store. "People bring me goods to sell. It's not like I'm hurting for inventory. I don't need to steal anything."

"Then it's someone affiliated with your business." Leya thumbed toward the warehouse doors. "What about Trevor?"

Fitzgerald barked a single laugh. "He wouldn't. He couldn't." He glanced at Truscott, then returned his attention to Leya. "Trevor's my nephew. He's a decent worker. The kid's got a five-cent head." He tapped his temple. "You know what I mean? The guy wouldn't have the smarts to put together something like you're describing."

"Your other employees, then," Leya said.

Fitzgerald smirked. "I've got a couple, yeah, but I'll be honest. None of them have the motivation to pull off what you're describing."

"We're going to need their names and addresses."

"Sure," Fitzgerald said. "Whatever you need." He walked over to his computer and sat. "It'll just take a moment." He moved the mouse around the screen. A new program popped up. In a moment, the printer started.

Fitzgerald grabbed a sheet of paper and handed it to Leya. Along with Fitzgerald's legal name, there were five employees listed—Trevor Crumbaker was one of them.

"And your security feeds," Truscott said.

"What's that?"

"You've got security cameras everywhere." Truscott waved his hand about. His voice hardened. "I want to see what's on them." He pointed at the computer. "Pull them up."

Fitzgerald stood. "Gimme a day and a time, I'll give you what you need."

Truscott snapped his fingers and pointed at the camera. "Monday night. From ten until two. Let's go."

"I don't appreciate your tone, Detective." Fitzgerald's face darkened.

Truscott's eyes narrowed. "I don't appreciate you running a criminal enterprise after all we've done to help you."

"A criminal enterprise?" Fitzgerald's brow furrowed. "Slander is against the law. And when have you ever helped me? All you do is interfere with my business."

"That wasn't your sister, was it?" Truscott motioned toward Fitzgerald's phone. "That was Webb. Or your attorney."

"You're delusional, Detective. If you're going to accuse me of being a criminal, I'm done with this conversation."

Truscott pointed at Fitzgerald. “You might think you’re smart hiring Bryce Harmon to represent your criminal buddies, but he can’t represent you all. It’s going to come back and bite you.”

Fitzgerald crossed his arms. “You’re crossing a line, Detective. I’d like you to leave.”

Leya held up a calming hand. “How about we schedule a time for you to come down to the station so you can answer some questions?”

“What planet do you live on?” Fitzgerald shook his head. “I haven’t done anything wrong.”

“You have a business license,” she said. “We can have the city compel you to come down and speak with us.”

“I’d like to see you try.”

Leya cocked her head. “What about the video?”

“You can have the video,” Fitzgerald said. “But I’m not going to let you call me a criminal.” He placed his right hand over his heart and raised his left. “I swear to you, Detective. Whatever you think I did, it wasn’t me.” His jaw tightened. “If you insist we do this through my attorney, we can. Have a nice day.”

***

As soon as Truscott dropped into the passenger seat, he said, “It’s got to be him, right?”

Leya pulled her door closed. “I don’t know. Are we barking up the wrong tree?”

Truscott spun slightly in his seat to face her. “Now you’re the one who is unsure?”

“Quaid Webb never said he knew Lucky.”

“So?”

“The connection we’re building is the men standing outside that back door.”

“That *open* back door,” Truscott corrected.

"Still. Quaid never said he knew Lucky."

Truscott shifted in his seat and faced forward. He leaned back against the headrest. "Maybe we muddied our investigation."

Leya started the car and entered the westbound traffic on Sprague Avenue.

"But there's Bryce," Truscott said.

"What about him?"

"How's a guy like Webb get a high-priced attorney like him?"

She glanced at him.

"Bryce Harmon doesn't fit into the story," he asserted.

Leya shrugged. "Maybe he's hard up for money."

"If not Fitzgerald," Truscott said, "then what was going on at that store in the middle of the night? What's up with the fake Camp Faith IDs?"

"Assuming that's what they were."

Truscott eyed her.

"I'm just saying. Maybe they were something else."

"The back door was open, and someone was inside. It was Fitzgerald or one of the workers." Truscott waggled the list of employees. "Someone who had access."

Leya said, "But let's not rule out Lucky. People lie all the time."

Truscott banged his knuckles against the inside of the door. "Fitzgerald would certainly have the juice to hire a guy like Bryce Harmon."

"Let's say Lucky is the guy. What's his motivation?" Leya waved a hand at the pawn shop parking lot as she spoke. "It's not like he's hurting for business. You saw the line in there today. It's that way all the time."

"That's the surface." Truscott looked at her. "We need to figure out what's going on with Fitzgerald's life behind the scenes. I bet that's where we'll find the truth."

***

The phone rang for the third time and Leya wondered if Bryce Harmon was letting the call go to voice mail. His receptionist had stated he was in his office before she transferred the call.

It rang once more before the line activated. "Bryce Harmon."

"Mr. Harmon, this is Detective Navarro. We met earlier."

"Yes."

"We'd like to re-interview your client."

"Which one?"

Leya frowned. There was no need for the man to be purposefully obtuse. "Quaid Webb."

He harrumphed. "For?"

"Follow-up."

"He doesn't want to talk with you."

"We're hoping he'll change his mind."

"What about precisely?"

"We'd like to show him some more photographs," Leya said.

"Of."

"Others we believe are involved in the burglaries."

Two seconds passed before Bryce exhaled heavily. "I'll ask him, but it's unlikely he'll change his mind. When are you hoping to do this?"

"Now."

Bryce harrumphed a second time. "That won't happen. I'm leaving for a meeting." Papers rustled in the background.

"What about tomorrow?"

"I'll be in Colville for a client meeting."

Leya pinched the bridge of her nose. "Monday?"

The papers rustled some more. "I could make ten a.m.

work at my office. I'll contact my client to see if he's available and if he wishes to speak with you. My assistant will confirm with you."

"Fine," Leya said, and jotted a note onto her desk calendar.

He ended the call.

***

Truscott appeared at her cubicle. He carried five papers, each contained six photographs spaced out evenly three by two.

"Here are the photo arrays," Truscott said. He dropped the small stack of papers onto her desk.

On the top paper, Grady Fitzgerald was in the furthest slot in the bottom row. All the other men looked vaguely like the pawnshop owner. They were all pasty white, of similar age, about the same weight in the face, and had comparable facial structures.

The second paper contained Trevor Crumbaker in the closest slot on the bottom row. Men of similar age and appearances filled the other boxes. All of them were grinning.

She flipped through the three remaining pages and found all were similar. Since she didn't know the names or faces of the other employees, Leya had no idea who she was looking for. Each page had six random men staring back at her.

"This is optimistic," Leya said.

"Proper preparation prevents piss poor performance."

"The hell is that?"

Truscott straightened. "A petty officer once told me that in the Navy."

"Well," Leya said, "all that proper preparation might go to waste if we can't convince Quaid Webb to roll on the guy behind the burglary ring. Did all the employees have records?"

"No." Truscott shook his head. "I pulled their DOL pictures, which created its own problems." He tugged Trevor Crumbaker's photo array out and moved it to the top. "Look at that stupid grin. What kind of moron is that proud to renew his license? Try matching that to a booking photo. Do you know how many idiots have smiled while getting booked? Not a lot of them, I'll tell you that much."

Leya studied the paper. The other five men smirked or sneered back at her. "We better hope the brains of the outfit doesn't end up being this idiot," she said, "because you know it's getting challenged in court."

Attorneys often objected to photo arrays as being biased. This frequently had to do with where an officer placed a suspect on the paper. The upper left corner was an almost immediate disqualifier. The middle of the upper row was strongly challenged since a person's gaze often went there naturally. The middle slot on the lower row was challenged normally for the same reason, too. Those were just the challenges based on placement.

Then there were the objections based on a photograph's background color. A suspect with a blue background couldn't be lined up against five others with beige backgrounds. They would obviously stand out like a sore thumb.

Some challenges were based on how the accused appeared. Did they negatively stand out in any way? Was the suspect's hair messy while everyone else's was combed? Did the suspect have a face tattoo while everyone else had ink-free skin? Crumbaker's smiling photo would surely get tossed as prejudicial evidence because of five sneering and smirking individuals in the other pictures.

So many things could go wrong with photo arrays they weren't considered a smoking gun in a criminal trial. At best, they were circumstantial evidence since they couldn't be counted on to make it past an evidentiary hearing.

"When are we meeting with Webb?" Truscott asked.

"Monday morning, maybe."

"But it's Thursday." He tapped his watch. "There's no way to talk with him sooner?"

"Not a chance," Leya said. "His attorney's got a client meeting in Colville tomorrow. Then it's the weekend."

Truscott's lips pulled back and revealed clenched teeth. He looked like a dog about to growl.

"Don't blame me," Leya said. "He wanted a lawyer. Now, we've gotta play nice. And Webb might even say no."

"Great."

She checked the clock on her computer. "We might as well call it a day."

"What about writing the warrant for Fitzgerald's security video?"

Leya frowned.

"He didn't give it to us when we asked for it," Truscott said.

"But he said he would. The guy was adamant he wasn't involved."

"So why didn't he give us the video at that moment?"

"The conversation went sideways."

"Are you blaming me?" Truscott asked.

Leya shrugged. "Things happen. But we're not getting overtime to write a warrant. Do you want to hang out and do it?"

Truscott sighed. "Not really."

"Let's follow up with Fitzgerald in the morning. If he doesn't come through, I'll write one up then."

"Fine." Truscott knocked twice on the side of her cubicle. "I'll see you in the morning."

"You all right?"

"I hate losing my cool," he said over his shoulder as he walked away.

***

"But the guy owns a pawnshop." Ernie stood at the kitchen counter and chopped a bell pepper.

Leya sat on the opposite side of the counter and lifted her wineglass in salute. "Crazy, right?"

Violet and Rose ran into the room. Benny, the Jack Russell terrier, closely followed them. "Is it done?" Violet asked breathlessly.

"Yeah," Rose chimed in. "Is it done?"

Ernie eyed the girls. "Soon."

She grabbed her belly. "I'm so hungry. My stomach is eating my kidney."

"Mine, too," Rose said.

Ernie stopped chopping. "Do you even know what a kidney is?"

Rose glanced at Violet. Instead of responding to her father's question, Violet threw her hands into the air and yelled, "Spaghetti!"

"Spaghetti!" Rose echoed, although she pronounced it "Ba-sketti."

The girls bolted from the kitchen. Benny barked as he rushed to catch up.

Ernie lifted the chunks of green and threw them into a pot on the stove. He was making the girls' favorite tonight. Leya wasn't a fan of the pasta dish, even if Ernie doctored it up. She kept her opinion to herself, especially when her husband did the cooking, and the girls were likely to ask for seconds.

Ernie grabbed an onion and turned back to the cutting board. “Why would he do something like that?”

“Greed, probably.” Leya swirled the wine in her glass. “We don’t know.”

“I’d guess greed is what you come into contact with most on your job.”

She shrugged. “There are other emotions. Revenge sometimes. People take from others to make them hurt.”

Ernie sliced a hunk of onion off, then looked up. “This pawn guy wants to hurt everyone in the corridor?”

“Nah.” Leya returned to swirling her wine. She liked the hypnotizing motion. “I’m sticking with greed.”

The knife bounced off the cutting board. “So you got him.”

“I wish.” She sipped now, deeper than she should have, and held the liquid in her mouth a moment before she swallowed. “The guy we had as a witness never actually identified Lucky before lawyering up. And the pawnshop guy denied any knowledge of a burglary ring.”

“Would you expect any less?”

His question irritated her, and she was about to argue when she watched him struggling through tears to finish chopping the onion. Leya held her tongue and listened for the girls. They were oddly quiet now.

“What do you think those two are up to?” she asked.

“I’m sure they’re fine.” Ernie squeezed his eyes closed and looked away from the cutting board. He grunted, then sniffed.

“Want me to take over?”

He shook his head. “Almost done.”

She did not expect him to accept her half-hearted offer. They split the cooking duties, although he admittedly did more since she promoted to detective. When she was on patrol, Leya cooked on her weekends, which was great because of the five-days-on, four-days-off rotation. Ernie was a better cook, and he ended up with one more day in the kitchen than she did back then, yet he never seemed to mind.

Ernie blinked away the last tears. "Do you have probable cause to search his house for any of the stolen items?"

"You sound like my boss."

"So that's a no?"

She swirled her remaining wine. "That's a no, Sergeant."

Ernie picked up some onions and tossed them into the pot. The rest he scraped into a small plastic container. "If he's truly behind this ring and he wants to sell the stuff they've stolen, how hard will it be to bring it into his store?"

Leya considered her husband. He often asked good questions. It was one reason she enjoyed her time with him. So why had she gotten irritated by the earlier one? Maybe because this string of burglaries was getting to her.

"To sell anything through the store," Leya said, "he needs to create a paper trail. If he's going to claim someone sold it to him, he needs to show who that person was and get a copy of their ID."

Ernie stood at the stove and stirred the sauce. "Does it have to be a valid state ID?" he asked over his shoulder. "Like current?"

"I know what valid means and it can be expired."

He waved a hand. "Doesn't that seem like a lot of work?"

Leya slumped over the counter and cupped the wineglass in her hands. "What do you mean?"

Ernie turned to face her. "I'm imagining it this way. If this Lucky guy—"

"Lucky," she interrupted. "Plain Lucky."

"Huh?"

"Never mind. Please continue."

Ernie peered into the pot. "So if this Lucky guy has a ring of thieves breaking into businesses and stealing stuff, then those guys will bring it all back to him and he pays them for it."

"All right."

"So he stores it somewhere other than his pawnshop."

Leya sipped her wine. Ernie wasn't telling her anything she hadn't considered herself. But he was making dinner, so she let him go on talking. She did this sometimes, too, when he let her weigh in on his work problems.

Ernie tapped the wooden spoon on the edge of the pot. "Maybe he has a garage full of stuff somewhere."

"That's what we're assuming if he's involved. Without probable cause, we're not getting into his house."

"Maybe he already got rid of the stuff."

Leya cocked her head. "But we checked his store. There was nothing inappropriate there."

Ernie set the spoon into the tray and reached for a box of spaghetti noodles. "Why does he have to sell it?"

"Say that again," Leya said.

Her husband looked over his shoulder as he ripped open the box. "Which part?"

"About selling it. What do you mean?"

"I don't know."

"You just said it." She set her glass down. Thoughts danced at the back of her mind. "What are you thinking?"

Ernie shook half the box of noodles into his hand and yanked them the rest of the way out. "I was thinking maybe his motivation isn't for the reasons you believe."

The words confused her, and she shook her head. She hadn't had that much wine. "I'm lost."

“What if—” Ernie let the words hang there as he turned to the stove and dropped the pasta into a second pot. He slapped his hands together twice. When he faced her again, he restarted. “What if this Lucky guy burglarized those places for some other reason than taking stuff?”

Leya cocked her head. “But there was stuff taken.”

“Okay, but maybe the point wasn’t to keep it.”

She frowned. “If it wasn’t about the stuff, then why burglarize those places in the first place?”

“How would I know? I’m not the detective. I’m just the cook.”

Leya lifted her glass and returned to swirling the wine in her glass. Her eyes unfocused as Evan Barkuloo’s admonishment drifted back to her. *Who benefits from what’s going on?*

The girls ran back into the room and pulled at their mother’s free arm. The Jack Russell barked at them.

“Protect us!” Violet called.

“Yeah,” Rose said. “Help us. Benny is going to eat us!”

The dog hopped on his back legs and happily turned around.

Leya put down her glass. She’d consider the string of burglaries later.

***

Leya awoke with a start. The room was dark, and Ernie snored lightly on his pillow next to her. The red lights on the alarm clock said 01:34 a.m.

She hadn’t been dreaming, or at least she didn’t think she had, but she knew why Lucky Fitzgerald was behind the break-ins.

Initially, her heart raced with excitement, but after

several moments of lying in the darkness, she calmed. Hadn't she seen something like this on an episode of *Castle*? Or was it *Monk*?

She opened her eyes again. The clock read 01:47.

As quietly as she could, she slid out of bed and tiptoed from the room. She walked into the office she shared with Ernie and closed the door. When she flicked the switch, she squinted against the harshness of the light.

Leya tapped the keyboard, and the computer whirred to life. It sounded awful right now, as if the machine protested the early morning intrusion into its CPU. Once it finished its booting sequence, Leya jumped onto the internet and sought out the state's business license search.

Her fingers hovered over the keyboard. What was the name of the entity?

She closed her eyes and envisioned Lucky standing next to the large cardboard sign. Unfortunately, she couldn't recall the business name.

Leya entered *Spokane security businesses* into the search bar. Even before she hit Enter, she remembered the company's name. Seeing it on the screen confirmed it for her.

She went to Washington State's business licensing page and entered *Security Solutions of Spokane*. When it returned with its result, Leya clicked on it, confident she had solved the burglaries.

Her shoulders slumped as her hopes dissipated. The registered agent for the company was Mervin Longwill. Leya hesitated only a moment before she opened another tab on the browser.

She searched for Mervin Longwill and was rewarded with several entries that showed he was an attorney on the South Hill. For ten minutes, she bopped around the internet looking up information about Longwill. She didn't learn a lot except he appeared to be in his mid-sixties and seemed to be involved in a lot of real estate transactions.

Leya eventually turned off the computer and left the office.

It would be another hour before she finally fell asleep.

# Chapter 10

Leya had hoped to get into the department early that morning, but that wasn't possible even before the interruption to her sleep. Ernie had a breakfast meeting with some of the STA staff, so he was out the door by 6:30 a.m. She should have gotten out of bed while he showered and dressed, but she lingered under the covers, drifting in and out of sleep as she tried to make up for the time lost in the wee hours.

The girls added to the morning's stress. Violet decided on a disaster of an outfit—rabbit ears, a pink sweater she insisted on wearing backward, green shorts, and red Converse high tops. Leya didn't fight it since the child was covered. Rose, on the other hand, filled a second lunch box with a variety of trinkets she had collected from family trips. Leya eventually convinced her to leave those items at home only to discover her daughter had replaced them with three yo-yos, a Rubik's cube, and a broken fidget spinner. She let Rose win that battle.

There was no time for Leya to drive her personal car to the school and return home for the department-issued vehicle. So the girls rode in the backseat of her Chevy Impala.

"Turn on the siren," Violet demanded.

"No."

Besides, there was no need for the siren because Rose wailed like a European patrol car racing to an emergency. Leya wondered where she might have heard that sound.

Violet leaned forward. "Then put us in handcuffs."

Rose stopped wailing now. "Yeah. Like bad guys. Pew-pew!"

Leya was thankful for the teachers who wrangled her

daughters for several hours and then the daycare operators who watched over them afterward. They were saints.

She arrived at the department after eight and tossed her keys onto her desk. Leya didn't bother starting her computer. Instead, she headed for Truscott's cubicle. It looked as if he was only getting settled in. His computer's login screen popped up while he shifted in his seat.

"Hey," she said.

"You look rough."

"Rough night. Something came to me in my sleep."

"Let me guess."

She frowned. "Did you dream about it, too?"

"Are we talking about the security company?" He shook his head. "No. Came to me while I was shaving."

It irritated her that he hadn't lost sleep to come up with the same realization.

Truscott set his fingers on the keyboard and typed in his password.

"Mervin Longwill," Leya blurted.

"What?"

"The registered agent of the LLC. He's an attorney." She pulled a piece of paper from her pocket. "Here's his number."

"Look at you."

She felt slightly vindicated for her loss of sleep. "Let's call him."

"Before we go out to the business?"

She shrugged. "Might save a trip."

Truscott slid his desk phone toward her. "Do the honors. You found the legal beagle."

She picked up the receiver and dialed. A woman answered on the second ring. "Longwill Law. How may I help you?"

"This is Detective Navarro with the Spokane Police Department. May I speak with Mr. Longwill?"

"And what's this regarding?"

"Security Solutions of Spokane."

"Okay," the receptionist said. "Please hold."

The line went silent.

Leya looked at Truscott. "She's getting him now."

He turned to his computer. "The suspense is killing me."

Truscott started his email. He didn't worry about her looking over his shoulder. Even though it was a city system, a lot of officers were weird about others seeing what emails they got. Leya did nothing unethical or immoral, but she didn't like people reading over her shoulder. She didn't even like Ernie doing it and she loved the man. She averted her gaze so as not to see anything.

The phone line activated. "Merv here."

"Mr. Longwill, this is Detective Navarro."

"Of which agency?"

"Spokane Police. I'm calling about Security Solutions of Spokane."

"That's what my assistant said." Mervin Longwill had a deep, resonating voice that might have had a home on a radio station. Papers shuffled in the background. "Listen, I only have a few minutes. I'm headed for a meeting."

"You're the registered agent for that LLC, correct?"

"That's right." Longwill tapped some papers onto a hard surface.

"Can you tell me who the members are?"

"No."

A stapler slammed and Leya quickly pulled the phone from her ear.

Truscott turned to her with his eyebrows raised.

She moved the receiver back into position. "We're

investigating a series of burglaries."

"What's that got to do with my client?"

"Your client's name has come up recently."

"As a burglary suspect?" Longwill asked. "Unlikely. They're a security company." There were two metallic snaps now like a briefcase closing. "Are we almost done? I really need to go."

"We'd like to talk with your clients."

"So call them. I'm not stopping you."

"I haven't made myself clear. We want to know who the ownership of the company is."

Longwill cleared his throat. "I appreciate the difficultly of your job, Detective, but people have a registered agent expressly for this reason."

"To commit crime?" she asked and immediately regretted the words.

Truscott grimaced. Leya's face warmed, and she shook her head.

"I'm not a criminal lawyer," Longwill said, "but surely you're not accusing my client with no proof."

Leya inhaled deeply before calmly saying, "I apologize. I misspoke."

It sounded like Longwill was moving about his office. "I don't have the time to list the myriad reasons people want a layer of protection from the public, Detective. I'm sure you can figure that out for yourself. If not, google it. But I can assure that owning an LLC is completely legal and doesn't imply any criminal behavior."

"I can get a warrant for the information," Leya said.

"I imagine you can. Now, if there's nothing further…"

She shook her head even though the lawyer couldn't see the gesture. "No, thank you."

"I'll await your arrival, Detective," Longwill said. "Have a nice day."

The call ended.

Leya stared at the phone's receiver. "That went well."
Truscott stood. "Screw it. Let's go to the source."

***

Security Solutions of Spokane sat in a Third Avenue strip mall on downtown's periphery. Its neighbors included a podiatrist, a small property management firm, and an alcohol testing project run by a regional college.

It was a simple office—a receptionist counter sat out front while two desks hunkered behind. The aroma of new carpet and fresh paint hung in the air. Framed posters for various security systems hung on the walls. A cardboard advertisement like the one in Lucky's Pawn stood near the front door.

A twenty-something woman with long blond hair sat at the receptionist counter. She chewed on the end of an ink pen as she concentrated on her computer. Her head swiveled toward Leya and Truscott when they entered the business. A name plaque on the desk read Meghan. She casually removed the pen from her mouth and said, "Good morning."

Leya swooped her jacket away from the badge and gun on her hip. "Detective Navarro." She motioned toward Truscott. "Detective Truscott."

The receptionist sat up straighter. "Yes?"

"We'd like to talk with the owners of the company."

Meghan looked over her shoulder before saying, "The manager isn't here."

"But the owners?" Leya asked.

She shrugged. "Cameron hired me."

"Where's Cameron now?"

"On a sales call with Juan. He's new." Meghan's head bobbled. "Cameron's training him to handle sales."

"Can you call him?" Leya asked.

Meghan reached for the desk phone but hesitated to lift the receiver. "They're on a presentation." Her smile was embarrassed. "I'm not supposed to interrupt unless it's important."

Leya glanced at Truscott. "It's important," they said simultaneously.

Meghan reluctantly nodded. She grabbed the receiver and dialed a number. After a moment, she said, "It went to voice mail. Want me to leave a message?"

Leya motioned for her to hang up. "Call Juan. See if he answers."

The receptionist shrugged. She consulted a sheet before dialing a second number. After a moment, she hung up. "It went to voice mail, too. Cameron makes the guys turn off their phones during presentations. They're on commission so he wants them focused."

Leya pulled her notebook from her jacket. "What are their full names?"

The receptionist swallowed with some difficulty. "Cameron Jacobson and Juan Rails. Am I going to get in trouble for telling you that?"

"Do you know where they are now?"

"If they put it into their calendar, I will." Meghan consulted her screen. "Here you go. They're at a presentation not too far from here—East Sprague Small Engine Repair."

***

Evan Barkuloo stood on the sidewalk in front of his store while he considered a colorful tri-fold pamphlet. His dirty apron protected a yellowish plaid shirt and brown slacks.

A handsome mid-thirties white man stood next to Barkuloo and towered over the older man. He wore a blue Polo shirt, black slacks, and black shoes. He gestured toward the brochure as he spoke. A twenty-something Hispanic man stood to the side and watched with earnestness.

Leya and Truscott approached from the west. Juan Rails noticed the detectives and stepped back. Both Leya and Truscott nodded at him. He smiled and returned the gesture.

"You can't go wrong with this system," Cameron Jacobson said. His attention remained on Barkuloo as he tapped the pamphlet. "Even if you don't get the monthly monitoring, the audible alert and automatic calls to your cell phone are worth the peace of mind."

The shop owner clacked his teeth together. "It's a lot of money."

Truscott moved closer to the tall man. "Cameron Jacobson?"

"Yeah?"

Barkuloo smiled at Leya. "Is this good news? Did you find who broke into my shop?"

"We're working on it," she said.

"I'm Detective Truscott," Truscott said to Jacobson. "This is Detective Navarro. We'd like a moment."

Jacobson motioned to Barkuloo. "We're in the middle of something."

"Take a break."

"Yeah, all right." Jacobson turned to Barkuloo. "I'm sorry about this. Gimme a couple minutes and I'll be right back. Juan will take care of you."

The shop owner studied the detectives with curiosity. "Maybe I'll go inside."

Cameron motioned for Rails to follow their prospect. "Go with Mr. Barkuloo. Answer his questions."

Rails stepped into the building.

Truscott shifted his position so Jacobson couldn't run

to the east. Leya blocked his escape to the west. They did it without communicating. It was a natural movement they both had developed from their time as patrol officers.

When it was just the three of them, Jacobson frowned. “If this is about my ex-wife, I’m gonna be pissed if she cost me a sale.”

“It’s not about your ex-wife,” Truscott said.

“It’s not?” Jacobson looked to Leya. “She keeps accusing me of stalking her and I’m not.” His attention swung back to Truscott. “I don’t want nothing to do with the crazy bitch. Trust me. I’ve had my fill of that one.”

“We want to know about Security Solutions.”

Jacobson cocked his head. “If you wanna buy a system, you gotta set an appointment.” He thumbed over his shoulder. “I’m already with a potential customer.”

“No,” Truscott said. “We want to know who owns your company.”

“Huh?”

Truscott stared at him.

Jacobson glanced at Leya. “What’s going on?”

“It’s a simple question,” Truscott said. “What are you hiding?”

“I’m not hiding nothing.” Jacobson threw his hands into the air. “You guys bust up a sale and for what? Nothing. Grady Fitzgerald owns the business. Big fucking deal.”

Leya and Truscott exchanged glances.

“What?” Jacobson said. “You know the guy?”

“We know Grady,” Truscott said.

Leya pointed at the small engine repair business. “How’d you get the lead on Mr. Barkuloo?”

“Maybe I cold called him.”

Her eyes narrowed. “You knew he was broken into, didn’t you?”

Jacobson lifted his hands in mock surrender. "Listen. All I know is Grady gave me a lead. He said, 'Call this guy. Sounds like he might have had some trouble.'"

Truscott moved closer to Jacobson. "That's what he said?"

"Easy, guy." Jacobson lifted a hand. "I'm not giving the old man the strong arm. If he doesn't want the system, he doesn't have to buy it."

"How'd he come by the lead?" Truscott asked.

"Grady?" Jacobson shrugged. "He said some guy on the police department is feeding him leads on burglaries and stuff." The salesman grinned. "Sounds like someone is earning a spiff on the side."

Truscott cocked his head.

Jacobson rubbed his fingertips together. "You know? Special incentive. What do they call it in the police department? Wetting the beak."

Truscott's expression flattened. "That's bribery."

"Relax, man. I'm not doing it." Jacobson glanced at Leya then returned his attention to Truscott. "For all I know, Grady isn't doing it either. Maybe he's talking out his ass. You know how people are."

Leya asked, "Are most of your leads from Grady?"

Jacobson shrugged. "Not all." His protest was weak. "Sometimes I cold call and sometimes folks set an appointment."

She nodded. "But mostly the leads come from Grady?"

"Lately, yeah."

"How long has Spokane Solutions been in business?" Truscott asked.

Jacobson waggled a hand. "I don't know. Three years, I think. Maybe four. I've only been here for two. Why?"

"Has it gotten busier since Camp Faith opened up?"

"Oh, hell yeah." Jacobson chuckled. "That place has

been a gold mine for us. I hope the city never shuts it down."

***

Leya pulled into the parking lot of Lucky's Pawn. Only a few cars were in the lot at this time of morning. She parked and turned off the engine. Truscott popped open his door.

"Hold on," she said.

He glanced at her.

"If Lucky won't answer our questions," she said, "what's the plan?"

Truscott settled back into his seat. "We don't have enough to arrest Fitzgerald since we don't have any corroborating evidence or witness statements. The video we got of the alley doesn't show him at all. We're still running on supposition."

"Hey," she said, "he hasn't given us the security footage from his store yet."

Truscott snapped his fingers. "Let's attack that now. If we don't get it, we go back and write a warrant."

Leya studied the exterior of Lucky's Pawn. "So we're thinking the motive for the burglaries was to help promote the growth of his security business?"

Truscott sniffed dismissively. "Shit. It's like the plot of a Steven Seagal movie."

She eyed him.

"I mean bad."

"I got that, but criminals aren't smart. Their plan doesn't have to make sense."

Truscott shook his head. "It's just that I thought Fitzgerald would have been smarter than that."

"Me, too," Leya said. She slid out of her seat and slammed the car door. Truscott's door slammed a moment behind hers.

Inside Lucky's Pawn, the store was quiet as compared to the previous visits. Only a single customer was inside, and he browsed the jewelry section.

A man Leya had met several visits prior stood behind the counter. He had thinning gray hair and a handlebar mustache. He wore the green bowling shirt all employees did. His name tag read *Jerry!*

Truscott pulled his jacket to the side. "Is Grady in?"

Jerry shook his head. "We haven't heard from Lucky today."

"Would you mind calling him? Tell him Detectives Truscott and Navarro would like to speak with him."

Jerry noticeably swallowed before grabbing the telephone. He consulted an index card and dialed. After a moment, he shook his head. "Voice mail."

Truscott motioned for him to hang up.

"Is it like him not to come in?" Leya asked.

"Not without calling first. He's usually pretty good at letting one of us know if we gotta handle the opening by ourselves." Jerry leaned to see the guy at the jewelry counter. "I'll be over inna minute."

The customer waved his hand. "Take your time."

Jerry looked at Leya again. "Lucky says the morning sets the course of the ship." His forehead scrunched. "That's how you say that, isn't it?"

She shrugged. "Maybe. Is it abnormal to open alone?"

"I've done it a few times, but like I said, Lucky usually calls ahead to say we're on our own." Jerry leaned again to watch the customer at the jewelry counter. "I left him a couple of voicemails but still no call back."

Truscott said, "When Lucky arrives, have him call us. He knows the number."

"Should I tell him what it's regarding?"

"Tell him we want to buy a security system."

***

Grady Fitzgerald lived in far north Spokane off Rutter Parkway. Clusters of trees guarded the house like a phalanx of soldiers. They found the home with the help of Truscott's phone.

"Turn there," he said and pointed.

Leya entered a long, winding driveway. A large two-level house with a three-car garage sat several hundred feet back from the roadway. A red BMW 4 Series was parked in front of it.

"Maybe he ran to Mexico," Leya said.

"Because of a burglary ring?"

"You said the plan was like a Steven Seagal movie."

He eyed her. "Have you ever seen one?"

"Are they like Chuck Norris movies?"

"Sort of."

"Then no." Leya shook her head. "Definitely not."

Truscott clicked his tongue against the back of his teeth. He leaned forward to study the looming house. "Dealing in people's weaknesses certainly pays well."

They exited the car and approached the front door.

Even though it was chilly, the morning was pleasant. The sky was free of clouds and a light wind blew from the west. Something chattered in a nearby cluster of trees. A squirrel making last-minute preparations for winter, Leya thought.

Truscott rang the doorbell. He turned to study the BMW. "Maybe he can't park it in the garage because it's full of hot goods."

She angled her head. "Hot goods? Your movie should be on Lifetime."

Truscott waved her off. "They don't show Steven Seagal movies but think about it. If they're bringing the stolen items up here, that's a helluva drive." Grady Fitzgerald's home was twenty minutes from downtown.

Leya glanced around. The nearest neighbor wasn't within shouting distance. "It's a pretty good place to hide stolen stuff."

Truscott rang the doorbell again. He looked through the glass alongside the door. "Maybe he's out back."

"I've got it," Leya said.

She left the front steps and walked around the house. Even though it was November, the lawn was still green, and the shrub beds were filled with lush bark. Grady Fitzgerald took pride in his landscaping. A large deck jutted out from the second story of the house. A concrete patio was built underneath.

Leya took a moment to peer into the windows on the lower level. The first floor looked tidy. She ascended the deck stairs to the second level. Fitzgerald had an incredible view to the south, but Leya wouldn't allow herself to appreciate it. Maybe later, but there was always an officer safety concern with patio doors. A gunman could stand on the other side.

That turned out not to be an issue today, though.

Lying near the dining room table was Grady 'Lucky' Fitzgerald.

Blood pooled around his body.

# PART II

## Chapter 11

Detective Andrew Parker scratched his chin as he studied the case notes on an unsolved South Hill murder. He wasn't ready to give up on it and have the file moved to a cold status, but the crime was almost a year old now. The method of killing—the victim on his knees, a single gunshot to the back of the head—led Parker to believe it was a hit, the kind of murder not usually seen in Spokane.

Murders-for-hire had happened in town, of course. He'd had a meeting with his lieutenant and captain early on to discuss the history of such a thing. According to his chain of command, one of three precursors usually happened in local contract killings. The hiring party talked too much, the killer was too inexperienced and bungled the event, or the victims feared for their lives and warned their families.

Yet none of those had happened in this case. It was an efficient murder with no evidence or witnesses left behind. The victim's associates offered no reasonable explanation why the death occurred.

In the neighboring cubicle, Jessie Johnson clacked away on his keyboard. He'd just gotten off the phone on a follow-up interview. It sounded like it had gone well. He even laughed a couple of times with the witness. Maybe the partners would get to close another case and keep the brass believing in their ability to do their jobs.

Parker hated when cases went too long without viable leads. He pinched the bridge of his nose and turned the page. Every week, Parker pulled this same binder out and reread its contents in hopes something would jar loose. Perhaps a creative spark would ignite. Yet nothing like that had happened this morning.

Even with evidence and witnesses, he couldn't solve every case. Per FBI statistics, the national average for solving a murder was about fifty percent. The Spokane Major Crimes unit was slightly higher and Parker didn't want to do anything to bring that number down. Unfortunately, he might if he cried 'no joy' on this case and turned it in.

Lieutenant George Brand appeared at Parker's cubicle. He was the head of Major Crimes and a fussbudget. Brand reminded Parker of a toy his daughters played with—an enormous bear with a chubby face and kind eyes. Although the lieutenant hid his eyes behind round spectacles.

Parker occasionally wondered what drew a guy like Brand to a career in law enforcement. Was it the promise of helping the community? The man seemed more likely to collate budgets for a non-profit agency than run a Major Crimes division.

The lieutenant set a piece of paper on top of Parker's opened case binder. On it, in neat cursive handwriting, was an address.

"You're up," Brand said. He looked over his shoulder at Johnson. "You, too."

Parker snatched the note and studied it.

"Where's it at?" Johnson pushed his chair closer to

join the conversation.

"Rutter Parkway," Parker said.

"That's BFE."

Brand frowned disapprovingly.

"Bum Fuck Egypt," Johnson clarified.

"Yes, Johnson. I know." The lieutenant pointed at the note. "Two Property Crimes detectives are up there now."

Parker looked up at Brand. "Who?"

"Navarro and Truscott."

Johnson flashed a disapproving look. Parker suspected he knew why—Truscott.

"The victim," the lieutenant continued, "was the owner of Lucky's Pawn. He was shot to death."

Parker set the note on his desk and began rolling down the sleeves of his white shirt. "Why were Navarro and Truscott there?"

Brand glanced around to see if anyone was listening. It was an odd behavior from the lieutenant since he wasn't prone to gossip. He bent and lowered his voice before speaking. "They're assigned the Sprague Corridor burglaries. The ones associated with Camp Faith." He eyed both detectives. "The ones the press are having a heyday with."

Parker nodded. He read the paper and knew the fallout from the city's lack of response to the homeless epidemic.

"It's their suspicion—" Brand said after another glance around. He looked like a prairie dog poking its head out of the ground to search for danger. "That this Fitzgerald fellow might have been involved."

Parker didn't understand why Brand's statement of suspicion needed to be handled with any level of privacy. Far more salacious rumors were openly said in the department—unless it had something to do with an officer.

Damien Truscott was involved, so maybe the lieutenant's attempt at confidentiality had to do with that. Plenty of innuendo floated around the guy. Who knew what kind of problem he might have created? Maybe the department was trying to keep a lid on the case to reduce its liability.

Great, Parker thought. *They're handing us a turd.*

His jaw flexed as he fought against saying the first expletive that came to mind.

Brand straightened. "So, there you go," he said at regular volume. "Let me know what you find after you get there."

Both Parker and Johnson nodded.

"All right," the lieutenant said. "I'll update the captain."

Parker relaxed as Brand walked off. The man wasn't being quiet for any confidential reasons. The obsequious bastard was doing so because he wanted to be the first to notify the chain of command. He enjoyed controlling the flow of information. George Brand was an administrative choke point. Parker had run into his kind in the Army, too.

"Look at him," Johnson said. "The guy loves his job."

Parker shrugged—he was glad someone in the department did. He stood and grabbed his suit jacket from the back of his chair. "Ready?"

Johnson's jacket hung from a hook on the side of his cubicle. He lifted it, then slipped an arm in. "Tuck yourself in."

The back of Parker's shirt had come free from his pants. He tossed his jacket onto his desk and hurriedly adjusted himself.

"Wanna drive together?" Johnson asked. "Maybe hit a drive-through on the way and grab some lunch?"

"Let's drive separately in case we need to split up

afterward. Rutter Parkway is almost in Stevens County." Parker grabbed his jacket. "Besides, Brooke made me lunch."

"Jesus," Johnson said with a shake of his head. "She spoils you."

"I can't help it if I married right." Parker reached under his desk for his lunch box.

"I married right, too," Johnson said. He sounded defensive. "Ashley is great at other stuff."

The two men headed for the exit.

Johnson eyed Parker's lunch box. "What'd she make you?"

"Wouldn't you like to know?"

"It's always chicken."

"Not always."

Johnson grunted. "Almost always."

Parker pushed the door open. "Well, like I said, I married right."

***

Grady Fitzgerald lay face down with his arms splayed out. His feet were tangled in the legs of a tipped over dining room chair. His head was turned sideways and blood pooled underneath it.

Parker squatted and studied the dead man. It appeared a bullet had entered the left eye and blown a hole out the back of the skull.

A chair was pushed away from the end of the table. Beyond that was the sliding glass door to the back deck. Parker moved to the chair and squatted, carefully not to sit and transfer any potential evidence. He extended his arm as if he were holding a gun. If a bullet were to pass through the victim's head, it might have gone to the far wall, which was covered in pictures.

If the bullet was not sent on a different trajectory.

"What do you see?" Johnson asked.

"Gimme a minute."

Parker stood and carefully stepped around the fallen body. He walked across the room until he got to the wall. Sunlight shone through the sliding glass windows and reflected off the picture frames. Parker cocked his head left and right as he searched the various photographs. All the pictures were of the victim in locales around the world.

Eventually, he found a black framed picture with a jagged hole in its upper right. The photograph was of Grady Fitzgerald standing next to one of those red phone booths the British use.

Parker wanted to lift the frame and look at the wall. It was natural curiosity. However, it was best to wait for the forensic team to photograph it in place. Besides, what would he learn from seeing a bullet hole? He'd seen a deformed slug lodged in a wall before. It's not like he could guess the caliber.

He turned to Johnson. "The round passed through the victim and lodged in here."

His partner nodded and continued to work on his sketch pad. Johnson was a master at sketching scenes. Parker had once asked Johnson if he ever drew anything else—comics or still life. The guy was that good. Johnson had dismissed the question with a flippant "Don't be gay" response. Parker assumed Johnson did draw but didn't want anyone to know about it. He never asked his partner about it again.

Parker stepped back and studied the monstrous house once more. Five bedrooms, three baths, three-car garage. It stood on nearly four acres. No one lived with Fitzgerald currently. Had someone lived with him previously? Is that the reason he bought such a big house?

He jotted that question in his notebook. A former lover or spouse would be someone to follow up with. They might also carry a grudge of some sort.

The house was clean, excluding the dead body in the dining room. Did Fitzgerald have a cleaning crew? Parker jotted another note. He would need to look for evidence of such. Invoices or payments would suffice. If he found out a cleaning service was used, what days did they clean? Could someone have been here and seen the body? Or could one of the cleaning members be involved?

Parker wondered what a home this size cost. Even before the recent spike in housing prices, it likely was a huge number. He couldn't imagine what it would go for now.

"You ever meet the guy?" Johnson asked.

Parker looked over his shoulder. "Fitzgerald? Yeah. While I was in Property Crimes."

"Me, too. What'd you think of him?"

"He was a dick."

Johnson lowered his pad. "So the front door was unlocked."

"Sliding glass, too." Parker waved his hand. "But what's it matter? We're out here in the middle of nowhere."

"BFE," Johnson reminded.

"The guy probably didn't lock his doors while inside the house."

"Maybe he didn't fear his attacker."

Parker shrugged. "You done with the sketch?"

Johnson nodded.

"Let's wander through the house once more before we let everyone in."

The two detectives slowly worked their way through the Fitzgerald residence. For a house of such magnitude, each room was slightly underwhelming. Bedrooms had the requisite furniture, and everything was in its place. Nothing appeared disturbed as they walked through.

They headed down to the lower level. The first room they came to had a pool table, two pinball machines, and a vintage Pac-Man. No balls sat on the felt and the machines were quiet. It should have been a cheerful room, but it wasn't.

The rest of the lower level consisted of a laundry room, a weight room, and a pantry. When they finished the tour, Parker eyed Johnson. "Anything catch your eye?"

"Pawn brokering pays better than I thought."

"Ain't that the truth." Parker stepped by his partner. "Let's check the garage, then get forensics started."

The two men ascended the stairs and entered the garage. The light was already on, as someone had likely cleared it for suspects.

Had Parker expected this part of Fitzgerald's life to be messy, he would have been disappointed. The garage was neat. Three cars were parked side by side—all late sixties classics—a Chevrolet Corvette, a Ford Mustang, and an Oldsmobile 442. Parker liked cars, but he didn't know them well enough to pinpoint their years.

Johnson asked, "How much are those worth?"

"More than our annual salary."

Parker pushed a square button on the wall and the garage door slowly ascended.

"You stay here," he said, "and run evidence with the forensic team. I'll interview the Property Crimes detectives."

"Good luck with Truscott."

Parker grunted and headed for the driveway. Once outside, he pulled the cloth booties away from his shoes. He also removed the latex gloves from his hands. Parker walked to the edge of the inner perimeter. That line of yellow police tape designated only investigators and forensic personnel were allowed inside.

An officer with a clipboard stood nearby the tape. He logged anyone who entered or left the area.

Geri Utley and several crime scene technicians approached. She was the leader of the county's forensic unit. She carried a camera bag over her left shoulder. The team members behind her carried several toolboxes. Prior to entry, they'd slip into white hazmat suits. They were the ultimate professionals.

Parker lifted the line of yellow tape and Geri ducked underneath. He held it so the others could follow her.

"Johnson's waiting for you inside," Parker said.

Geri didn't stop walking. She called over her shoulder, "Always a pleasure, Andrew."

Parker turned to the officer. "You got them all?"

"Yes, sir."

Parker liked it when a crime scene went according to plan. His eyes shifted toward the Property Crimes detectives as they lingered near a Chevy Impala. Damien Truscott watched him with suspicion.

Well, Parker thought, it was going mostly according to plan.

***

"That's when I saw him on the floor," Detective Leya Navarro said.

"Then what did you do?" Parker asked.

"I opened the sliding glass door and went inside."

Parker glanced over her shoulder at Detective Damien Truscott as he chatted with Sergeant Ryan Yager. Both men stood near the forensic team's van, about thirty feet away. "And Truscott was at the front of the house?"

"Uh-huh. That's correct."

"How'd you know the sliding door was unlocked?"

"I didn't. It was instinct to try it."

"And when you opened it?"

"I pulled my gun. I didn't know if maybe the killer was still inside."

Parker nodded. "Then what?"

Navarro shrugged. "I called Truscott."

"On the radio?"

"My cell. We didn't bring our radios."

Parker didn't comment. He often left his radio in the car. In fact, it was on the passenger seat now. For officer safety reasons, it was a bad habit. The boxy piece of equipment was a pain in the ass to carry around, especially when a cell phone could easily fit in a pocket.

She continued. "He answered right away, and I told him what I found. He entered the house, then."

"Through the front door?"

"That's right."

Parker angled his head. "How'd he know it was unlocked?"

"He must have tried it like I did."

"What did you do then?"

Navarro shrugged again. "We searched the house for officer safety. We didn't locate anyone. Afterward, we called dispatch."

Parker made another note. "Did you touch the body?"

Navarro smirked. "He had a hole in his head. There was no reason for me to touch him."

"Had to ask."

"I understand, but it's not my first rodeo."

Parker looked around the property. "What were you doing up here?"

"Looking into Fitzgerald's involvement with the Sprague Corridor break-ins."

"Involved how?"

"We don't know that yet."

"You've seen his house." Parker motioned toward the opened garage. "And those cars aren't exactly cheap. I'd say the guy wasn't hurting for money."

Navarro rolled her eyes. "Regardless, we were looking at him."

"And now he's dead."

She crossed her arms.

"What evidence did you have against him?" Parker asked.

"A witness saw a suspicious group gathered behind his store. We also have video confirmation the group was working with someone inside his business."

"Did you ID Fitzgerald as that someone?"

"No."

Parker frowned. "That's pretty thin."

"When we approached Fitzgerald about it, he acted strange."

"How so?"

"Evasive." Navarro waved a hand. "He has security cameras in and around his store, but he still hasn't given us footage of the night in question."

Parker tapped his notepad. "Your proof was still circumstantial."

"He's also the owner of Security Solutions of Spokane."

"That's a problem because?"

Navarro's shoulders slumped. "Our working theory is he's burglarizing homes and businesses to promote his security company."

Parker couldn't contain his smile.

"Why is that so hard to believe?" Her face reddened. "He has—*had*—the perfect fall guy for the crime."

"And who is that?"

"Camp Faith. It's taking the blame for all the crime in the area."

Parker turned a palm upward. "Your theory is sound. Your proof weak."

"We know," Navarro said. "But I've struggled for months to put something together. We finally found a connection to Fitzgerald and the theory sort of fit."

Parker smiled. "Sounds far-fetched. Like some straight-to-video bullshit."

"That's what Truscott said, too."

His smile melted.

Leya jerked her head toward the house. "But there's a dead guy in there that makes me think maybe we were on to something."

"Be careful," Parker admonished. "You're making connections before weighing all the evidence."

"I already know the facts," Navarro said. "You're the one playing catch up."

Parker was playing catch up. "Thank you for your time, Detective."

***

Detective Damien Truscott crossed his arms. "That's when Leya called and said Fitzgerald was dead."

Parker grunted. "And you went inside?"

"You think what I did was wrong."

"I didn't say that."

"The look on your face did." Truscott hooked his thumbs around his ridiculous belt buckle. "I'll tell you something, Parker, and I'll stand by it if you want to quote me in your report, but I wasn't worried about destroying any fingerprints on the door handle. Leya was inside and Fitzgerald's killer might have been in there, too. If it was locked, I would have kicked the door in. I would have taken a dump in the middle of your crime scene if it meant protecting her."

Parker studied Truscott. The jerk looked like he listened to John Denver music—tweed sport coat, light blue dress shirt, and blue jeans with a white crease down each leg from repeated ironing. The only other guys who ever did that type of foolishness were the country boys Parker served with while in the Army. The guy's boots even looked like he shined them. All Truscott needed was a hat and he would have looked like that actor who starred in *McCloud*, that show from the seventies that Parker's mom watched on reruns. Truscott was just asking to be mocked.

"I'm not judging you for entering the house," Parker said.

Truscott briefly pinched his lips. "I apologize for misreading the situation."

However, Parker judged the man for leaving the Special Victims Unit. If the rumors were true, he abandoned the team because he couldn't handle what he'd seen. At least, that's what some of the SVU detectives had told Parker after Truscott rotated out. Parker disliked being a Major Crimes detective—not for the work, but the hours. He hated how it affected the time with his family and his pursuit of bodybuilding.

But he was stuck. Major Crimes was the big leagues. There was no higher honor in the department. Parker would never admit failure by stepping down from the assignment. The Special Victims Unit was a rung lower than Major Crimes—a Triple A league, to continue the baseball metaphor. Truscott supposedly gave it up to return to Property Crimes, which had to be Single A in this comparison.

Parker knew Johnson felt the same way about the man since they had talked about it. He imagined most of the other investigators would think Truscott was weak. How could they not? But what about the administration? Was Truscott tainted goods in its eyes? Were the brass hoping the man would keep his head down and stay out of trouble? If so, stumbling on a dead body linked to such a high-profile case couldn't be good.

Parker tapped his pen against the top of his notepad. "Do you know anyone who might have wanted to kill Fitzgerald?"

"Not really."

"Navarro said you suspected him of being involved with the Sprague Corridor burglaries."

Truscott grabbed the lapels of his coat. Now, he looked like a college professor, about to make an important point. Were there cowboy professors? Surely some existed in places like Wyoming and the Dakotas. "It was starting to look that way."

Parker tilted his head. "But you're not convinced."

"Not really."

"Want to elaborate?"

Truscott held onto the lapels and flapped his elbows twice—a cowboy bird. "There were some dots we still needed to connect."

Getting the man to give him any information was like pulling teeth. "Navarro mentioned that. Why don't you fill me in?"

Truscott's face tightened.

"Something wrong?" Parker asked.

"Feels like we're about to lose our case."

"We're not prosecuting a case here."

"No," Truscott said, "it feels like you're about to take it from us—lock, stock, and barrel."

Parker understood now. This was about territorial pissing. He pointed his pen at Truscott's face. The man stood several inches taller than him. "Listen, asshole.

This is a homicide investigation. If it wraps yours into it, tough shit. Murder trumps burglary. Got it? Push in your chips and leave the table."

Truscott nodded twice, then shook his head. It wasn't a confusing signal to read. He had accepted Parker's explanation, but he didn't like it.

"So about those fucking dots," Parker said.

"Yeah." Truscott glanced around. Parker thought the man was looking for either Navarro or Sergeant Yager. "We suspected Fitzgerald might have hired the men responsible for the burglaries, but we haven't been able to confirm that."

"You're assuming the burglaries are a concentrated effort."

"That's correct," Truscott said.

"Because of the lanyards Navarro mentioned."

Truscott watched Parker for a moment before nodding.

"What's it going to take to connect that dot?"

"More detective work."

Smart ass, Parker thought. He scratched his chin with his notepad to buy time to calm himself. He'd gotten angry, and that only gave power to the interviewee. Had this been a suspect, Parker would have misplayed his hand. He was lucky it was only Truscott. "If you connect that dot, what's that do for us?"

"Us?"

"The department." Parker waved a hand. "The city. Take your pick."

"Linking Fitzgerald to the burglaries solidifies the means. Then we've got to work out the motive."

Hollywood loved to talk about motive, but it was a bonus in Parker's world. Means and opportunity were the only prongs truly needed to convict. However, prosecuting attorneys loved knowing a motive, since it helped sway a jury.

"What was the opportunity?" Parker asked. "The businesses and homes in the corridor?"

"Camp Faith." Truscott scuffed the bottom of his boot across the ground. "Just waiting to be the scapegoat."

"Back to motive. You're linking Fitzgerald to the burglaries because he owns a security company."

"That's a theory," Truscott said, "and not a strong one, I'll admit."

Parker's gaze drifted to the open garage and the three classic cars parked inside. "Let's say I buy this story. What did Fitzgerald do with the stolen property?"

"He wasn't running it through his store. We checked."

If Grady Fitzgerald wasn't fencing a cache of stolen goods through his store, what was he doing with it? An image came to Parker of a pirate's cave stocked with chests brimming with gold coins and shiny jewels. He could see it clear as day as he and his friends had watched *The Goonies* a dozen times while growing up. One-Eyed Willy's shimmering haul had thrilled him every time he saw it.

"So if the guy didn't fence the goods through his store—" Parker waved his hand toward the house. "And if he didn't keep it here, then he's hiding all that booty somewhere else."

Truscott grinned.

"What?"

"You said booty, like a pirate." Truscott waved a dismissive hand. "It reminded me of a movie, is all."

Parker's face warmed again. He didn't want to have anything in common with this guy. "So, he's keeping the goods elsewhere?"

Truscott's smile faded. "Maybe. Again, we're assuming."

Which led Parker back to his initial question—who would want to hurt Grady Fitzgerald? If the man was indeed involved in a string of burglaries, then any victim of a break-in was a potential suspect in the murder. It was a tenuous argument, Parker admitted, but one that should still be put on the board if a suspect didn't quickly emerge.

"I need you to write up what you saw and did here," Parker said.

Truscott nodded.

"You'll keep working these burglary cases?"

"Unless you take them away from us."

Parker's brow furrowed.

"Of course, we'll keep working them," Truscott said. "They're open until we prove who was behind them."

"If you find anything pertinent to Fitzgerald, I'd appreciate it if you'd keep Johnson and me in the loop."

"Sure."

"Thanks for your time, Detective."

Truscott walked toward Navarro and Sergeant Yager. Parker watched the three of them for a few moments. How could Truscott be okay with moving down to Single A? It had to be like going back to high school. A real man would have kept his mouth shut and sucked it up. Or he would have quit and gone to a different department.

There was no way the guy was happy, Parker thought.

Truscott smiled when the sergeant clapped his shoulder. Then he shared a laugh with Navarro.

Parker tsked, then went in search of Johnson.

***

Parker leaned against the hood of his car and reviewed his notes. He looked up when an engine softly revved. A black Chevy Impala wound its way up the driveway.

"Shit," Parker muttered. He closed his notebook and tucked it inside his jacket pocket.

The Impala stopped and Captain Gary Ackerman soon climbed out of the driver's seat. The silver-haired man assessed the scene. Ackerman oversaw the entire Investigations unit, which meant he was not only Parker and Johnson's boss but Navarro and Truscott's as well.

He wore a dark tailored suit, light blue shirt, and yellow printed tie. Ackerman always looked ready to step onto the set of one of those political talk shows. Rumors abounded about the captain—he had political aspirations beyond the department, he had ties to the mob, and he was a silent partner with some real estate developers. Parker listened to all the scuttlebutt but chose to believe the only story he knew for certain—Ackerman controlled the career path of every detective within the Spokane Police Department.

The captain's gaze landed on Parker. He stepped out of the path of the car door, shut it, and strolled over like he didn't have a care in the world. Or perhaps it was as if he was on camera. But there was no media present. The jackals had yet to get a whiff of the murder.

If the press had heard about Fitzgerald's death, would they have cared? They did not know about his potential involvement with the burglaries. At worst, a reporter from the local paper would call with questions and they would write a small article about the death of a local business owner.

As Ackerman approached, Parker registered something was wrong. The tightness in the man's face didn't match his carefree walk. "Parker," he said when he neared. "Where's your partner?"

"Inside with the evidence techs."

Ackerman's gaze drifted about the scene. It seemed to stop on the Property Crimes team. "They confirmed the victim as Grady Fitzgerald?"

"It's confirmed."

Still not looking at Parker, the captain asked, "Did you interview Navarro and Truscott?

"I did."

"They filled you in on their investigation?"

Parker nodded. "That's correct."

The captain continued to survey the crime scene. "What did you think of them?"

"Sir?"

Ackerman looked directly at Parker now, but he didn't elaborate on his question.

Parker cleared his throat. "They seem fine."

"As in competent?"

"Yes."

Ackerman's brow furrowed. "Did you get the sense they were holding anything back?"

"Sir?"

The captain studied Parker for an uncomfortable moment.

"No," Parker said. "They seemed forthcoming."

"Competent and forthcoming." Ackerman looked toward Navarro and Truscott.

Parker also stole a glance at the Property Crimes detectives. They talked with Sergeant Yager and didn't seem the least bit concerned by the captain's presence. That would surely change if they knew the questions he was asking. Ackerman had never shown up at a crime scene before with questions like these.

"Is something wrong?" Parker asked.

Ackerman's gaze returned to him. "Have you heard the name Fred Zimmer?"

"Sounds familiar."

"He's been on the news lately. He's outspoken about Camp Faith and the negative impact on the neighborhood."

Parker snapped his fingers. "Lug Nutz."

“Right,” Ackerman said. “He has accused the department of knowing a local business owner was behind the Sprague crime spree, but we refused to make an arrest. He stopped short of naming names, yet it was clear he had inside information. Probably Councilwoman Hembree. They’ve gotten chummy lately.”

Parker didn’t respond. A business owner spouting off didn’t bother him, neither did a council member. He figured it was the way the world worked, especially with politicians. The city council often said publicly they supported the police, but they frequently threw the department under the proverbial bus when it suited their needs.

Ackerman continued. “The press said we didn’t return their phone calls, which might be true. I don’t know with our PIO system.”

The department had an officially designated Public Information Officer who handled all forward-facing communications with the press. However, SPD also empowered twelve other officers to handle these duties on an as-needed basis. Those specially trained officers handled low-level media contacts and after-hours emergencies. The purpose of decentralizing the communication was an effort to improve the relationship with the press. The unfortunate result was an occasional hiccup, like a reporter not calling the officially designated Public Information Officer and leaving a message for one of the part-time PIOs instead.

“A reporter called me for a follow-up quote after the interview posted,” Ackerman said. “That’s how I became aware of Zimmer’s interview. I couldn’t say what he accused of us wasn’t true, otherwise, I’d be called a liar later. So, I said what we always do.”

Parker knew the words almost by rote, even as Ackerman said them.

"'We're in the middle of a continuing investigation and I'm unable to comment at this time.' As soon as I ended the call, I hunted down Zimmer's interview."

"And you think Navarro and Truscott gave the guy some inside scoop?"

Ackerman shrugged. "I don't know what to think. I only know you're late to the party."

"I've already heard that today."

"Take that as a positive. It means you're above suspicion."

"Suspicion of what?"

"We have a leak."

Parker glanced at Navarro and Truscott again. He didn't know either detective well. He'd worked with Truscott a little while on patrol, but mostly knew the man because of the recent rumors. However, Parker couldn't imagine either detective leaking information to Fred Zimmer.

"What's that mean for us?" Parker asked.

"For a while," Ackerman said, "the information goes one way in this investigation." He jerked his thumb upward. "Don't share anything with Property Crimes until we know the leak didn't come from them. Got it?"

"Sure." Parker's voice must not have held the conviction the captain wanted.

"Listen," he said, "we're up to our asses in political alligators right now. Everybody wants to take a bite out of us with this Camp Faith fiasco. We don't need some loose-lipped sons-of-bitches making it worse."

Ackerman rarely swore. For him to do so now showed how frustrating the homeless situation had grown for the administration.

The captain continued. "When I get back to the department, I'll send Navarro and Truscott's report on Fitzgerald to you."

Parker kept his face impassive. He didn't have a problem keeping elements of a case secret. He did it all the time. However, this wasn't a normal investigation. If Grady Fitzgerald was indeed involved in a string of burglaries, he'd want to talk with Navarro and Truscott. Restricting the flow of information would make getting to the truth difficult.

"You need anything from me?" Ackerman asked.

"No, sir."

Jessie Johnson stepped out of the house then and made eye contact with the captain.

"Looks like your partner is done. Get him in the loop."

"Yes, sir."

Ackerman walked off.

Johnson peeled off his latex gloves as he approached. He tucked his sketch pad under his right arm. "What'd Ackerman want?"

"To promote us."

"Yeah? To what?"

Parker smirked. "Spies."

# Chapter 12

Parker dropped into his swivel chair. He rolled up the sleeves of his shirt as the computer whirred to life. The internal fan wheezed as if it were about to give out. Parker wondered how much longer the department would continue to operate on these antiquated systems. He had a flat screen monitor to give the appearance of modernity, but the computer tower was several generations old.

All the other Major Crimes detectives operated on similar systems; Parker had checked one quiet rainy afternoon when he was restless. Considering the unit's mission, the department should want to upgrade their computer hardware. Major Crimes wasn't Volunteer Services. The team handled the most prominent cases, and its investigators were supposedly the best. So why were they relegated to substandard computers?

The monitor flickered and changed from black to a background image of the department's badge. However, he still wasn't prompted with a login screen. He imagined the CPU chugging through its calculations as it tried to finish the boot sequence.

Maybe Parker could write a children's book—*The Little Computer That Could.* People wouldn't buy it, though. It would remind them of their work problems every time they read it to their kids.

New computers ranked low on the department's hierarchy of needs, Parker thought. It was the only explanation for working on such dated equipment. If SPD was forced to rank their spending priorities, Parker guessed that life safety items like guns and ballistic vests came in at number one. Obviously, human life was more important than computers. It was an argument Parker couldn't refute. SWAT and Tactical Team needs ranked next because command staff liked flashy toys and they were a great recruiting tool. Annual training demands for all officers required a chunk of money which brought that category in at number three. And cars, Parker thought. What about those? Cops couldn't respond to calls for service without those.

He glanced at Johnson who seemed to wait for his computer to boot up as well. Had the city's IT geeks decided it was time to shove an update on them? Parker looked toward the ceiling.

Replacing old computers with new ones for some deskbound detectives would rank so low it probably wouldn't even be a budgetary line item, Parker decided. They'd never make it a systemwide job. Instead, it would be done one computer at a time. A bubblegum and chicken wire solution. Even the Army wasn't this bad.

The login screen finally popped up and Parker muttered, "Thank God."

He entered his password and gained access to the various programs. Parker should have transferred his notes to the file, but Parker jumped to the internet first. There was something he wanted to see. Ackerman hadn't said which local news channel had interviewed Fred Zimmer, but there were only four choices. It took a few minutes for Parker to find it.

The video had a clickbait worthy headline: ARSON VICTIM ACCUSES SPD OF WITHHOLDING INFORMATION. Parker felt dirty for rewarding the news channel with a click. He was only one person, but he didn't want to encourage them to do more of this.

An advertisement for a local appliance company started. The spokesmodel, an attractive blond woman, smiled as she stood next to a refrigerator. The sound was louder than Parker expected, and he turned down his speakers.

Johnson leaned back from his desk. "What're you watching?"

Parker motioned him over. "That interview Ackerman told me about."

When the advertisement finished, the news clip started. An establishing shot of Camp Faith came on while a woman narrated.

"*Crime of all sorts has spiked in the East Sprague Corridor.*"

Johnson scooted his chair over to Parker.

The narration continued. "*Burglaries, assaults, property damage, and graffiti are common occurrences. Many in the community have correlated this increase in crime to the presence of Camp Faith. A vocal proponent of this belief, Fred Zimmer, had his business and property torched yesterday morning. Today, he has a different stance.*"

The video cut to an image of a female reporter and Fred Zimmer standing in front of the burned-out Lug Nutz building. Zimmer wore a red polo shirt with his business logo on the left breast.

"*I was led to believe,*" Zimmer said, "*members of Camp Faith were behind all the crime in our neighborhood. I no longer believe that. While some Camp Faith members may commit crimes, they are certainly not behind all the criminal activity.*"

The reporter pulled the microphone back to her. "*What made you change your mind?*"

"*It's come to my attention,*" Zimmer said, "*the police know who is responsible for the break-ins and it's someone within our own business community.*"

Johnson shook his head. "Here we go."

Parker shushed him.

"*Have they made any arrests?*" the reporter asked.

"*No,*" Zimmer said, "*and that's the problem. I want to know why the department is protecting this business owner. What does this person have on the chief? What kind of loyalty is owed them?*"

"*Who is this individual?*"

Zimmer squinted at the screen. "*I'm not at liberty to say, but the police know. Ask them.*"

"*Where did you get this information?*"

"*From a source within the department.*"

The camera cut to a shot with the reporter talking with Councilwoman Marjorie Hembree. She was a thin woman with a mannish haircut. Her angular features were free of makeup. Her brown pantsuit seemed more suitable to the 1980s, but she wore it well.

"*If this is true,*" Hembree said with a look of stern disapproval, "*that the police department is protecting a business leader while they run a criminal enterprise, then heads will roll. I promise you. I've staked my reputation on being a reformer and I won't hesitate to go after the SPD leadership.*"

The picture changed and suddenly the reporter was outside city hall. Citizens walked behind her on their way into the building. "*Calls to the police department were unreturned at the time of this story. This is—*"

Parker paused the video. His gaze drifted into the narrative provided by the website. There was a statement at the bottom of the story.

NOTE: SPOKANE POLICE CAPTAIN GARY ACKERMAN CLAIMED THE DEPARTMENT, "WAS IN THE MIDDLE OF A CONTINUING INVESTIGATION" AND WAS UNABLE TO PROVIDE FURTHER COMMENT.

Johnson mumbled, "Loose lips sink ships," and scooted back to his desk.

Parker closed the internet browser. "If they knew it was Fitzgerald, why didn't they out him on the camera?"

"They could have gotten sued if it wasn't true."

"Good point. You think either of them would have said his name if they knew the man was dead?"

***

It was almost five when Parker's desk phone rang. He didn't pick it up but continued to focus on the sentence he was trying to construct for his report. No matter what he wrote, the words failed to convey the message he wanted to deliver about the positioning of Grady Fitzgerald's body. He could take the lazy way out and simply write "face down" since the photographs would do a more than adequate job of telling the story. However, Parker always worried that a day might come that the pictures would disappear prior to his testimony, and everyone would be forced to rely on his narrative.

The phone rang again.

He pressed the delete key, and the cursor zoomed backward. An alternative description wasn't leaping at him. He should just write three or four choppy sentences and be done with it.

Once more, the phone rang. Johnson leaned back in his chair. "Hey, yo."

Parker snatched the receiver from the cradle. Irritated, he said, "Parker." His attention remained on his report; its lack of clarity bothered him.

"Yes. Hello? This is Bryce Harmon."

Parker cocked his head and looked at the binders on the upper shelf of his cubicle. They were the open cases he was working. No suspect in them had retained Harmon as legal counsel. Parker's mind spun through the active cases grinding their way through the court system. Harmon wasn't counsel on any of them—at least, he hadn't been.

"And?" Parker said. It seemed the least offensive thing to say. The two had sparred on cases in the past.

"It's my understanding you've been assigned the Grady Fitzgerald case."

Parker pulled the receiver from his ear and stared at it. How did Harmon know about that? No press release had been issued yet. Parker put the phone back to his ear. "That's right."

"In that case," Harmon said, "my client would like to speak with you."

Parker leaned back in his chair. Was Harmon's client Fitzgerald's murderer? Did he want to turn himself in? Could it be that easy? "Who's your client?"

"Quaid Webb."

"Who?" Parker asked.

"He has information that might be helpful to your case."

"Would you two like to come in now?"

"Right now would be troublesome. I'm on my way back from Colville." Parker picked up the traffic noise then. "Would tomorrow work?"

Saturday, Parker thought. He scratched his chin. He hated taking time away from Brooke and the kids. Parker grabbed his pen and tapped the top of it against his desk. "Fill me in on how your client fits in with this murder."

"He has information." The attorney's tone was clipped.

"Did I do something to annoy you?"

"No." Harmon expelled a large breath of air. "I apologize. Things have… changed on my end. We were supposed to meet with Detectives Navarro and Truscott on Monday."

Parker's face tightened. "What for?"

"It might not matter anymore. So, tomorrow at ten? We'll come to you."

"Is your client confessing?"

"To what?"

"Murdering Grady Fitzgerald."

Harmon clucked. "Not if I have anything to say about it."

The call ended.

Parker held the receiver for several moments until a beeping started on the line. He placed the phone back into its cradle and stood.

Johnson leaned back in his chair. "Where you headed?"

"Property Crimes," Parker said over his shoulder as he walked away.

***

Parker searched for Leya Navarro, but she wasn't at her desk. It looked orderly as if she might have already shut down for the day. It was Friday after all. Maybe she had called it quits and went home. Parker remembered how it was when he was a Property Crimes detective. He liked those times. Unfortunately, it didn't help him now.

"Shit."

He didn't want to talk with Damien Truscott again. From the country boy attire to the rumors concerning his departure, too much about the man bugged Parker. Yet, he needed some background information on Quaid Webb.

Parker moved deeper into the Property Crimes unit and found Truscott sitting at his cubicle. The man hunched over his keyboard with a half-eaten apple stuck between his teeth. He looked up when Parker asked, "Got a minute?"

Truscott bit into the fruit and pulled it from his mouth. "Yup," he said as he chewed.

"Bryce Harmon called about some douchebag named

Quaid Webb."

Truscott swallowed. "What'd he call you for?"

"He asked if I'd been assigned the Fitzgerald murder then suggested we meet in the morning."

"That's cute." Truscott tossed the apple into his trash can. "Webb is our prime suspect in the string of burglaries."

"I thought that Grady Fitzgerald was."

"We've got video of Webb outside Lucky's Pawn."

Parker cocked his head. "He's one of the guys you think Fitzgerald hired?"

"That's right."

"You haven't arrested him?"

"We don't have enough proof." Truscott rubbed his hands together. "Standing outside a pawnshop at night with what looks to be a fake Camp Faith ID is hinky as hell but not illegal."

"You couldn't get him to admit to anything?"

Truscott shook his head. "No, then Harmon shut down our questioning."

Parker crossed his arms. "This Webb character must be pretty good to afford a guy like Bryce Harmon."

"That's the thing. He's not. Navarro and I thought—" Truscott motioned in the direction of her cubicle. "—Fitzgerald had provided Harmon as counsel for Webb. Now that he's dead…" He let the thought taper off.

Parker shrugged. "That shouldn't change anything. The legal relationship has already been established."

"But who's going to pay the bills?"

"Fitzgerald's estate, I guess." Parker's head bobbled. "Assuming Fitzgerald hired him in the first place."

Truscott stood. "The bigger question is how did Harmon hear about the murder? Have you released his name to the news?"

Ackerman's admonishment to not share anything of

importance with Property Crimes came back to Parker then. Anything that might be shared with the public didn't seem to be something he had to keep from Truscott. "We haven't released anything about the crime yet."

Truscott rapped his knuckles on his desk. "Maybe Webb killed him and called his attorney to get in front of it."

Parker shrugged. "Or maybe he thinks he has something of value. Something to trade."

"He wants to do it with you instead of us. Why?"

"I already told you—murder trumps property crimes."

Truscott rolled his eyes. "Thanks for the reminder."

"Get pissy if you want," Parker said, "but you know how the system works."

"Better than you, I'd imagine."

The statement gave Parker pause.

Truscott continued. "Leya set up a meeting with them for Monday morning."

"Yeah. Harmon confirmed it."

"I wonder if they'll cancel."

"Maybe they'll keep it," Truscott said.

"And see what comes of my meeting?"

Truscott nodded. "Playing both ends against the middle?"

"Attorneys are always looking for an angle. Did you have a plan for your Monday meeting?"

"We have some photo arrays ready to go." Truscott grabbed a file from his desk and handed it to Parker. "We were hoping Webb would identify the inside man."

Parker flipped through the pages. "Why are there six?"

"That's the number of employees at Lucky's Pawn including Fitzgerald."

"Why not bring in each of the employees?" Parker asked. "Sweat them old school."

“A group of guys hanging in an alley isn’t a crime.”

“But the fake Camp Faith IDs show some nefarious intent.” Parker gave the file back.

“Nefarious. I like that word.” Truscott set the folder on his desk. “We gotta be careful. I’m sure you’ve heard how political this whole mess is. Every which way we turn, we’re bumping into someone telling us to watch our tails.”

Ackerman’s warning rang in his ears.

“Navarro and I don’t want to be wrong about Fitzgerald,” Truscott said. “We pushed on the guy, but he didn’t say squat.” He tapped his sternum. “I wanted him to be involved. Trust me. Maybe he wasn’t. It never felt right.”

Parker shoved his hands into his pockets. The Property Crimes detectives had knowledge on the burglaries. He didn’t want to internalize all that information while trying to keep his eye on Fitzgerald’s murder.

“Listen,” he said. “Harmon and Webb are coming in tomorrow morning at ten. Why don’t you join in?”

“Yeah, thanks. I appreciate that.”

“Invite Navarro, too.”

Truscott nodded.

He pointed at the file. “Bring those six packs with you.” Parker took a step and paused.

“Something else?” Truscott asked.

There was. Parker wanted to ask about the rumors that swirled around the man. Why had he left SVU? Had he stepped down from one of the most highly coveted units in the department or was he kicked out? If it was the former, was it worth the judging eyes and whispered comments?

Parker didn’t ask. Better for him not to know. When the days got bad for him in Major Crimes, Parker didn’t want the temptation of knowing Truscott might be happier back in Property Crimes. That would eat at him and might encourage him to do something stupid.

He lifted a hand. “It’s nothing. See you in the morning.”

***

Parker entered the house and braced himself for impact. Nothing happened, though.

“Hello?” he called. “I’m home.”

No one answered.

Parker suspected his wife was around somewhere because the aroma of cooking beef wafted to where he stood. An electronic voice softly drifted from the kitchen. Brooke often listened to an audiobook while she prepared dinner.

He closed the front door and tossed his keys into a wooden bowl that sat on a nearby stand.

Parker hunched with expectation when someone giggled from the other room. Several hushes followed and the giggling stopped. Parker smiled and he tiptoed forward.

A squeaky floorboard often irritated him, and he had learned to step over it at night so as not to wake anyone. However, he purposefully settled his weight on it. The floor creaked loudly.

From around the corner, the youngest of his girls popped out. Willow’s hands were together, and her index fingers extended like a mock gun. “Hands up, buster!”

Parker feigned shock as he lifted his arms into the air. “I give!”

The other girls jumped out now. Hailey, the oldest, threw her hands into the air with exasperation. “You were supposed to wait!”

“Yeah,” cried Charlotte. “Why didn’t you wait?”

Willow shoved her fingers further out and proudly proclaimed, "I got him!"

Parker lowered his arms to touch the heads of his girls. "You got me," he said. "All of you."

"Mom!" Hailey shouted toward the kitchen. "Willow ruined our ambush."

"Yeah," Charlotte said. "She ruins everything!"

"Give your father some space," Brooke called from the other room. "He's not even in the door yet."

The three girls looked questioningly at him.

"I'm in the door," Parker said. "How about a hug?" He opened his arms but none of the girls moved toward him.

Hailey glared at Willow. "I'm never playing with you again." She scampered up the nearby stairs before Willow could reply.

"Ruiner," Charlotte added then thudded behind her older sister.

"Mom!" Willow called, but she didn't wait for a response. She pursued her sisters up the stairs. Their bedroom door slammed but quickly reopened. Bickering immediately started.

When Parker entered the kitchen, Brooke tapped her digital tablet with a knuckle and silenced her audiobook.

"Can you believe they schemed on that for more than thirty minutes?"

"It went flawlessly." Parker leaned on the nearby counter. "What are you making?"

"For us—grilled steak salad. I've got a side of ravioli for the girls. You know how they are with the greens."

Brooke was exceptionally caring when it came to ensuring Parker followed a clean diet. When he was younger, he ate more bulking foods. However, he couldn't dedicate as much time for adding weight then shredding. The demands of his career didn't allow it. If he wanted to continue to body build, he needed to be more disciplined. Therefore, he ate a regimented diet. It wasn't exactly kid friendly.

"How was your day?"

"Caught a new case," Parker said.

"But you're home on time."

He shrugged. "I have to go in tomorrow."

Brooke's shoulders slumped. "I have a hair appointment. You were going to watch the girls."

"Consider it a call out. Besides, it won't be all day."

She rolled her eyes. "I guess I can ask my mom to watch them."

"There you go."

"For a guy who wanted three, you sure act cavalier about their care."

Parker touched his chest. "I worry about them."

"Uh-huh." She nodded. "Then what's this about going in on a Saturday? The weekend is family time."

"Couldn't be helped. We got a late tip and could only meet with the guy and his attorney tomorrow."

"Likely story." She smiled as she sliced some vegetables.

Parker would have preferred to spend his Saturday with his family. He hadn't confessed to Brooke how much he hated working in Major Crimes. If she found out, she would simply suggest he leave the assignment.

Only it wasn't that simple. She had no idea how a stigma would follow someone after stepping down from an assignment like Major Crimes. Damien Truscott carried a patina of failure now. It would forever discolor the rest of his career. Parker fought hard for his reputation. He would never move down from this assignment. He'd bury his feelings until he determined a way out—either by transfer or promotion. Unfortunately, he couldn't figure out a better assignment within the department and a promotion to sergeant would likely send him back to graveyard.

If Brooke knew about his unhappiness, she'd focus on his well-being as if it were her singular mission. Brooke might even suggest he leave the job to the detriment of their finances. She'd find ways to further tighten their budget, or she'd reenter the workforce.

Parker never stopped her from returning to her former employer, but he knew how much she enjoyed being around the girls. Having a stay-at-home wife might have been old-fashioned, but it gave Parker a strange sense of pride. He liked that the girls had their mom with them daily.

The couple had already tightened their budget to the point where it felt like they strangled it. They hadn't been on a real vacation in years and several house remodeling projects were already on hold until they could save up for them. Every overtime dollar Parker earned went into a separate savings account. Unfortunately, it had been raided several times for one unforeseen expense or another.

Parker lightly tapped the counter. "Hey, I'm sorry about the overtime tomorrow."

"I think you're addicted to it."

"It's definitely not that."

She put the spatula down and crossed her arms. "I don't have anything to worry about, do I?"

"What do you mean?"

"I hear the stories the other wives tell."

Parker straightened. "Don't be weird."

"You're not keeping a badge bunny on the side, are you?"

He chuckled. "Definitely not. And nobody says that."

"The other wives do. Why? What do your buddies call them?"

"I don't know, but not that." Parker moved toward

Brooke and slipped his arms around her. “Jessie and I’ve got to meet this guy and his attorney along with some Property Crimes detectives. Shouldn’t take long. When we’re done, I’ll head home.”

“Are any of these detectives hot?”

“Jessie, but you’ve met him.”

Brooke’s eyes narrowed. “You know I’m crazy, right?”

Parker patted her butt. “Baby crazy.”

“No.” She wriggled out of his arms. “No more.”

“You say that now.”

She pointed out of the kitchen. “Get changed. Dinner’s almost ready.”

He backpedaled. “We could try for a boy.”

“With our luck, we’d get another girl.”

“And that would be a bad thing?”

“Out!”

# Chapter 13

Damien Truscott glanced at Leya Navarro before asking Parker, “Where’s your partner?”

He jerked his head in the general direction of the restrooms. “Indisposed.”

Truscott wore a red plaid shirt, a pair of pressed Wranglers, and brown boots. Parker imagined the guy driving a pickup with a gun rack in the back. It probably had an American flag in the back window with some silly saying like *These Colors Don’t Run*. In his right hand, he held a folder and a notepad.

“How do we want to do this?” Truscott glanced at Navarro. “There’s not enough space in one of the interview rooms for all of us.”

Navarro wore a tan shirt, blue jeans, and soft boots. She would have looked like a woman about to spend a day shopping at the mall if it weren’t for the gun and badge on her hip. She carried a notepad and pen. She asked, “Is there somewhere else we could interview him?”

Had this been during the regular week, Parker would have contacted one of the geeks from the IT department and asked them to set up a camera and microphone in the conference room. That way, everyone could be present, and the interview could be properly recorded.

Unfortunately, it was Saturday morning, and the Public Safety Building was quiet.

“I’d like to have the interview recorded,” Parker said, “so we need an interview room.”

Truscott looked to Navarro.

Parker continued. “Webb and his attorney will be in there. I’ll be there, too. That’s three. Normally, I’d say

Johnson runs with me and we would kick the two of you out."

The Property Crimes detectives spoke at the same time.

"This was my case!" Navarro blurted.

Truscott smacked the file. "Fucking bullshit."

Parker lifted his hand to stop them from going further, but he didn't speak. He wasn't going to fight to be heard.

The Property Crimes detectives said a few more words before their indignation petered out.

"I would suggest," Parker said slowly, "Johnson watch from the viewing room. That way, one of you could be in there to address the burglaries."

Truscott lifted his chin toward Navarro. "This is her case first. She should be in there with you."

Navarro remained stone faced.

"Besides," Truscott said, "she'd probably do better with Bryce Harmon."

Parker nodded. "Are those the arrays?"

Truscott handed the folder to him.

On the top paper were six photos of white men positioned in two rows of three. In the furthest spot on the bottom row was Grady Fitzgerald. Parker spread the pages wider, but he did not know who he should have been looking for on the other pages. He tucked them back together and handed the file to Navarro.

"All right," Parker said. "When we get in there, I'll start the interview. Then I'll pass it to you. Understand?"

Navarro nodded.

Parker checked his watch. "Shouldn't be too much longer."

The three detectives stared at one another. Each forced an awkward smile.

"Navarro," Parker said. "Got any kids?"

"Two girls."

He smiled. "No kidding. I've got three." Parker looked at Truscott. "What about you?"

"I don't have any girls." He thumbed over his shoulder. "I'm gonna start some coffee." He wandered off.

They watched Truscott leave.

Parker wouldn't comment on the other detective, not to the woman who was now his partner. That was just asking for trouble. He wondered what the hell was taking Johnson so long.

"It's too bad we have to be here on a Saturday," Navarro said.

Parker had lost plenty of nights and weekends to the job now. The worst part about today was he made the choice to do it. The call outs to crime scenes were never his decision.

"Maybe you get to catch a killer," Navarro said. "That's pretty cool, right?"

It was the same attitude Parker had prior to joining Major Crimes. After a while, the reality of his situation set in, but she didn't want to hear about his woes. So he said, "Yeah, pretty cool."

Jessie Johnson walked over and dropped into his chair. "When are these douchebags showing up?"

Parker's cell phone rang, and he answered it. "All right," he said and immediately hung up. "Harmon and his client are at the west entrance."

Navarro glanced in the direction of the doors. "I'll go get them."

"I've got it," Parker said, but he made no move to get out of his chair. The frustration at meeting with Bryce Harmon and his client this weekend remained in his gut.

She hesitated but took a step in that direction. "It's no problem."

"No." He held up a hand to stop her. "I've got it."

Navarro glanced at Johnson.

Parker knew making the attorney and his client linger at the west entrance was petty, but it made him feel better. They were taking time from his family this weekend. He didn't feel like hopping to his feet upon their arrival. Making Harmon and Webb wait hurt Parker, too. It took additional time away from him, but the spiteful act made Parker feel good.

He languidly arose from his chair and gathered his files from his desk. "I'll meet you in the interview room."

Parker ambled off down the hallway.

***

"We're being recorded." Parker flicked a switch and a light on the wall above him glowed red. "Both audio and visual. Do you understand?"

Quaid Webb nodded. "Oh, yeah. Totally."

Webb wore a blue hooded sweatshirt unzipped to reveal an Insane Clown Posse T-shirt underneath. He had tucked a partially smoked cigarette behind his right ear.

Bryce Harmon sat next to Webb. A briefcase lay open on the floor and a notepad rested on the corner of the table. Harmon had dressed down for today's interview. He wore a buttoned shirt, blue slacks, and brown shoes. It might have been a stylish outfit on a slimmer man.

Leya Navarro shifted her stance as she observed from the corner. She chose not to lean against the wall. Parker appreciated her officer safety awareness, but he had no concerns either Webb or Harmon would do something stupid.

Parker opened his file and removed a Miranda Warning card. "I'm going to read your rights."

"I'm good." Webb dismissively waved his hand.

Harmon harrumphed. "Let him."

"But they already did." Webb leaned around the attorney to see Navarro. "Her partner."

"You have the right to remain silent," Parker said.

"Whatever." Webb's gaze drifted to the ceiling.

Parker followed the Miranda Warning word for word until he reached the end. Once he finished, he asked, "Do you understand each of these rights I have explained to you?" It was a required question from the card.

"He does," Harmon said.

Webb's attention returned to Parker. After a moment of silence, he said, "I do. Yeah. Geez."

"Having these rights in mind," Parker said, "do you wish to talk to me now?"

Webb eyed his attorney.

"I've already given my counsel," Harmon said. "This is your decision."

"Give it to me." Webb extended his hand. "Let's go."

Parker slid the card and pen to him but kept his eyes on the attorney. It was clear Harmon didn't want his client here. The attorney shifted the briefcase on the floor.

In the confines of the room, Parker picked up on Webb's body odor and a hint of sweet cologne which he imagined came from Harmon. The air wasn't moving since the HVAC was off because of the weekend.

Quaid Webb signed the Warning card and pushed it back to Parker.

"You called for this interview," Parker said. "Why?"

Webb tried to affect a casual posture. "I heard Lucky got got."

"You heard that, huh? How?"

"You know how it is." Webb set his hands on the table. "People talk."

"Which people?"

"I don't remember."

Parker put the Miranda Warning card into the file and closed it. He set the pen on top of his notepad. He was already tired of Webb's game. "Why are we here?"

"I've got information." Webb glanced toward his attorney.

"No, you don't," Parker said. "This is a circle jerk."

Webb nervously laughed. "I promise."

Harmon lowered his eyes as he rubbed his hands.

Parker leaned forward. "Counselor?"

The attorney lifted his head and pulled his shoulders back. "My client has information."

Parker looked at Navarro, who shrugged in return. They'd only been in the room for a couple of minutes, and it all felt wrong, like Webb was trying to run a con. The room's lack of air movement was getting to Parker. Webb's body odor was doing a number on his sinuses.

He looked at Navarro. "Would you mind cracking the door?" As an afterthought, Parker said to Harmon, "The air system is off, and it's a bit stale in here."

The attorney nodded once but Webb said, "I didn't notice."

Navarro cracked the door. A waft of cool air entered the room.

"Tell me," Parker said to Webb, "who told you about Fitzgerald's murder?"

"It was on social media."

"I call bullshit."

"For real." Webb looked at the attorney. "You saw. Tell him."

Harmon nodded. "This I can confirm. My assistant verified the social media comment."

"What platform?"

"Twitter."

Parker cocked his head as he studied Webb. "You have a Twitter account?"

“Not me, no.” Webb waved a hand like putting out a match. “A friend has one. She showed me the picture. Some rando posted it and did a hashtag thing.” He crossed two fingers over two others. “You know what I’m talking about? Anyway, it said lots of police cars were on Rutter Parkway.”

“How’d you know it was Grady Fitzgerald’s home?”

“You mean Lucky?” Webb smirked. “I didn’t know it was his place.”

Parker started to roll his eyes but stopped. He inhaled deeply before asking, “How did your friend know it was Fitzgerald’s?”

“Because she knew him.”

“Your friend had been there?”

Webb paused several seconds before answering. “Yes.”

“What’s this friend’s name?”

“I’d rather not say.”

Navarro’s shoulder thudded against the wall, and she glared at Webb.

“What?” he said. “Don’t look at me like that. I don’t have to reveal my sources.”

“You called this meeting,” Parker said. “You’re Detective Navarro’s prime suspect in the Sprague Corridor burglaries.”

She nodded. “When we asked about Lucky, you wanted a lawyer.”

Harmon looked toward Navarro. “My client has a right to an attorney, but we’re not here to argue that. What he’s doing today—” Harmon shifted in his seat to consider his client. “He has come forward to confirm your suspicions about Mr. Fitzgerald.”

Webb nodded. “That’s right. Yeah. That’s what I’m doing.”

Normally, Parker would have expected a surge of

adrenaline right then—they were about to get confirmation a murder victim was involved in a burglary ring. This new information might lead them to a killer, but Parker couldn't get over the feeling everything felt wrong. "Your client hasn't asked for anything in exchange for this information."

Harmon turned his hands upward. A pained expression crossed his face, but he quickly buried it with a forced smile. "Quaid… Mr. Webb is doing this of his own volition."

"Meaning what?" Parker asked. "He's proceeding against your advice?"

"Meaning—" The attorney held up a hand and paused as if searching for the right words.

"Lucky hired us," Webb interrupted.

Harmon curled his fingers and looked at his client.

"Relax." Webb leaned back in his chair. "That's what I came to tell 'em."

"All right, then." Harmon lowered his hand. "Go ahead."

Quaid Webb nodded several times. "Yeah, so Lucky hired us. He brought the team together like they do in those movies, but I didn't know any of the other guys."

"You're admitting to participating in the burglaries?"

"That's right, but I don't know anybody else."

Parker opened his file and removed the photo of Quaid Webb and several others in the alley behind Lucky's Pawn. "You don't know these other guys?"

"We never learned names." Webb nodded. "That's the way Lucky wanted it. Just like those movies."

"Why was Lucky breaking into businesses and homes in the area?"

Webb shrugged. "Hell if I know. I was just muscle."

"What were you doing in the alley?"

"Planning a burglary."

"Which one?"

"I don't remember."

Navarro pushed off the wall. "What were the lanyards for?"

Webb looked at her. "The what?"

She motioned around her neck. "The ID cards."

"Oh. They were so we'd look like the bums at that camp."

Navarro looked at Parker and nodded. She was done with her questions.

Parker tapped the tip of his pen against his notepad. Harmon concentrated on it as if it were a hypnotist's swinging pocket watch. Webb shifted in his seat, waiting for the next question.

The whole moment was wrong. It should have been confrontational, more argumentative. The only way this meeting made sense was if Webb was taking the blame for the others. Or perhaps he was shielding someone not known yet.

Part of it was Webb's demeanor. Part of it was in how Bryce Harmon sat idly by. If Parker followed this interview to its logical conclusion, Webb would take the fall for the burglaries and his friends would get away free.

But why would a man like Webb do that? There was a mistaken belief there was no honor among thieves. That wasn't true. If another connection existed more powerful than the money, there was honor.

"What can you tell me about your partners?" Parker asked.

"Nothing."

"Gimme some descriptions."

"I'm here to tell you about Lucky. That's it."

Parker scratched his face.

"Who's paying for your attorney?" Navarro asked.

Webb leaned back in his chair to get a better look at her, but Harmon lifted a hand to stop him from speaking.

"That's outside of the reason we're here," the attorney said.

"If it was Lucky—" Navarro said.

"Detective," Harmon said forcefully, "we're not answering that question."

Parker faced Webb. "Quaid, if you don't want a deal, why is your attorney here?"

"He has a right to an attorney," Harmon said.

"But why meet with me?" Parker asked Webb. "You haven't given me anything to help with a murder investigation." He motioned toward Navarro. "You could have met with the Property Crimes detectives and told them all of this."

"That's what I figured," Webb said, "but this guy—" He thumbed toward his attorney. "—said we should meet with you."

Harmon's lips pinched. "Damien Truscott and I do not have the best working relationship. I believed Mr. Webb would find a more sympathetic ear with you."

Parker motioned Navarro closer.

"We're going to show you some pictures," he said. "If you see someone you know, tell us."

Webb rolled his eyes. "Yeah, yeah."

Parker turned the folder before opening it so Webb couldn't see inside it. He didn't want to start with the photo array containing the Grady Fitzgerald picture. That seemed almost a formality now. Instead, he slid the array from the bottom of the stack and placed it on the table. Webb studied each picture, then pushed it back. "Nope."

Navarro pulled the document from the table.

Parker removed another photo array from the bottom of the stack and put it in front of Webb. Harmon leaned over to study the photos as well.

Parker didn't know why Webb was taking his time. For that matter, Parker could have ended the charade right then and put the array with Fitzgerald down. His wife and kids were waiting. He had better things to do on this day.

"Nope," Webb said and casually flicked the paper away.

Navarro slid that paper from the table.

Parker continued the farce by pulling another photo array from the bottom of the stack. Webb pulled the document closer and stiffened. His gaze flicked to Harmon, who watched the detectives. Webb casually said, "Nope," then and pushed it across the table.

Navarro looked at Parker and he nodded. She slid it off the table and held it separate from the earlier documents.

Webb quickly dismissed the next two arrays. On the final document, Webb confidently stabbed Grady Fitzgerald's picture. "That's Lucky. Right there. That's him."

Parker slid his pen to Webb. "Circle the picture you pointed to, then initial and date the paper."

Webb did so. "There you go," he said with a smile. "I told you. Lucky was behind it all."

Parker looked at Navarro. "Well?"

She lifted the photo array Webb had keyed on earlier. "Who did you see on here?"

Webb shook his head. "I don't know what you're talking about."

"I don't believe you," Navarro said.

"Neither do I," Parker added.

A silence descended over the room.

Harmon eyed his client. "What do you want to do now?"

"I think I'd like to stop talking."

The attorney abruptly stood. “This interview is over.” He grabbed Webb by the arm.

“Hold on.” Parker stood and looked at Navarro. “You can have him for the burglaries.”

She seemed to consider something before facing Webb. “You just admitted to your involvement in a series of crimes.”

Webb’s eyebrows rose. “Which one?”

Parker saw the problem immediately. Navarro had a photo of Quaid Webb behind Lucky’s Pawn but no physical evidence tying him to any crime. Just because the man admitted to the crime didn’t mean she’d be able to get a conviction.

Navarro said, “We’re going to want to talk with you again.”

Bryce Harmon glared at his client before turning back to Navarro. “Call my office, Detective. We’d be happy to schedule something.” The attorney lifted his briefcase, then pulled his client from the room.

Parker and Navarro followed them down the hallway until the two men exited via the west doors. A moment later, Johnson and Truscott arrived at where they stood.

“We came in on a Saturday for that?” Johnson asked.

Truscott shook his head. “Bryce must be losing a step.”

Parker pointed to the photo array that Navarro still held. “Who did he key on?”

She lifted it to show the others. All the men in the array were smiling. Navarro tapped the picture in the closest slot in the bottom row. “Trevor Crumbaker,” she said. “Fitzgerald’s nephew.”

# Chapter 14

Parker pulled into the parking lot of Lucky's Pawn but couldn't find a spot.

Damien Truscott glanced around. "Never seen it this busy."

"It's Saturday."

Parker left the lot and found an opening along the side street. He climbed out of the car and waited for Truscott to walk around before crossing.

Johnson and Navarro were traveling together to check out Trevor Crumbaker's listed residence. The four detectives split their teams since both Property Crimes detectives had recently seen Crumbaker. Johnson had called Navarro like they were kids picking teams on a playground.

"If Crumbaker's watching the camera feeds," Truscott said, "he'll see us approaching. There are cameras all around the building."

"Nothing we can do about that. Besides, if they're busy, he's unlikely to be watching the screens."

The detectives cut through the parking lot.

Truscott said, "Fitzgerald denied having anything to do with the break-ins. Maybe he was telling the truth."

Parker paused outside the front door. "What if Fitzgerald confronted his nephew and was murdered as a result?"

He felt sort of foolish bouncing the idea off Truscott, but Parker usually did that with Johnson. He enjoyed giving air to an idea, letting it into the world so it could breathe. Sometimes it blossomed. Other times, it suffocated almost immediately.

"Makes sense," Truscott said. "The nephew would

know where his uncle lived. He could have gone there under the guise of apologizing."

Parker liked the word "guise" and almost complemented Truscott for using it. Almost.

He yanked the front door open and waved Truscott forward. "After you."

The two men entered the store and weaved their way to the front. Parker had been in most of the city's pawnshops and Lucky's was one of the nicer ones. An oldies song played through the speaker, something about tainted love.

A line of customers waited as two men in green bowling shirts bustled behind the counter. Someone whispered, "The hell is this?" as he and Truscott walked by.

"Which is Crumbaker?" Parker asked.

Truscott shook his head. "Neither."

The closest man glanced up from a form he was filling out. He was in his mid-forties, with thick black hair and a pleasant face. "Sorry, fellas. You're gonna have to wait."

Parker didn't fault the guy for the dismissal. Since it was overtime, Parker had dressed down in jeans and a long-sleeve shirt. He currently wore a light blue windbreaker. Truscott wore a lightweight vest over his plaid shirt. Neither man particularly looked like a cop.

"Spokane Police," Parker said. He lifted the hem of his windbreaker to expose his gun and badge. "We'd like to ask you a few questions."

The guy behind the counter straightened and looked toward his counterpart.

"Go ahead," the other man said. "I got this."

The nearest employee looked at his customer. "I apologize," he said, then moved toward the detectives. His name tag read *Eric!* "What's this about?"

"Is Trevor Crumbaker in?" Parker asked.

Eric frowned. “He doesn’t work here anymore.”

Truscott shifted his stance. “When did he quit?”

“Trevor didn’t quit.” Eric crossed his arms. “Lucky fired him.”

Parker and Truscott glanced at each other.

“When did this happen?” Parker asked.

“Thursday.”

“Do you know what for?”

Eric shook his head. “Lucky didn’t say. He just called and said Trevor was out and I was the new assistant manager.”

Parker pulled his notebook from his back pocket. “What’s your full name, Eric?”

“Eric Sebastian,” Truscott supplied.

The assistant manager’s face pinched. “That’s right. Am I in trouble for something?”

Parker forgot Truscott put together the photo arrays. He would know the names of the Lucky’s Pawn employees.

“We hate to tell you this—” Truscott said.

“About Lucky?”

Parker looked up with some surprise.

Sebastian mashed his lips together. “Yeah, we heard.”

“How’d you hear?” Truscott asked.

“How could we not?”

Parker cocked his head. The department had not issued a press release, yet Quaid Webb had discovered it via a tweet on Twitter. Had the rest of Spokane already found out, too?

Sebastian must have picked up on Parker’s confusion because he said, “Someone who lives up near Lucky must have seen all the cops—” The assistant manager’s head bobbled apologetically. “I mean, the police. Anyway, whoever it was must have gone up his driveway to look—”

“You’ve been out Fitzgerald’s place?”

Sebastian nodded. “Oh, yeah. We all have. He was a pretty good boss. He threw a couple parties every year—Fourth of July, Christmas, that type of get together. Anyway, one of his neighbors must have seen the cops—the police, I mean—and snapped a picture to a friend.”

“Snapchat,” Truscott whispered. “Social media.”

Parker glared at him.

“My sons use it.”

“I know what Snapchat is,” Parker said.

Sebastian continued. “And that other friend screenshotted that and probably posted it to Instagram or something. Then someone else posted it on Twitter. Before long, someone’s mom posted it to Facebook.” Sebastian turned to the customers in line. “How many of you heard about Lucky?”

Everyone in line raised their hand. Several made sad faces.

“See?” Sebastian said.

Truscott asked, “Do you have access to the security system?”

“I do.”

“Lucky was supposed to have sent us some footage from a few nights ago. We never got it.”

“You’re not getting it now.”

“How come?”

“The system was wiped.” Sebastian spread his hands. “When I came in on Friday morning, the system had a reset notice. I called Lucky about it, but he never called back.” Sebastian frowned. “Well, obviously.”

“Could Trevor have done that?” Truscott asked.

Sebastian shrugged. “I guess. Everything was saved to the cloud. If Lucky forgot to cancel the guy’s access, it’s entirely possible Trevor could do it. He seemed cooler than that, though.”

"Did you ever see Trevor do anything illegal?"

"Illegal how?"

Truscott thumbed over his shoulder. "Like maybe running a burglary ring out of the shop."

"Are you serious? Not while I was here."

"How can you be sure?" Parker asked.

Sebastian smirked. "Because I would have seen it."

Parker made a note in his file. "Why are you here?"

"What do you mean?"

"Lucky's dead."

"So? There's still a business to run."

"Who's going to pay you?"

Sebastian knitted his brow. "We input our hours into the computer, and it generates a check. That's how it works."

Parker stared at the man. Even Truscott seemed confused by the comment.

"I figure we'll keep working until some attorney tells us not to."

Parker eyed the other detective. "Anything else?"

Truscott shook his head. "I'm good."

Sebastian said, "Do you need Trevor's address and phone number? I can give those to you."

"We already have them," Parker said.

Prior to leaving the department, Navarro had called Trevor Crumbaker's cell phone number. She didn't leave a message when it wasn't answered.

Parker motioned toward the other employee. "Why don't you send him over?"

Sebastian nodded, then walked over to the other employee. They exchanged a few words. Soon, the second guy ambled over. His name tag read *Matt!*

"Matthew Butler," Truscott whispered.

Parker nodded, then asked, "Have you heard what happened to Lucky?"

Butler nodded. "Eric and I talked about it before the store got busy. It's crazy, you know."

"Have you heard from Trevor?"

Butler shook his head. "Why would I? Lucky fired his ass."

"Do you know where he might be now?"

"Why are you asking?" Suspicion clouded Butler's eyes. "You think he might have had something to do with Lucky's death?"

"We don't know. We're just asking questions."

"That sucks if he did. They're like related, you know. Uncle and nephew. I would never hurt my uncle."

Truscott lifted his chin. "Did you ever hear talk about Trevor being involved with something hinky?"

"Like what?"

"Running stolen goods out of the back of this store."

Butler glanced at Sebastian, then returned his attention to the detectives. "Just because I know a thing doesn't mean I can get in trouble for it, does it?"

"What do you know?" Truscott asked.

"I promise I wasn't a part of it."

"Tell us."

Butler nodded. "I caught Trevor talking to a guy one time outside. I could tell whatever they were doing wasn't right. They were all huddled together like this." Butler moved in close to Parker.

The detective gently pushed him back. "I get the picture."

"Yeah, anyway, it looked like they were maybe doing a drug deal or something. I asked Trevor what he was up to, but he told me to fuck off."

Parker jotted a note on his pad.

"Did you tell Lucky about it?" Truscott asked.

"No."

"Why not?"

Butler appeared embarrassed. “Trevor had something over my head.”

Truscott frowned. “Well?”

“He caught me—”

Both detectives stared at him.

“In the bathroom.” Butler widened his eyes. “On my break.”

Parker and Truscott frowned as they looked at each other.

Butler continued. “You made me tell you. Look, I thought I locked the door.”

“We get it,” Parker said. He raised a hand for Butler to stop talking. “That’s why you didn’t question him any further and why you didn’t go to Lucky with it.”

“Trevor would have ratted me out,” Butler whispered, “and Lucky would have fired me for doing that in the store. I need my job.”

Parker eyed Truscott before saying to the clerk. “Thanks for your help. We’ve got what we needed.”

Butler started away but stopped. He spun back to the detectives. “Uh, hey. You don’t need to put what I told you into any report, do you? I mean, the stuff about what happened in the bathroom.”

“Your secret is safe,” Parker said.

The clerk breathed a sigh of relief. “Oh, man. I appreciate that.” He extended his hand to Parker. “I really do.”

“Have a nice day,” Parker said. He turned without touching the man’s hand.

***

“We struck out,” Jessie Johnson said. “We went to Crumbaker’s listed residence, and he wasn’t there.”

The four detectives were in the Major Crimes section.

Johnson sat in his chair while Leya Navarro leaned against his cubicle. They had returned to the department before Parker and Truscott.

Parker bent forward in his chair and rested his elbows on his knees. “The address he had on file with Lucky’s matched his DOL record?”

Johnson nodded. “And get this. Crumbaker lives with his mother. Talk about failure to launch.” He motioned to Navarro. “Leya charmed the old gal like a champ.”

She shrugged. “It wasn’t that big of a deal.”

Johnson waved a hand. “Don’t let her fool you. I wasn’t getting anywhere. The woman had her guard up before she opened the door. Social media had broken the bad news about her brother’s murder.”

Truscott clicked his tongue against the back of his teeth. “Digital tattletales.”

“That’s right,” Johnson said and snapped his fingers. “Exactly. What a world, right? Nothing stays quiet. Anyway, ol’ moms thought we were there to lay the blame on her son.”

“Why’d she think that?” Parker interrupted.

“Because he’d been recently fired,” Navarro said.

Johnson shrugged. “And we’re the cops. It’s not like we’re welcomed into every home.” He looked at Navarro. “That’s when Leya spun the whole case on its head. She said we had to know her son was all right so we could focus on finding her brother’s killer—the real killer. The whole story was beautiful.”

Truscott nodded. “Nice work.”

“I connected with her as a mother,” Navarro said. “That’s all.”

“She let you search the house?” Parker asked.

“Yeah,” Johnson said. “Trevor’s room looks like he’s stuck in high school. Posters of bands and video games on the wall.”

“Neat and clean,” Navarro added. “The mother said she tidies up on Saturday morning.”

“Did she tell you where he was?” Truscott asked.

Johnson shook his head. “She stated he doesn’t have any friends or a girlfriend, but she confirmed his phone number.”

“Hard to deny that,” Truscott said, “since we got it from his work.”

“I’ve called the number several times,” Navarro said, “but no answer on any of them. I didn’t leave any messages.”

“What do you think?” Johnson asked. “Maybe we should leave one now and have him call us?”

“If he was involved in Fitzgerald’s murder,” Parker said, “he’s not calling us back. He’s on the run.”

Truscott shoved his hands into his pockets. “Maybe Quaid Webb told Crumbaker he saw his picture in a photo array.”

“What’s he going to say?” Parker leaned back in his chair. “He didn’t point him out. Maybe Webb told the truth and Fitzgerald was really behind the burglaries. Maybe we’re chasing our tails here.”

“You believe that?” Truscott asked. He turned to the others. “Do any of us believe that?”

Both Johnson and Navarro shook their heads.

“So,” Parker said, “no luck at his last known.”

Johnson smirked. “By the look on your face, you had the same luck at the business.”

Parker pulled his notebook closer to him. “A big zero. The closest we got is one employee thought he caught Crumbaker talking about something inappropriate with a customer.”

“Yeah?” Johnson said with a glance at Navarro. “And?”

“And nothing,” Parker said. “The employee never told

Fitzgerald, so it didn't go anywhere."

"Why not?" Navarro asked. "Was the guy in on the scheme?"

Parker's face pinched. "Not exactly."

Truscott chuckled. "Crumbaker caught the guy jacking it in the store's bathroom."

"You're kidding," Navarro said.

"The threat of his indiscretion being revealed kept the guy quiet."

Navarro frowned. "Gross."

Truscott shrugged. "Don't go anywhere near SVU if that's all it takes to make you sick."

At the mention of the Special Victims Unit, a heavy blanket dropped over the moment. Parker watched Johnson and Navarro's expressions flatten.

Truscott must have felt the tenor change, too. The smile slipped from his face, and he cleared his throat. "What's next?"

"I'll contact dispatch," Parker said, "and put out an Attempt to Locate, then let's call it a day. There's no reason for us to chase our tails around for the weekend."

While everyone said their goodbyes, Parker turned to his desk. He snatched the receiver from his phone and dialed police radio.

It was answered on the first ring.

***

Parker lay on the ground in the living room. He flipped over the top card on the deck.

"Three!" Willow said.

She grabbed his green playing piece and tapped the board three times. It landed on top of a red piece and Willow bopped it out of position with more force than was necessary. She said, "Sorry!" before dropping her head onto Parker's shoulder. She clutched a well-worn teddy bear in her left arm.

"This is a baby's game," Hailey said as she put the red piece back into its starting position.

"Is not!" Willow shouted in Parker's ear.

"Girls," he said half-heartedly. He had played enough games with his daughters to know they all eventually devolved into chaos.

"Is, too," Charlotte chimed in. "It's totally a baby's game."

Beyond them, the local news started on the television. The national news broadcast had just ended. The sound was off on the set and the closed captioning ran. There was a delay between the newscaster and their dialog, but it was better than having the sound on in the background. An image of Camp Faith flicked onto the screen.

"It's your turn," Willow said.

"I don't wanna play anymore," Hailey said. "This game is dumb."

Charlotte rolled onto her upper back and kicked her feet into the air like she was riding a bicycle. "Look what I can do."

Hailey swatted at her sister's legs but missed.

Willow looked up at Parker. "Dad! Make them play."

"Take your turn, Hailey."

Fred Zimmer and Councilwoman Hembree appeared on the screen. The closed captioning box read, THE SPOKANE POLICE DEPARTMENT IS WITHHOLDING INFORMATION FROM—

Charlotte flipped over onto the board and scattered the pieces everywhere.

"Hey!" Willow cried as she hurriedly got up. She swung her teddy bear at Charlotte. "I was winning!"

"Nuh-uh," Hailey said as she now stood. "I was winning." She glared at the middle sister. "Why'd you do that, you big, fat loser?"

Charlotte scrambled to her feet, which sent the game board spiraling across the carpeted floor. "I'm not a loser!"

Parker pushed himself upright to his knees. He couldn't see the television around the commotion of his daughters. "Girls," he said.

Willow waved her hands at the board. "You did that on purpose."

"I didn't!"

"I'm never playing with you again," Hailey said. She ran up the stairs.

Willow swung the teddy bear a final time. "You're a cheater!" She raced after her big sister.

"It was an accident!" Charlotte yelled and thundered up the stairs as Brooke descended.

The news coverage switched to the recent wing commander change at Fairchild Air Force Base. Parker grunted. He would have liked to have known what Zimmer and Hembree were complaining about. He set to collecting the scattered game pieces.

Brooke wore a pair of shorts and a T-shirt. She had just gotten out of the shower and was now drying her hair with a towel. "Another successful game, I see."

"It went longer than most."

"What caused this breakdown?"

Parker dumped the colored pieces into the game box. "Same as always."

"Why can some kids play together and ours can't?"

He shrugged. "Maybe they're too close together in age."

"I would think that's a good thing."

"Or maybe it's because we have an odd number."

Brooke smirked. "Here we go."

He hugged her waist. "I'm not saying we have

another."

"Then what are you saying? That we get rid of one?"

"That we stay in practice."

"Oh, no." She spun free of his grip. "My hair's wet."

"I don't mind."

"You don't mind anything."

Charlotte stepped out of the girl's bedroom and hollered, "Mom! They're being mean to me."

Brooke raised her eyebrows. "Duty calls." She headed up the stairs.

Parker's gaze flicked toward the TV. He didn't like thinking about work while he was at home. He wouldn't get on his computer to search for the news clip of Zimmer and Hembree's interview. It could wait until Monday.

He bent to collect the scattered playing cards.

# Chapter 15

On Monday, Parker diverted from his usual route to work. He was often on autopilot when he drove into the station. He liked routine, so he followed the same path to and from the Public Safety Building daily. There were some trips to the PSB or home he questioned how he even got there—his mind had been so full he wasn't aware of his drive.

Today, though, Parker wanted to drive by Camp Faith. The idea of doing so had come to him while he was at the gym. One television above the treadmills was tuned to the local news and a story about the camp had come up. Parker tried to ignore it, but he caught himself sneaking peeks at it. He even noticed Fred Zimmer spouting off again. It appeared to be a replay of the interview from Saturday's coverage. He would listen to it at the office.

After Parker's early morning workout, he returned home and ate breakfast as the girls regaled him with stories of their favorite TV show, *Teen Titans Go!* They jumped around the dining table and pretended to be different superheroes while Brooke made his lunch in the nearby kitchen. Camp Faith lingered in the recesses of his mind the entire time.

While driving down Ray Street, Parker changed course to swing by Lug Nutz. Fred Zimmer's news appearances had increased since the burning of his building. Parker wondered if the man had political aspirations. He pulled into the tire shop's parking lot. A white SUV with the fire department's logo was parked near the street. Parker stopped and got out.

Large swaths of white paint had melted down the side of the building's concrete facade. Soot danced along its upper edges. Plywood covered the storefront. Perhaps the glass had blown out from the fire. Maybe the firefighters had broken it for their entry.

Plywood even secured the bay doors. Someone went to a great deal of trouble to protect the building.

A side door was open. Parker approached it and noticed a warning sticker at eye level—*Premises protected by Security Solutions of Spokane*. He stepped around the door and discovered a large rock held it open. He stopped before entering.

He noticed the stench first. Burned rubber and other singed materials combined for a horrible aroma. Parker didn't want to enter the structure and smell that stink all day. He'd carried death's bouquet around often enough to know how odors stuck to clothing and inhabited his nostrils.

His gaze swept the building. The flat roof was mostly gone; only a few joists remained. The morning sky was visible above. It wasn't fully light yet, but the sun wasn't far off on the horizon. He felt the morning chill and wanted to shove his hands into his pockets, but officer safety dictated they remain out.

The floor inside the store was an uneven swell of debris. What remained of the ceiling and the roof—the charred remnants of drywall, insulation, and decking material—had fallen because of the fire and the subsequent water.

Parker tried to imagine what the tire store might have looked like before, but it was nearly impossible. The racks were empty, and the display counters were husks.

A man in a heavy fire coat and helmet wandered about the tire shop. He carried a clipboard in his left hand and a large flashlight in his right. A black Labrador with a yellow vest moved about the shop.

"Hey," Parker called.

The man looked over. “Don’t come in here.”

“I’m Detective Parker. Spokane Police.”

“Hold on.”

The man muttered something to the dog and the two carefully worked their way across the room. The flashlight swayed back and forth as the man walked. When he neared, the man appeared to be in his early forties with tired eyes and an unshaven face. The dog wagged its tail as it waited near the man’s side.

“Parker, you said?”

“That’s right.” He handed him a business card.

The man took it, studied it for a moment before slipping it under the board’s clip. “My friends call me Gabe.” He handed Parker a business card that identified him as Lieutenant Gabriel Lockwood, arson investigator for the Spokane Fire Department. He motioned toward the dog. “This is Adara.”

“Is she an accelerant dog?”

“I see they gave you a detective’s badge for a reason.”

Parker smiled. “Find anything?”

Lockwood lifted the clipboard and studied Parker’s business card again. “Major Crimes, huh? What’s this fire got to do with you?”

“I’m investigating a homicide linked to the corridor burglaries.”

Lockwood lowered the clipboard. “You think this is part of that?”

“I’m wondering.”

The lieutenant nodded but didn’t say anything.

Parker got the feeling Lockwood wasn’t in the sharing mood, so he asked the question he wanted to know. “Was the fire accidental?”

“My investigation isn’t finished.”

“So you haven’t found anything?”

Lockwood stared at him.

Parker opened his mouth to ask a question, but a grocery truck roared southbound on Thor Street. He waited until it passed. "Have I offended you?"

"If I showed up at your crime scene before you had a chance to fully assess the situation…?" Lockwood let the unfinished question hang in the air.

Parker nodded apologetically. "I'll leave you to it." He started for his car.

"I'll tell you this much."

He stopped and faced Lockwood.

"Tires are less likely to catch fire if they're stacked upright." Lockwood chopped his hand up and down like he was dicing an onion. "That's why it's an industry standard."

Parker looked back into the building to reconfirm that the tire racks were empty.

"Did someone stack them up?"

Lockwood shrugged. "I don't know what you're talking about. I haven't finished my investigation yet."

Maybe that's the way they played the game in the fire department. Or perhaps that's the way Lockwood played it with strangers.

"Can you tell me this much?" Parker asked. "Did your dog trigger on an accelerant? I just want to know if we need to monitor this incident or if we can cross it off our list."

Lockwood looked down at Adara. "Unofficially?"

"Yeah, unofficially."

"She alerted in multiple locations."

Parker nodded. "Thank you for your time."

Lockwood saluted with his clipboard. "I'll send you a copy of my investigation when I'm done."

Both men headed in opposite directions.

***

Parker's phone rang as he approached his desk. He picked up the receiver but only got a dial tone. He hung up and dropped into his chair.

The phone on Jessie Johnson's desk rang, but his partner wasn't there. A suit jacket hung from the cubicle hook. His partner's computer monitor was on, and a coffee cup sat next to his keyboard.

For a moment, Parker thought about answering Johnson's phone, but he quickly dismissed the idea. Dispatch would have dialed Parker's cell if he failed to answer his desk phone. They wouldn't have called Johnson. Either someone inside the department wanted to get the detectives or it was a coincidence the calls had arrived back-to-back.

The ringing ended.

He turned on his computer and let his mind return to his morning drive. The Camp Faith protest had grown larger. Demonstrators lined Second Avenue for nearly two blocks. They waved signs and hollered at passing cars. Fred Zimmer had a bullhorn and looked like their ringleader.

Three media vans had parked in the neighboring vacant lot, but their crews weren't visible. Perhaps they had already filmed their pieces for the earlier broadcasts and climbed back inside the vehicles. The camp wasn't exactly breaking news.

Parker waited for the computer to work its way through the boot sequence. While it did, he groaned and stared at the ceiling. Why did IT insist they shut down the machines nightly? How much time did detectives waste every morning going through this process? Was it because the computers were old?

"Not answering your phone?"

Parker looked over his shoulder to find Captain

Ackerman standing there. "Sir?"

He motioned to Parker's phone, then Johnson's. "I called you and your partner. No answers."

"I just got here."

Irritation flashed across the captain's face as he checked his watch.

Parker stood. If he was about to take an ass chewing, he wouldn't take it sitting. "I drove by Lug Nutz on the way in," Parker said, "and had a conversation with an arson investigator. Afterward, I drove by Camp Faith."

Curiosity replaced the captain's annoyance. "What did this investigator say?"

"Nothing official, but his dog alerted to accelerants."

Ackerman's brow furrowed. "So it's arson. We already knew that."

"We assumed."

The captain grumbled. "And the camp?"

"It's still there." Parker smiled, but Ackerman didn't appreciate his attempt at humor, so he pressed on. "The protest has gotten bigger. Fred Zimmer was front and center. I think he's running for office now."

"Hard not to think that with all the press coverage he's been getting." Ackerman rolled his eyes. "Hey, listen. I called you for a reason. We found the department's leak."

Parker kept his face flat. He'd forgotten about the captain's warning and openly communicated about the case with Truscott and Navarro over the weekend.

"It was the chief," Ackerman said.

Parker took a half-step back.

"Six degrees of separation and all that. The chief updated the mayor on the WSDOT Camp situation, and she updated a couple of council members who updated Councilwoman Hembree." Ackerman interlinked his index fingers. "And she and Zimmer have been joined at the hip lately. So, it wasn't the Property Crimes team."

The captain inhaled deeply and slowly exhaled. “I’m not prone to do that—think the worst of our people—my people. This business with the camp has us all looking over our shoulders for the next person to plant a knife in our backs.”

Parker cocked his head.

Ackerman motioned toward Johnson’s desk. “Where’s your partner?”

“No idea.”

The captain glanced around before continuing. “The governor is walking the camp at the end of the week.”

“What for?”

“A photo op. What else? Seattle and Tacoma have homeless camps up and down I-5, but ours is getting more attention right now because it’s in the heart of red country. Their media is rubbing our noses in it.”

Every election cycle was a reminder that two-thirds of the counties voted republican, but the state swung democrat because of the dense population living west of the Cascade Mountains.

The captain continued. “The governor is coming over to remind us how badly we’ve responded to the situation.”

“Like they’ve done any better on the left side of the state.”

Ackerman waved a hand. “It’s the optics, Parker. If the sheriff would shut his mouth—” The captain bit off an expletive Parker imagined the man wanted to say. “He’s up for reelection next cycle. The governor, too. So it’s all political posturing. Both men winding up their bases. John Wayne justice meets Mister Rogers caring. Even though the sheriff is right to want to bust up the WSDOT camp, he looks like a thug every time he threatens to ignore city and state laws to do it.”

Parker remained silent.

"Anyway," the captain said with a dismissive wave of the hand, "the chief doesn't have a lot of allies in this situation. We're adhering to the mayor's directive if it's within the law, no matter how bad it makes us look."

"Yes, sir."

"I was wrong to tell you not to trust Navarro and Truscott." Ackerman tapped his chest. "That's on me. I'll own it."

Parker nodded. "Understood."

The captain pointed at Johnson's desk and glanced around. "When you see your partner, pass along the message."

"Will do."

Ackerman rubbed his hands together. "All right, then." He turned and left.

Parker settled into his chair and opened his email program. He spent a couple of moments filtering through the clutter before getting to his latest messages. Someone slapped his left shoulder and Parker turned to look. No one was there.

Johnson snickered and Parker swung his gaze toward his partner.

"I didn't think the old bastard would ever leave," Johnson said, dropping into his chair. "Thanks for taking one for the team."

"Whatever," Parker muttered.

"Don't be that way." Johnson's brow furrowed. "What did he want?"

Parker set his hands on his keyboard. "He said I'm getting a new partner."

"Wait." Johnson leaned forward. "Why?"

Parker typed a series of random keys. It was an excuse to ignore his partner.

"Are you joking?" Johnson asked.

"Ackerman wants you to see him."

"Bullshit."

"I don't know what you did—" Parker glanced at his partner. "But dude seemed pissed."

"For real?"

"Like super pissed."

Johnson flopped back in his chair and looked toward the ceiling. "What'd I do?"

"He didn't say."

His partner looked in the direction of the captain's office. "Maybe I should let him cool off."

"Up to you," Parker said, "but if he finds out you're sitting around on your fat ass—"

Johnson abruptly stood. "You better not be messing with me."

"Kill the messenger if you want, but the truth remains."

Johnson's face whitened. "Ackerman wants to see me?"

"That's what he said."

"Son of a bitch."

As his partner walked off, Parker chuckled to himself.

***

Parker's desk phone rang. He had just shoved an overly large bite of banana into his mouth. When the phone rang again, he picked up the receiver and held it to his ear. He didn't speak, though. Instead, he hurriedly chewed.

"Hello?" a woman said. "Parker?"

"Uh-huh," he muttered through a mouthful.

"This is Annie."

Dispatch, he thought.

"You okay?"

His mind raced through the last few days. How many

callouts had there been since his? Two? Maybe three. There was no way she was sending him a new one.

He swallowed and cleared his throat. “Go ahead.”

“That Attempt to Locate you wanted,” Annie said. “The one on Trevor Crumbaker. Patrol is out with him now.”

Parker tossed the banana peel into the trash can and reached for a pen. “Where?”

“His girlfriend’s house.” Annie recited an address and Parker jotted it down. He repeated it for accuracy’s sake. “Let them know I’m on the way.”

After he hung up, Parker opened his desk drawer and removed a protein bar. It was shortly after ten and he had felt his blood sugar dropping. That’s why he had dipped into his lunch box and eaten the banana. If he was going out to interview Crumbaker, he did not know how long that would take. It’s not like he could bring his lunch box with him. Parker rolled down the sleeves of his shirt and stood.

He didn’t worry about his partner since Johnson had left twenty minutes prior for a dental appointment. He’d still been moping about being tricked into going down to the Captain’s office.

Parker grabbed his suit jacket from the back of his chair and hurried toward the Property Crimes office. Neither Navarro nor Truscott were at their desks. He was going to give one of them the option to tag along.

He found a sticky note on Navarro’s desk and wrote, *Call me. Found Crumbaker.* He stuck the note to Navarro’s computer monitor, then headed toward the exit.

***

Three patrol cars parked on Seventh Street, several

houses away from the target address. Parker didn't bother following the officer safety technique the others had. Any potential threat was already gone. He pulled to the curb directly in front of his destination.

Two uniformed officers—one black, one white—stood next to the porch. A white male with longish dark hair sat on the steps. Behind him, Officer Sophia Allen lingered in the opened doorway of the yellow and green Craftsman-style home. She appeared to be engaged in a conversation with someone inside.

When Parker approached, Officers Lucas Jefferson and Ron Rowe lifted their chins in acknowledgment. They were SWAT types—cops who always seemed ramped to ten even when the situation did not dictate it. They loved to act like they were in the military, although neither had spent a moment in basic training.

Jefferson stood several inches taller than Parker. He was a handsome man with the cocky demeanor of a former college football player. Rowe was a paler version of his friend—slightly taller, no less handsome, but with less of the football player's swagger.

Parker disliked them both.

"Crumbaker?" he asked.

"In the flesh." Jefferson smirked as he motioned toward the sitting man. "We're glad we could bird dog him for you, Parker."

Rowe chuckled. "That's us. Just a couple of hound dogs."

They barked and bayed for several moments.

The female officer turned to watch them. She rolled her eyes and returned to her conversation with the person inside the house.

"Who's the girlfriend?" Parker asked.

Rowe glanced toward the house. "Jocelyn Webb."

"Webb?" Parker raised an eyebrow.

"That's right," Jefferson said. He thumbed at Crumbaker. "Ol' boy out kicked his coverage with that one."

Trevor Crumbaker cocked his head. Longish dark hair fell in front of his eyes. "That's my girlfriend you're talking about."

"He's giving you a compliment, hotshot," Rowe said.

Crumbaker frowned. "Didn't sound like it."

Parker needed to be careful about how he asked his questions. Right now, Crumbaker wasn't under arrest, but he was detained for questioning. Parker didn't have enough probable cause to arrest him for anything. He needed to walk the man into giving him something to work with.

"Trevor?" Parker asked.

"That's right," he said. He crossed his arms.

"You warm enough? Want a coat or something?"

Crumbaker shook his head. "I'm fine."

"All right. I'm Detective Parker. I'd like to ask you some questions."

"About my uncle?"

"That's right."

Crumbaker's gaze flicked between Jefferson and Rowe.

Parker turned to the officers. "Why don't you guys step back? Give us some space."

The two patrol officers moved toward the sidewalk. A group of neighbors gathered at the property's edge to watch what was going on.

"You're a homicide cop," Crumbaker said.

"That's right."

Crumbaker relaxed and rested his elbows on the step behind him. "I hope you find whoever killed him."

"Me, too. Tell me what happened between you guys."

"What do you mean?"

"Why did he fire you?"

Crumbaker leaned forward again and looked down at his shoes. "He accused me of something I didn't do."

"Which was what, exactly?"

"Nothing."

"He had to fire you for a reason. What did he say you did?"

Crumbaker clasped his hands together. "He said I stole something."

"From the store?"

His head jerked up. "I wouldn't do that."

"All right," Parker said. He held up a calming hand. "What'd he think you stole?"

"It doesn't matter."

"Why don't you tell me, and we'll figure it out together?"

Crumbaker rubbed his upper arms. "Just leave it alone, man."

Parker would come back to that subject later. "What happened after you got fired?"

"I went home."

"To your mom's?"

Crumbaker's eyes narrowed.

"Got it." Parker pointed at the ground. "Sorry for the confusion. And did you talk with your uncle again?"

"Why'n the fuck would I do that? He fired me."

A Honda full of teenagers drove slowly by. Their rap music was so loud it rattled their license plate. Parker waited for the car to pass before continuing. Officers Rowe and Jefferson glared at the Honda.

Crumbaker's face hardened. "Are you trying to pin his death on me? I didn't have nothing to do with that."

"Relax, Trevor. I've got to figure out where everyone was when it happened. Understand?"

The man pinched his lips together, then reluctantly

nodded.

"How did you hear he was dead?"

"A friend messaged me on Instagram." He stretched his legs out. "Maybe it came out on Facebook first or some such shit. I don't know. I'm hardly ever on there."

"But you were on long enough to see the message."

"So?"

Parker shrugged. "Did you go up to your uncle's house?"

"No."

"What if I said we found your fingerprints?" It was a bluff. The fingerprint report hadn't come back yet.

"That doesn't mean nothing. I'd been there before."

"But not that day?" Parker asked.

"Stop trying to pin this on me. I had nothing to do with it."

"I'm not trying to pin anything on anyone. I just need to get the facts. Did you go up to his house the day before?"

"I don't know what day he was murdered." Crumbaker's face reddened. "I didn't do it. Listen to me."

"When was the last time you were there?"

"I don't fucking remember, but I'll tell you this much. I hated going up there because it was in Timbuktu. I only went for special occasions. Like the Labor Day party I took Jocelyn to. Most times, I just saw him at work."

Parker glanced around. Officers Jefferson and Rowe were still talking with the neighbors. The female officer in the doorway was engaged in a conversation with Jocelyn Webb.

"Where were you on Thursday night and Friday morning?" Parker asked.

Crumbaker pointed at the ground between his feet. "I was here."

"With Jocelyn?"

"That's right."

"What can you tell me about the burglaries occurring along the Sprague Corridor?"

He swallowed. "Why are you asking me about that?"

"I think you know."

"I don't know nothing."

Parker nodded. "Did a couple detectives talk to your uncle about the burglaries?"

"I guess."

"Don't guess. They did."

Crumbaker looked away. "What of it?"

"They told him a witness saw some guys hanging out back of Lucky's Pawn. It was late at night and there was an open door." Parker bent slightly to get Crumbaker's attention. "They accused your uncle of being part of the burglary ring, but that's why your uncle fired you. He worked it out and found you behind it."

"You got it wrong."

"Do I?" Parker asked. "They have a video—"

"No, they don't," Crumbaker interrupted. "They don't have video."

"Oh. You mean from Lucky's?"

"That's right. That system is rickety. It lost its footage from the last week. You didn't get anything from there."

Parker smiled. "I see where you could get confused about that. The video is from a neighbor's system."

Crumbaker cocked his head.

"Your uncle didn't tell you, huh? There's the audio/visual company behind Lucky's, across the alley. They have some cameras that look right into the back door of the pawnshop. That's the video I'm talking about. You know who they saw? Quaid Webb. How's he related to your girlfriend?"

Crumbaker leaned forward and put his head in his hands. "Fucking Quaid."

"Well, well, well." Parker fought back a smile. "Back to your uncle."

"We didn't kill him." Crumbaker looked up through his fingers. "I swear to God."

"If not you, who?"

Crumbaker dropped his hands. "How would I know?" His voice rose. "But we didn't. That's all I know."

"Maybe someone else figured out the burglaries were coming from Lucky's and—"

"They weren't coming from Lucky's."

"Maybe they took it out on him."

Crumbaker's face pinched. "That son of a bitch ruined it for us."

"Who?"

"Ask her." He thumbed over his shoulder.

"I'm asking you."

"Not until you talk with her."

"Okay, Trevor. We'll play it your way." Parker whistled to get the attention of Jefferson and Rowe. "Put him in your car until I'm done, okay?"

The two uniformed officers trotted over.

"Also," Parker said, "one of you call dispatch and see if they can locate Navarro and Truscott. Find out if they're on their way."

Rowe nodded and reached for his shoulder microphone.

Jefferson grabbed Crumbaker's elbow and pulled him to his feet.

Crumbaker leaned to Parker and whispered, "Hey, Detective."

"Yeah?"

"Don't tell Jocelyn I said nothing, okay? I don't want her to get mad at me."

***

"He said what?"

Jocelyn Webb sat cross-legged on a raggedy blue sofa. Her faded jeans were torn perfectly at the knees, as if she purchased them that way. The shabby Black Sabbath T-shirt she wore was probably bought at the same time as her jeans. A pair of unmarred Vans were underneath the coffee table. She inhaled on a purple vape pen, then pushed out a peppermint-scented plume of mist.

Parker jerked his head toward the open door where Officer Sophia Allen still stood. "Trevor said you were the ringleader."

"Behind some break-ins?"

"That's what he said."

Jocelyn clucked her tongue, then rolled her eyes. "Oh, Jesus." She barked a cruel laugh. "What else did he say? That I'm responsible for the Lindbergh baby, too?"

Parker glanced at Officer Allen, who shrugged in response.

"Don't you know what that is?" Jocelyn's face hardened. "Watch a documentary some time."

Parker's gaze dropped to his notepad. Not because he needed to remember anything. Rather, he wanted to defuse the moment and let Jocelyn calm down. He usually liked suspects to emotionally ramp up and spout off, but he didn't want her doing it so quickly. He had hoped to build some rapport and get some understanding of the situation first. He glanced around.

The carpet needed vacuuming and wear patterns had formed around the dated and mismatched furniture. Framed horror movie posters hung on the wall on both sides of a flatscreen TV. A bookshelf was filled with Stephen King novels and DVDs of the same titles. Two-half eaten egg McMuffins and a Styrofoam tray topped with pancakes lay spread out on the coffee table. It appeared as if the arriving officers had interrupted breakfast.

Jocelyn Webb was an attractive twenty-seven-year-old. However, she looked like many women her age these days—fake. Her golden tan was sprayed, her large eyelashes were purchased, and her teeth were unnaturally white. The highlights in her hair were new and her bare feet appeared as if they'd recently received a pedicure.

Jefferson and Rowe had been right. Crumbaker had outkicked his coverage; she was too flashy for him. Either Jocelyn came from money and was slumming with the man, or he was spending a lot of cash on her upkeep.

Parker asked, "Where do you work?"

"Is that important?"

He stared at her. Silence was often an effective tool for questioning.

She shrugged. "Hamilton Ship and Print."

Parker knew the business. They were a shipping business that also had monthly mailboxes for rent. They also offered custom printing services.

"Do you make good money there?" Parker asked.

"Minimum wage." Jocelyn sneered. "But it's a job."

"What do you do there?"

"Why's it matter?"

"I guess it doesn't." Parker's gaze drifted about the room again. "Do you know why I'm here?"

Jocelyn inhaled once more on the vape pen. "Haven't the foggiest." Mist escaped her mouth as she spoke. "That one—" She motioned toward Officer Allen. "—wouldn't tell me shit. So maybe you like harassing innocent citizens like all the other cops I've met."

"I'm a homicide detective."

Her lip curled again. "Oh. You're probably here about Trevor's uncle or something."

"That's right."

Jocelyn put the vape pen in front of her mouth but didn't inhale. She said, "Trevor's mom is going crazy now."

"I'd imagine."

She inhaled on the pen, then turned her head sideways to exhale. "So, why come around here harassing us when you've got a killer to find?"

The peppermint mist mingled with the aroma of egg McMuffins. There was another essence in the house that Parker couldn't place, but it gave the home a funky smell. It wasn't heavy like body odor, but it lingered like untreated mildew.

"Where were you last Thursday night?" he asked.

"Hold on." Jocelyn pointed the end of the vape pen at Parker. "You think we had something to do with that?"

"I don't know." Parker shrugged for dramatic effect. "Did you?"

"Aw, fuck no." She pointed out the window. "Hell no. I didn't even know the guy."

"That's not what I heard. Trevor said you were up at his house on Labor Day."

Jocelyn held up a single finger. "One party. Like months ago."

"So you knew him, and you knew how to get to his house."

She looked toward the open door. "Whatever he said—" She bit off the rest of her sentence, mashed her lips together, and turned her face away from Parker.

"A couple of detectives went to Lucky's Pawn and told Grady about a witness who saw illegal activity occurring out the back of the store."

Jocelyn didn't move her head, but her eyes shifted toward Parker.

"You already knew that," Parker said, "because that's why Trevor got fired."

"I don't know dick."

"The way I figure it, you and Trevor went up to Lucky's house for some revenge."

"Because he got fired? From a shit job?" She looked at him fully now. "That's bullshit."

"Maybe you went up there to tell him to keep his mouth shut about what you two had going on."

Jocelyn uncrossed her legs and stood. "That's not true. Stop lyin'."

"And you killed him," Parker said. "*Pop.* A single shot to the head. Nice and easy."

She pointed at him. "I would never kill anyone."

"Maybe you put Trevor up to it. He seems like a simple sort you could twist around your finger."

"Don't you call him that."

"Come on," Parker said. "It's obvious why you're with a guy like that."

Her mouth twisted with disgust.

"You push him around. Make him do what you want. You're the brains behind the operation. You can say it."

"We didn't kill Lucky!"

"What do you want to bet the CSI types found your fingerprints at Lucky's house?"

Parker hated the *CSI* shows. They gave all sorts of false representations about what evidence technicians could do and how investigations were carried out. However, they were a boon to detectives like him. All he had to do was drop the term CSI and everyone developed a mental picture in their heads about what might have occurred at a crime scene.

Jocelyn's face whitened. "I was there before. I already admitted it."

"But not since?"

"Ask Trevor."

"I already did."

"There you go."

Footsteps ascended the outside stairs and Parker turned to look. Detectives Navarro and Truscott appeared in the doorway. With a jerk of his head, Parker motioned them inside.

"Detectives Navarro and Truscott. I'd like you to meet Jocelyn Webb."

Perhaps the Property Crimes detectives had heard her name prior to entering the house, but both hid any surprise they might have had.

Navarro said, "We've already met your brother."

Jocelyn fell back into the couch. "Shit."

Truscott crossed his arms. "Yeah, we felt the same way."

Something wasn't right, Parker thought. Trevor Crumbaker hadn't asked for an attorney and, so far, neither had Jocelyn Webb. Usually, Parker would never think of doing what he was about to do, but he was going to bring an attorney to the forefront of the conversation. "What happened with Bryce Harmon?"

Navarro and Truscott looked at Parker.

Jocelyn rolled her eyes. "My brother. The stupid son of a bitch."

The three detectives remained silent.

"Bryce won't take my calls now." Jocelyn inhaled on her vape pen. "He's our cousin, you know? The one in our family who really made something of himself. And Quaid told him we didn't need him anymore, which was stupid because Bryce was helping us on the cheap. Whatever Quaid said must have hurt his feelings."

"What did your brother tell you about our interview?" Parker said.

Jocelyn's gaze flitted among the cops in the room. "He said it went cool." Her expression flattened. "But I can tell by you all being here that it didn't. Goddamn him."

"Why don't you start from the beginning?" Parker said.

Jocelyn's shoulders slumped. "How much did Quaid tell you?"

"He told us everything," Parker lied.

She sighed. "Yeah, that's what I figured." Jocelyn shook her head. "Whatever. We did it. What do you want to know?"

Parker eyed Navarro and Truscott. Neither seemed to grasp the gravity of her revelation. So he asked, "What did you do?"

Jocelyn inhaled deeply on the vape pen. She exhaled forcefully, then collapsed onto the couch. "We did those break-ins. Is that what you want to hear?"

Navarro and Truscott eyed each other.

"But we never killed Lucky!" Jocelyn pointed emphatically with the pen. "I swear on my life we never did that shit."

"Okay," Parker said. "Then let's go back to last Thursday. What were you doing that night?"

She shrugged. "I was here with Trevor, watching Netflix."

"On that?" Parker pointed at the TV on the wall.

"Yeah."

"Whose account?"

"Why's it matter?" Jocelyn asked.

"Because I need to verify it."

Parker could get a warrant and see what activity there was on the account. However, it wouldn't confirm someone actually sat in front of the television.

"My parents'," Jocelyn said.

"I need their names."

"For real?"

He stared at her until she rattled off their names and home address.

"Can anyone confirm you were here on Thursday night?" Parker asked.

"I don't know," Jocelyn said. "The pizza delivery guy, I guess." She threw her hands into the air. "You gotta believe me." She looked toward the Property Crimes detectives. "We wouldn't kill Lucky."

Parker asked, "What show did you watch? And where did you order your pizza from?"

Jocelyn didn't even hesitate. "We binged that documentary about Charles Manson. I don't remember the name of the show, but you can't miss it. As for the pie, we ordered it from Lunar Pizza."

"How'd you pay for it?"

"Trevor used his card."

Parker nodded. "If you're lying—"

"I'm not!"

"If you are, I'll be back."

Jocelyn rolled her eyes. "I'm telling the truth. We didn't kill no one."

Parker had enough to follow up on her story and pin down her location. Right now, if he had to make an educated guess, he'd say Jocelyn Webb and Trevor Crumbaker weren't involved in Grady Fitzgerald's murder. He wouldn't bet all his money on it, but he didn't have to—not yet, at least. There were still the matters of the burglaries for them to answer for.

He turned to Navarro and Truscott. "She's yours." Parker motioned toward the door. "Crumbaker is in Rowe's car."

"We saw him on the way in," Navarro said.

Truscott nodded in affirmation.

"I'm heading back to the department to write a warrant for their cell phones," Parker said. "I want to verify they were at home when they said they were."

# PART III

## Chapter 16

Jocelyn Webb fell back into the couch and crossed her arms. “I already know my rights.”

“That’s great,” Leya said, “but I’m going to read them to you, anyway.” She faced Officer Allen. “Is your camera on?”

The officer touched the body camera clipped to her shirt. “It is now.”

Leya had a white Miranda Warning card paper-clipped to the inside of her notebook. “You have the right to remain silent,” she read. “Anything you say can and will be used against you in a court of law.”

Truscott moved further to the left as Leya finished reading the card.

Leya could have done this at the station, but she figured it was better to do it right now while Jocelyn was comfortable and still in the habit of answering questions.

When she finished reading the card, Leya asked, “Do you understand these rights as I have read them?”

“I already said I did.”

“Will you waive those rights and talk with me?”

Jocelyn shook her vape pen. “This is some bullshit.”

"That's not an answer," Leya said.

"Yeah, whatever, but I don't know why I got to do this all over again. I already told that other detective everything."

"He was a homicide detective. We're investigating the burglaries."

"So, he's more important?"

Leya's face remained impassive. "Tell that to the person whose business you broke into."

"I never broke into anything."

"Who did then?"

Jocelyn crossed her arms. "I don't know. You tell me."

"Right now is your opportunity to tell us how it went down."

"Why should I do that? You cops are going to write what you're going to write. I know how this works. I've seen the shows."

"Yeah?" Truscott asked. "What shows?"

"The Seven-Five."

"That's a good one." Truscott nodded. "Pretty messed up what happened there."

Leya had no idea what the two were talking about.

Jocelyn snapped her fingers. "What about *We Own This City*? That's some messed up bullshit."

"That's a fictionalized account of what happened." Truscott's head bobbled from side to side. "Make believe, if you will."

Jocelyn's expression soured. "I know what fiction is. I'm not stupid."

Truscott lifted an apologetic hand. "Listen. I love movies." He covered his heart. "More than you'll know. We can talk documentaries all day long and they're going to show police departments screwing up. No filmmaker is going to make a documentary about any police doing the right stuff because it would be boring. Nobody would care about a cop making a clean arrest and writing a good report."

"Now, that shit's make believe," Jocelyn said.

Truscott chuckled. "Think what you want, but we care about the truth."

Jocelyn's attention shifted to Leya.

"If you want to tell us why you got involved in this," Leya said, "we'll listen. We'll put it in our reports."

Her gaze returned to Truscott. "It becomes official then?"

"That's right. It becomes official." He pointed to Officer Allen. "She's recording it, too. You can challenge what we write if it doesn't match."

Jocelyn nodded several times. "All right, all right," she said but fell silent after that.

Leya looked to Truscott, but his concentration remained on the woman sitting on the couch.

Officer Allen shifted her stance, which caused her leather duty belt to creak.

Jocelyn stretched her neck, then inhaled deeply, as if working up the courage to say something. "This is the God's honest truth—Trevor made me do it."

Truscott cocked his head. "He made you."

"That's right." Tears welled in her eyes. "He threatened to hurt me if I didn't help him."

"How did he threaten you?" Truscott asked.

"He grabbed me." Jocelyn held up her hands. "By the wrists."

"That's all?"

"And he yelled at me." She reached up and smeared a tear across her cheek. "He scared me. He said he would hit me. He can be intimidating when he wants."

"What did he make you do?" Truscott asked.

"He made me get my brother involved." It almost

sounded like a little girl admitting she'd been caught by her parents.

"Why didn't Quaid stop Trevor from hurting you?"

Jocelyn briefly lowered her head. When she looked up, she said, "I didn't tell him. I was afraid Trevor would hurt us both."

"Okay," Truscott said. "That's good. Real good. Wait here for a moment."

"What are you going to do?"

"Detective Navarro and I are stepping outside for a moment." Truscott eyed Officer Allen. "We'll be back."

Truscott didn't need to explain the pause. Leya understood immediately why.

The two detectives stepped outside. Three patrol cars were parked alongside the curb. Trevor Crumbaker sat in the back of the second unit. Officers Ron Rowe and Lucas Jefferson talked together near the first car.

Truscott headed toward the second patrol car. Ron Rowe hurried over and opened the front door. He popped open the second door with the security latch.

"Trevor," Truscott said. "Why don't you slide out?"

Because of the protective shield between the front and rear, there wasn't much room for a passenger to sit like a normal person. Knees would bang against the steel partition. Most arrestees turned sideways and extended their legs out as if they were sitting on a lounge chair.

Trevor Crumbaker had ignored the discomfort and was lodged in the patrol car's back seat. Truscott reached in, grabbed the man by the hand, and helped him wriggle free from his sitting position.

When Crumbaker stood, they escorted him to the back of the patrol car.

Truscott motioned for Officer Rowe to join them, then turned his attention to Crumbaker. "I'm Detective Truscott. This is Detective Navarro. We need to ask you some questions."

"But the other detective…" Crumbaker looked about.

"He's a homicide detective. We're here to talk about the burglaries."

Crumbaker's nose scrunched. "Shit."

Truscott removed a Miranda Warning card from the inner pocket of his jacket. "I need to read you these." He glanced at Officer Rowe. "Is your camera on?"

The officer touched the small box he wore on the middle of his chest.

"You have the right to remain silent," Truscott said.

Crumbaker's expression flattened, and he looked into the sky. It seemed as if he were struggling to hold back tears.

Leya often thought it odd that the reality of these moments didn't hit suspects until their rights were read to them.

When Truscott finished reading from the card, he asked, "With these rights in mind, do you agree to waive your rights and answer our questions?"

Crumbaker dropped his chin. "I don't know."

"Is that a no?"

"It's an I don't know." His face pinched. "I'm thinking about it."

"While you're thinking," Truscott said. "Let me tell you something. Your girlfriend said the break-ins were your idea."

"She said what?"

"That's right. She said you threatened her and assaulted her into cooperating with your crime."

Crumbaker looked toward the house. "What the shit?"

Truscott thumbed at the camera on Officer Rowe's chest. "That's the truth. The other officer recorded her putting the whole thing at your feet."

Crumbaker's face reddened.

“So,” Truscott said, “do you want an attorney, or do you want to talk with us now?”

“Yeah, I’ll talk.” Crumbaker balled his fists. “The burglaries were her and her idiot brother’s idea. They saw what was going on with the camp and thought it was an easy way to make a buck.” He turned to the house. “You fucking bitch!” he hollered.

“What about Lug Nutz?” Leya asked.

“Oh yeah. We broke into that place. Didn’t hardly get shit out of it, though.”

“You went along?”

Crumbaker turned his palms upward. “On some of them, yeah. It was sort of a thrill.”

“How’d you get past the security system?”

“Quaid and his buddies know how to get past that shit.”

“What were the names of the other guys with you?” Leya asked.

“Shay, Buzz, and Robs, but I don’t know any last names. I’d tell you if I knew. I swear on my mother’s eyes, I would. Fuck those guys.”

Leya jotted the names in her notebook. There would be time to circle back to them later. “Tell me about the Lug Nutz job.”

Crumbaker shook his head. “What a stupid idea that was. Like we were going to get much from a tire shop.”

“Why did you burn it?”

His gaze snapped between the two detectives. “We didn’t burn shit. Don’t pin that on us.”

Truscott held up a hand. “Hold on.”

“I’ll own the break-ins, even though they weren’t my idea.” Crumbaker turned again to the house. “Evil bitch!”

“Easy,” Truscott said.

“We didn’t burn shit.” Crumbaker pointed at Leya’s notebook. “Write that down.”

There was a commotion at the front of the house. "Quaid is gonna kill you, you dumb shit!" Jocelyn screamed from the open doorway. Officer Allen struggled to stop her from coming down the stairs. Jefferson ran toward them.

Crumbaker pointed at her. "I'd like to see him try!"

Officer Rowe grabbed the man and pushed him back. Crumbaker flopped against the rear of the patrol car.

"I should never have hooked up with her," Crumbaker said. "She was toxic from the jump."

Officers Allen and Jefferson moved Jocelyn back inside the house.

"That bitch and her brother." Crumbaker's gaze returned to Truscott and Leya. "Keep asking your questions. I'll tell you what I know."

***

Jessie Johnson looked up from his desk when Parker arrived. "Heard you found Trevor Crumbaker. Anything break loose?"

Parker removed his coat and hung it over the back of his chair. "Navarro and Truscott solved their burglaries." He sat and began rolling up his sleeves. "But it's not looking like they're connected to our murder."

He recounted the interviews of Crumbaker and Webb.

"Wait," Johnson said. "The girlfriend and her brother set this whole thing up?"

"That's what it sounds like. Navarro and Truscott are going to have a fun time peeling that onion." Parker opened his notebook.

"What're you working on now?" Johnson asked.

"We need GPS warrants for Crumbaker and Webb's cell phones and one for Webb's parents' Netflix account."

"I'll bird dog the cell phone warrants if you have the numbers and carriers."

Parker handed his notebook to Johnson. "Top of the page."

"That Netflix account is gonna be a pain in the ass."

"Yeah," Parker agreed. "And they take forever. That's why I'm gonna do it after I talk with Lunar Pizza." Parker reached for his keyboard.

"What for?"

"We need confirmation someone delivered a pizza to Crumbaker's house."

Johnson cocked his head. "That's a single point in time. Maybe they got the pizza and went out to Lucky Fitzgerald's house right after. Or maybe one of them stayed, and the other went. The pizza is the least valuable piece of information."

Parker started his internet browser. "All of it's circumstantial. They could have left their phones at home and gone up to Fitzgerald's house. If they did that, the GPS tracking is defeated. Same with the Netflix account, too. They could have started a movie and left."

"That's a lot of pre-planning," Johnson said.

"This isn't the fifties, man. Planning a murder is fairly easy now because of TV and the movies. All anyone has to do is pay attention and take notes. Hollywood has done the heavy lifting for them."

Johnson turned toward his computer. "So we're stacking the circumstantial to prove the truth?"

"Or as close as we can get to it."

Parker entered the words *Lunar Pizza* into the search bar and tapped Enter. A search result quickly returned.

***

"Oh goody," Jocelyn Webb said. She sat on the couch

with her legs crossed. "You're back."

Leya and Truscott stood on the other side of the coffee table. He looked at Leya, but she nodded for him to lead the questioning.

Officer Allen stood off to the left. Her body camera was rolling again.

Jocelyn sucked on her vape pen, then blew the mist downward. "Well, don't keep me in suspense. What'd the lazy prick say?"

"What do you think he said?" Truscott asked.

Her fist bounced on top of a knee. "He probably blamed it all on me."

"Of course he did."

Her lips pinched. "That bastard."

"What did you think he was going to do?"

Jocelyn pointed the vape pen at Truscott. "Some of it was his idea, you know."

"Yeah?" Truscott pulled his notebook from his pocket. "How'd it come about?"

"We watched that documentary about those Hollywood burglars. You know the one?" She sucked on the vape pen again but didn't bother to exhale. The mist escaped as she spoke. "One of us, probably him, made a joke we should do that, too. It sort of grew from there."

"Who thought it was a good idea to blame it on the homeless camp?"

Jocelyn's tongue traveled under her lower lip. "I don't remember. Probably Trevor." She nodded. "Definitely him. Yeah."

"When did you enlist Quaid?"

She uncrossed both legs and tucked them underneath her. She sat up higher now. "It's not like Trevor or me could pull it off. He doesn't know how to break into anything except a bag of cookies. My brother had some trouble with the law. Nothing too big, but he had some friends who knew a thing or two."

"What did you do with all the goods you stole?"

"Took them to a dealer my brother knows." She motioned toward the window. "That's where Trevor was smart. He told us how pawnshops track everything. It would be stupid for us to sell anything in town, and it would have been suicidal for us to try it through Lucky's."

"What about the ID cards?" Leya asked.

Jocelyn smiled proudly. "That was my idea. I saw them on the news, like in a report, you know? The TV people were making a big deal about how they were going to stop the crime. As if? We were working to blame everything on them, right? So I made up some fake badges at my work. I even gave the guys fake names." She laughed. "Trevor's was Michael Rotchburns. Get it?"

"Yeah." Truscott nodded. "Hilarious."

Leya scrunched her face. She didn't get the joke.

"Mike Rotchburns," Truscott said, then repeated it slowly. "My crotch burns."

"Oh."

"See?" Jocelyn asked. Her smile remained.

Truscott scratched his chin. "Why were the guys at the pawnshop on Tuesday night?"

"What are you talking about?"

"There was a video of them standing in an alley behind the pawnshop, getting something from the back door."

"Huh." Jocelyn waved her hand. "That night you're talking about is probably after I made the cards. Trevor said he had some necklaces to hold them. He and Lucky went to these conventions where they got them. That's the only time I know they went inside the building because he forgot to bring them home with him. It figures it would be the one time Trevor goes into the building late at night that sinks us."

"What do you mean?" Truscott asked.

"They'd done a lot of break-ins by then and we were worried the guys might get sloppy since no one seemed to catch on."

"Who's we?"

"Trevor, Quaid, and me. Like we talked about how good it was going. We couldn't believe we were getting away with it. The cops and everyone seemed so focused on the camp. We wondered how long it could last. So we started to think far ahead, like if something bad happened, because it felt like we were pressing our luck."

"Is that when you suggested Bryce Harmon as the group's attorney?" Truscott asked.

"He was my mom's cousin," Jocelyn said, "so he knew Quaid and me. It's not like we had family get-togethers or nothing, but he knew we existed, if you know what I mean. Anyway, I told the guys to call him if they got jammed up and drop our family's name. We'd figure out how to pay Bryce later." Jocelyn shook her head. "My fucking brother had to go and ruin that for everyone."

"Tell us about the tire shop," Leya prompted. She wanted to leave the conversation about an attorney.

"Lug Nutz? What about it?"

"Why'd your guys decide to burglarize it?"

She shrugged. "Hell if I know. I didn't pick the buildings. Quaid and his friends did. They knew how to get past certain systems. Sometimes they did a smash and grab. Other times, they would finesse them." Jocelyn motioned toward the window. "I don't know what Trevor said, but he went along on most of them. He was getting his kicks by going."

Leya nodded. "Did they tell you why they set fire to it?"

“Oh, no. That wasn’t us.” Jocelyn sucked on the vape pen and forcefully blew out a plume of mist. “Did the boys break into it? Yeah, sure. We’ll own that. They took some tools and got some cash. That’s about it. But we didn’t set that place on fire.”

“How can you be so sure? You weren’t there.”

“Because Trevor and Quaid said so. I believe them. Besides, what did the tire guy ever do to us?”

“Maybe it was an accident.”

“Not a chance.” She tapped the vape pen against her knee. “Listen to what I’m saying. The building was safe when they left it. Besides, why would I admit to breaking into a joint and lie about not burning it down?”

Truscott looked up from his notepad. “Which brings up a good point. Why are you admitting to this?”

“What do you mean?”

“You rolling on Trevor and your brother.”

“Trevor rolled first.”

“But your brother?”

She shrugged. “Quaid said if I ever got caught to own up to it.”

“He said that?”

“That’s right. He said to throw him under the bus if I had to.”

“But why?”

“Quaid’s smart. He’s been in jail before and knows how the system works. He said, since we didn’t hurt anybody, we’re golden. The judges never prosecute anyone for stealing stuff. They only zap someone if people get hurt. That’s why I swear to you we didn’t kill Lucky and we didn’t burn that building down.”

“All right. Who are Quaid’s friends—Shay, Buzz, and Robs.”

Jocelyn paused, as if considering a lie or avoiding the question all together.

"Don't think about it," Truscott said. "Just tell us."

She sighed. "Shad Puryear, Brandon Lightfoot, and Kyle Robles."

"Do you know where they live?"

"They're Quaid's friends. I think they live out in North Idaho."

Truscott eyed Leya questioningly.

She knew what he was silently asking; did she have any further questions? She would after she returned to the station, but right now, they had strongly linked Jocelyn and Crumbaker to the tire shop burglary. They could snatch up Jocelyn's brother and his cohorts and work on further ratcheting all the burglaries down.

Leya shook her head. "I'm good."

Truscott turned to Jocelyn. "Please stand up. You're under arrest for Second Degree Burglary."

"I figured." She tossed her vape pen onto the coffee table and stood.

Officer Allen removed a set of handcuffs from the case on her duty belt and stepped forward. Jocelyn put her arms behind her back and faced the detectives. The officer moved closer to the woman and ratcheted a pair of cuffs around her wrists.

"You know," Jocelyn said, "it's not like Lucky was so innocent in all of this."

Leya moved to the opposite side of the room so she could observe Officer Allen's search of the woman.

Truscott shifted his position for the same reason. He asked, "How so?"

Officer Allen ran her hands up and down each of Jocelyn's legs.

"Trevor gave every address the boys hit to Lucky so he could turn it over to that security company."

"Why'd he do that?" Truscott asked.

"Trevor got a spiff whenever the security company

sold a system."

"A spiff?"

Jocelyn smirked. "Look who's never worked retail."

Leya said, "It's a special incentive. A bonus."

Truscott asked, "Did Lucky know Trevor broke into those properties?"

"I don't think so. Trevor told him he had a friend in the police department who was giving him some inside information."

Officer Allen straightened and grabbed Jocelyn by the arm. "She's clean."

"Lucky had to be smart enough to figure it out on his own," Jocelyn said. "Don't you think? I mean, he had to know we were breaking into all those places."

***

Parker hung up the phone and stood. "I'm headed out," he said to Johnson.

His partner glanced in his direction. "To where?"

"Lunar Pizza."

He left his cubicle and retrieved two Department of Licensing photographs from the color printer. Parker didn't bother putting the pictures into photo arrays since he wasn't trying to assign guilt. He was simply trying to pin down a part of Trevor Crumbaker and Jocelyn Webb's alibi for Thursday night.

He returned to his cubicle and continued speaking as if he hadn't left. "The manager said the delivery driver who worked that night is coming on shift in a few minutes. She also said I could look through that night's receipts. No warrant necessary."

Johnson nodded appreciatively. "That's nice of her."

Parker grabbed his jacket from the back of his chair. "Believe it or not, there are a few nice people out there.

I'll see you in the morning."

When Parker stepped into the hallway, Captain Gary Ackerman almost bumped into him.

"Leaving?" the captain asked.

"Running to verify an alibi."

"Something to do with the pawnbroker's murder?"

Parker nodded as he rolled down a sleeve.

"Any movement on that?" Ackerman glanced over his shoulder toward the chief's office. "It would be great if we had some resolution before the governor's arrival."

"Nothing yet," Parker said, "but it looks like Navarro and Truscott might have caught the two behind the burglary ring."

"Yeah?" Ackerman's eyebrows rose. "How's that?"

Parker's phone rang, and he pulled it from his pocket. The ID screen revealed Navarro was calling. "Speak of the devil." He motioned toward the phone.

"Answer it."

Parker clumsily swiped his finger over the screen since he still held his suit jacket and the photographs in the opposite hand.

Ackerman pointed at the phone. "Put it on speaker."

He did as ordered. "Parker," he said. "Captain Ackerman's with me."

"Hey," Navarro said. "Truscott's with me, too."

Parker waited a moment for Truscott to acknowledge himself, but the man didn't bother. He respected the other detective for remaining quiet.

"Yeah, so," Navarro said. "We got verbal confessions from both Trevor Crumbaker and Jocelyn Webb about their involvement in the burglary ring."

Ackerman cocked his head. "Who?"

"Lucky Fitzgerald's nephew," Navarro said, "and his girlfriend. She and her brother were the masterminds behind the whole burglary ring. We also got the names of the others involved."

"That's great news," the captain said with a satisfied nod. "Just great. Are you booking those two now?"

"We are," Navarro said.

"What about the others?"

"We'll write up arrest warrants since we believe they're out of state."

Parker was antsy. He didn't want to stand in the hallway acting as the captain's phone valet. He wanted to be on his way to the pizza company. He glanced around and hoped no one saw him standing there holding the phone like a waiter presenting a wine menu.

"After you get done," Ackerman said, "one of you come by and brief me so I can get the chief in the loop."

"Yes, sir," Navarro said. "It's going to be a while."

"Totally understand. I won't keep you long."

"Parker," Navarro said.

He turned his attention to the phone. "Yeah?"

"They both denied burning the tire shop."

"But they admitted the burglaries, right?"

"Yeah," Navarro said, "but they were adamant about not being involved with the fire."

Parker looked up at Ackerman but didn't speak. There was a pause on the phone and traffic noise came through the speaker.

"You still there?" Navarro asked.

"Yeah."

"Are you thinking what I'm thinking?"

"Maybe."

Leya asked, "Are you going to bring him in?"

"Not tonight," Parker said. "Thanks for the heads up."

"You bet."

The call ended, and he slipped the phone back into his pocket.

Ackerman's face tightened. "Were you talking about

Fred Zimmer?"

Parker nodded.

"Remember, he's in tight with Councilwoman Hembree."

"And?"

"And nothing. If he's the guy, bring him in. Just be right. Remember who his friends are."

Parker slipped an arm into his suit jacket. "Of course."

"I'll make sure the chief doesn't pass anything on to the mayor. We don't need the councilwoman giving her friend a warning he's become a person of interest."

# Chapter 17

Lunar Pizza sat near the corner of Pines and Main in Spokane Valley. The business was in a converted home. Its garish yellow and orange coloring allowed it to stand out amongst its more conservative neighbors.

Before he entered the business, Parker texted Jessie Johnson. DO ME A FAVOR. RUN A BACKGROUND ON FRED ZIMMER. TALK TO YOU TOMORROW.

Once inside, Kathy Thompson ushered Parker into a small back office. "It's not much," she said, "but we make it work."

She wasn't kidding. The office was about half the size of a normal bedroom, just large enough for a desk, a chair, and a single four-drawer cabinet. Hanging on the wall were various posters required by state agencies and a Year-at-a-Glance calendar.

On the floor was a small cardboard box with its lid cut off. Inside were many rolls of receipts with rubber bands wrapped around them. Thompson lifted the box and set it on the cluttered desk.

She was in her mid-forties with short, sandy hair and a doughy figure that hinted at a career spent around the pizza industry. Parker imagined it would be hard to maintain healthy habits working around food like this. Thompson, however, seemed like a gracious person. When Parker walked through the kitchen, she complimented the two cooks and they appeared to appreciate her.

"This is old school," Kathy said and lifted a roll of receipts, "but it still works for us. Why change? What date are you looking for?"

Parker told her.

Kathy dropped the roll back into the box and resumed digging. In a moment, she said, "Got it." She removed the rubber band and set a small stack of receipts onto the desk. "What address?"

Parker consulted his notebook for that information.

Kathy licked her index finger before flipping through the receipts. When she found what she wanted, she tugged it out. "Here we go. A large Hawaiian ordered at nine seventeen. Paid with a credit card in the name of Trevor Crumbaker. We delivered it less than thirty minutes later. Not bad if you ask me."

She handed the receipt to Parker.

He pulled out his phone and photographed it. This did not clear Trevor Crumbaker or Jocelyn Webb of Grady Fitzgerald's murder. All it did was prove a pizza was ordered and sent to her home. It was paid with his credit card. In today's world, a person could have placed this order from Abu Dhabi.

Parker returned the receipt to Kathy.

"That's it?" she asked.

"I'd still like to talk with the driver who delivered the pizza."

"That's Cory. He's waiting for you outside." She rolled the receipts and wrapped the rubber band around them again. "We really appreciate what you do, Detective. Everyone in the law enforcement community. We have a first responders' discount. Available year round."

"Thank you."

"Would you like us to make you something? My treat. Take it home for the family."

"Oh, no." He smiled politely. "My wife is already making us dinner."

Kathy nodded. "Well, think about us the next time you want a pizza."

***

Cory Lenz leaned against the hood of his souped-up, cherry red Toyota Corolla. He was a skinny white guy with short hair and two lines cut into his left eyebrow. His faded blue jeans fell below his waist and bunched above his bright white Adidas. Several gold chains hung outside his Tu Pac sweatshirt. He seemed overdressed to deliver pizzas.

He cocked his head and waved his hands as he spoke. “Yo, so you’re like a murder cop or something?”

Parker fought back a smirk. “That’s right.”

“And these two—” Lenz motioned to the DOL photographs that Parker held. “—they killed somebody or something?”

“All I’m asking is do you remember delivering a pizza to them on Thursday night?”

“What was the address again?”

Parker recited it.

Lenz crossed his arms and held his chin like he was posing for the cover of a rap album. “Yo, I don’t know. I mean, it would help me a lot if I knew what they did.”

“How’s that help?”

“Don’t mean mug me, bro. I’m a working man like you.” He stuck out his tongue and laughed. “Know what I’m saying?”

Parker inhaled deeply. Cory Lenz was an idiot.

“You delivered a pizza to the woman’s house,” Parker said. “I need to know if you saw either of them there.” He lifted the photographs for a third time.

“Can any of this blow back on me?”

“What are you talking about?”

“I don’t know, man.” Lenz motioned toward the photographs once more. “Maybe they’re stone-cold killers—you know what I'm sayin'? If I say I saw them, will it end up in a court report somewhere? If so, maybe they see it. Maybe they come after me."

"They're not going to come after you."

"How do you know?" Lenz pointed at Parker. "They don't make those movies for no reason. That's why they always start off, based on a true story." He tapped his temple. "You ever think where that shit comes from? I do. It comes from moments like this." He flicked his wrist. "Nah. I ain't saying shit about shit."

Parker looked over his shoulder. "What do you think Kathy would say?"

"About what?"

"Your lack of cooperation."

"The fuck are you talking about? I'm cooperating."

"She promised full cooperation. What you're giving is considerably less than that. And based upon your clothes and this car, I'm thinking you need this job."

Lenz swallowed. "I got bills. What about it?"

Parker lifted the photographs.

"You only need to know if they were there?"

"That's what I need."

Lenz leaned in and studied the photographs. "Yeah. I seen them. Both, in fact. I never forget a motherfucker who doesn't tip."

***

"Daddy!" Willow cried from the corner of the living room. "Save me!"

Parker closed the front door behind him. "What seems to be the trouble?"

"They've locked me up." Willow anxiously bounced up and down. Plastic toy handcuffs were around her wrists, but nothing blocked her from simply walking away from that area.

Hailey and Charlotte stood in the middle of the room. They both wore toy duty belts with plastic blue guns in their holsters.

"She's under arrest," Hailey, the oldest, said.

"For what?" Parker asked.

"Tattling." Charlotte pointed at her younger sister. "She's a tattletale."

Willow lifted her handcuffed wrists into the air. "Am not!" She sprang about in righteous indignation.

"Are, too!" Hailey shouted.

"What did she tattle on?" Parker asked.

Hailey and Charlotte stared at their father.

He looked at Willow. "Well?"

"They took some of mom's chocolates."

Parker grimaced. "Not her secret stash?"

Willow nodded. "Uh-huh."

He looked at his two oldest. "So what happened?"

"She grounded us for an hour," Hailey said.

"And made us clean our room," Charlotte added.

Willow smiled. "And she gave me a piece of chocolate for not stealing."

Now, Hailey pointed. "That's why she's under arrest, too!"

"All right," Parker said. "Let your sister out on good behavior."

"Aw," Hailey and Charlotte whined together.

Willow jumped out of the corner. "Yeah!"

Parker left the girls to sort out the rest. He found Brooke in the kitchen assembling five plates. It appeared they were having steak, asparagus, and a salad.

"Hello, handsome stranger," she said.

He leaned his elbows on the counter. "Sounds like you're going to have to move your stash."

"I should probably quit."

"Not for me."

"You say that, but I worry someday you're going to drop me for one of those fitness girls."

"Never."

Parker didn't go for the hard angles the women at the gym developed. Instead, he liked his wife's curves. They were pleasing to look at and more delightful to the touch.

"How was your day?" she asked. "Any headway on that case?"

Parker shrugged. "Maybe, but let's not talk about it. Tell me about your day."

She waved a hand. "I did the same routine as always. I wake up. I take care of the girls. I go to bed." Brooke eyed him. "Don't get me wrong. I'm thankful I get to stay home, but my days are boring."

"I don't think so."

She rolled her eyes. "You don't want to hear about the chores I did."

Parker rested his chin in his hands and smiled. "Try me."

***

"And this is my wife, Tessa," Truscott said, "and these are my boys, Jace and Cole."

Leya shook Tessa Truscott's hand. She was an attractive woman about the same age as Truscott. The boys were lanky teenagers, all length and no mass.

Leya and Truscott had expected to work late on the arrests of those involved in the burglary ring and decided their families should get together for dinner. They set seven o'clock as their breaking time. The detectives drove in separate cars to the restaurant.

They were at Bennidito's Pizza in the heart of the East Sprague Corridor. It seemed a fitting place for them to celebrate their success.

A server pushed two tables together and motioned for the families to take them. Ernie and Leya sat together with the Truscotts across from them. At the nearby table, Rose and Violet sat side by side and watched the teenagers like they were rock stars. Jace and Cole seemed thoroughly bored by the entire event. The server handed everyone a menu and stated she would be back in a few minutes to take their order.

"What are we celebrating?" Ernie asked as he perused the menu.

Leya said, "We broke the burglary ring."

Tessa glanced at her husband. "You nicked them?" She turned to Leya. "We watch a lot of British crime shows. You ever watch any?"

"We don't get much alone time." She thumbed toward the girls.

Rose and Violet huddled together and giggled. They gazed at the boys as the two fiddled with their phones.

"You'll get more as they grow," Tessa said. "We got into the British shows a couple years ago. So much better than American TV." She set her hand on Truscott's arm. "Am I right?"

He covered her hand with his. "Totally."

Ernie set down his menu. "What now?"

Both Leya and Truscott faced him.

"I mean, about the burglaries. What will the administration do? Is the heat off Camp Faith? Are you still partnering up?"

Truscott pulled back. "That's a lot of questions."

Leya smiled proudly. "Ernie is on the executive team at STA. He tends to take the thirty-thousand-foot view of things."

Ernie turned his palms upward. "What can I say?"

"Well," Truscott said, "they partnered us up for this

burglary ring. Once we finalize this case, we'll go back to our own cases." He looked to Leya for affirmation.

She nodded. "As for the heat being off the camp, I don't think this is going to move the needle much. Not with the politicians and local business owners beating the drum about increased crime and decreased property values."

"But that's all true," Tessa said. "Isn't it?" It wasn't an argumentative question. Her expression was open, and she seemed to look for answers.

Truscott remained silent.

Leya shrugged. "It's hard to tell what the truth is."

"What's the solution, then?" Ernie asked.

No one answered.

Ernie rested his forearms along the table's edge. "How do we solve a problem no one wants to take ownership of?"

Truscott pointed at himself. "I'm just a detective. I have no answer for that."

"But you live in the city," Ernie insisted.

"We live in the valley."

"Okay, but you work here," he said. "You have to have an opinion."

Truscott and Tessa remained silent. Even the kids looked at Ernie.

Leya put her hand on her husband's arm. Ernie glanced down and his face relaxed.

"I'm sorry," he said. "I get excited about policy discussions when they don't seem to be going anywhere."

Truscott shrugged. "I'll tell you this much. It's not an official policy, but it's probably the policy of everyone who lives in the county. I don't want any camp or its solution in my backyard."

Ernie leaned back in his chair and crossed his arms. "If I'm being honest—" He glanced at Leya. "I wouldn't want it in our backyard either."

The server approached. She smiled and clasped her hands. "Are we ready?"

Leya and Truscott glanced at each other before saying in unison, "We're gonna need another minute."

# Chapter 18

"Did you see the news?" Jessie Johnson asked.

Parker set his phone on the desk. "The fire?"

"That's it."

A garage fire had occurred overnight at a house on Riverside Avenue, about ten blocks from Camp Faith. Parker caught the news while at the gym that morning. The footage showed firefighters battling the blaze, but the sound was off. He read the captions but there wasn't much the on-scene reporter knew.

Johnson spun in his chair to face Parker. "They alluded it was tied to the camp."

The reporter had mentioned the Lug Nutz arson and an RV fire as recent blazes in the neighborhood.

Parker slipped off his suit jacket and hung it over the back of his chair. "I'm not sure why they even mention the RV fire when it was ruled an accident caused by faulty wiring."

"Hey, why'd you ask me to run Fred Zimmer?"

"The burglars that Navarro and Truscott arrested denied burning the building."

"So? They denied the burglaries at first, too."

"I know," said Parker. "But these denials had a different flavor to them. More adamant, almost self-righteous." He glanced at Johnson knowingly. "They rang of truth."

Johnson rolled down his lower lip. "Interesting."

"So what did you find?"

"His record is clean."

"We should have guessed," Parker said. "Anything else?"

"He's got a concealed carry permit and a Smith &

Wesson .45 caliber registered to him."

Parker opened his mouth to respond, but Lieutenant Brand appeared from behind their cubicles.

"Gentlemen," he said, "be prepared."

"For what?" Johnson asked.

Brand rolled his hand. "Fred Zimmer and Councilwoman Hembree are out at Camp Faith right now with the press. They're making a stink about our lack of response to the burglary epidemic."

Parker cocked his head. "They haven't heard about yesterday's arrests?"

"The chief is playing it close to the vest with the mayor. The captain mentioned you want to bring in Zimmer for an interview."

"That's right."

A smile hinted at the edge the lieutenant's lips. "Well, I'm certain this day is going to have quite a bit of drama." He patted the edge of Parker's cubicle. "Keep me informed of any progress."

Brand walked toward his office.

"There goes a happy man," Johnson said.

Parker faced his computer. "Happy Tuesday."

***

"Happy Tuesday," Leya said.

Truscott leaned away from his computer. "What's so happy about it?"

"There's plenty to feel happy about." She leaned against Truscott's cubicle. "The burglary ring for one."

He nodded, but he didn't smile. "I'll give you that."

"What's going on?"

"Nothing." Truscott motioned toward his computer and frowned. "I've got the big case blues."

She cocked her head.

"What have I got now?" He leaned into his computer. "A thrift store burglary up north where someone stole a vintage typewriter."

"For real?"

"Can't make that up."

Leya dismissively waved her hand. "Remember that warrant we wrote for the registered agent?"

His eyes narrowed. "Remind me."

"For Security Solutions of Spokane."

Truscott snapped his fingers. "That's right. We couldn't find the ownership group because it was blocked by—" Truscott snapped his fingers several times. "Melvin—"

"Mervin."

"Longwill."

"I emailed him the warrant yesterday morning," Leya said. "He just sent me the LLC formation paperwork."

"Yeah, so? We already know Fitzgerald owned the business. The manager told us so."

Leya smiled. "You're never going to guess."

"Never going to guess what?"

"He had a partner."

Truscott cocked his head. "Who?"

***

"Here's the way we're figuring it," Parker said. "Trevor Crumbaker and Jocelyn Webb ran a criminal enterprise with her brother, Quaid."

To Parker's left sat Johnson. On his right were Navarro and Truscott. Across from him were Lieutenant Brand and Captain Ackerman. They were seated in the department's conference room.

"We already know this," Ackerman said. "Navarro and Truscott arrested those individuals yesterday." The captain eyed Navarro. “That’s correct?”

She nodded. “Yes, sir, but Parker was instrumental in us locating them.”

“Have you located their accomplices yet?”

“Only Quaid Webb. Patrol booked him this morning. We’re still working on the others.”

Ackerman’s gaze swung back to Parker. “Continue.”

He set his hands on the table. “Crumbaker provided locations his crew burglarized to his uncle.”

“Why’d he do that?” Ackerman crossed his arms. “I thought we said Fitzgerald wasn’t involved in the burglaries.”

“He wasn’t,” Navarro said.

Parker motioned her to carry on.

“Crumbaker told his uncle that a friend in the department was feeding him information on recent burglaries.”

“But that was a lie?” the captain asked.

Navarro nodded. “Correct.”

“Why was he giving the addresses to Fitzgerald?”

“So he would earn a spiff.”

“For what?” Ackerman grunted.

Lieutenant Brand leaned in slightly. “What’s a spiff?”

“A special incentive,” Navarro said. She glanced at her partner who took over the explanation.

“When Leya and I first visited Lucky’s Pawn together,” Truscott said, “there was a standing advertisement for Security Solutions of Spokane. It seemed out-of-place inside the pawnshop, but it had a special listed. Fitzgerald said the company gave him a discount for allowing them to advertise in his store.”

Lieutenant Brand’s face pinched with impatience. “We already know this.”

Ackerman lifted a hand. “It’s all right. Let them lay it out.”

"So Fitzgerald owned the security business," Truscott said, "and every victimized business was a potential customer."

Ackerman eyed the various detectives. "Hold up a minute. You've all said Fitzgerald wasn't a part of the burglaries, but he clearly benefitted from them if the victims bought a system from him."

Navarro shook her head. "Crumbaker and his girlfriend insisted Fitzgerald didn't know."

The captain frowned. "I'm not buying it. He had to have known or, at least, figured it out."

Truscott rested his arms along the edge of the table. "If anything, I'd lean toward willful blindness. When we approached Fitzgerald about our suspicions of his involvement, he probably realized right then what was going on, but he didn't roll on his nephew."

"But he fired him," Navarro said.

Ackerman lightly tapped the table. "He had to, right? To protect his business and cover his own ass." The captain leaned back in his chair and studied the detectives. "So why are we here? Why did the lieutenant ask for us to meet?"

"There's been a development," Parker said. "We want the department on the same page before we act."

The captain met his gaze. "That would be nice."

"It's about Security Solutions of Spokane."

"What about it?"

"Turns out Fitzgerald had a partner."

The captain stiffened. "This partner have a name?"

Parker nodded at Navarro.

She said, "Fred Zimmer."

Ackerman's eyes narrowed. "There's one degree of separation between Zimmer and Fitzgerald?"

"Yes, sir."

"Do you suspect him of Fitzgerald's murder?"

"We don't know," Parker said, "but we ran Zimmer's name. He's got a concealed carry permit and a Smith & Wesson .45 registered to him."

"Do we know the caliber of the bullet that killed Fitzgerald yet?"

Parker shook his head. "Ballistics haven't come back yet."

"What about the arson?" Ackerman's eyes swept over the various detectives. "You said the burglars denied setting the fire, correct?"

Navarro and Truscott nodded.

"There might be something there," Parker said, "but we need to tread lightly. It's not our case."

Ackerman drummed his fingers on the edge of the table. His attention turned to Johnson. "You've been quiet."

"Yes, sir."

"Anything to add?"

He shrugged. "Some days you're the lead dog. Other days, you get the bad view."

The captain fought back a smile.

God damned Johnson, Parker thought. The guy stayed quiet the whole time, and yet the captain was going to remember him fondly when they left the meeting. Guys like him had all the luck. At least, he was Parker's partner and not someone else's.

Ackerman turned his attention back to Parker. "What's the plan?"

"We'd prefer not to come at Zimmer head on. Navarro and Truscott are going to bring him in for follow-up questioning about his break-in. Once he's here, I'll join the interview."

The captain seemed to consider the strategy before standing abruptly. "I'll brief the chief. Good luck."

# Chapter 19

Leya sped up around a slow-moving Subaru as she descended Monroe Street toward the bridge crossing the Spokane River.

"What part of the South Hill does Zimmer live on?" Truscott asked.

She glanced at him. "Upper east. Why?"

"What route are you taking?"

Leya rolled a hand from the steering wheel. "Are you my FTO now?" The last person who questioned her route to a destination was a Field Training Officer. She pointed ahead. "I'm running up Monroe to Twenty-ninth, then I'll head east. That work for you?"

The light at Spokane Falls Boulevard turned green. They passed through the intersection unimpeded.

"Take Sprague," Truscott said. "We'll run by the camp and see if he's still there. If not, we can run by his business on the way up the hill."

Leya slapped her blinker. She hated to admit his suggestion made sense. She waited for the car next to her to pass by, then Leya cut over two lanes and turned left onto Sprague Avenue.

They rode in silence for a few minutes, which took them to the other side of downtown. A red light stopped them at the intersection of Sprague and Browne. A cluster of four homeless men shuffled through the crosswalk. All wore blankets draped over their heads and wrapped around their bodies.

"Right of Way funds," Truscott muttered.

"What's that?"

He turned to her. "The state set aside another five million in money for the camp. Came from something called the Right of Way Safety Initiative. You hear about that?"

"Must have missed it."

"Saw it in the paper today. The number being thrown at this problem is massive now. Something like twenty-four million." Truscott shook his head.

"They need housing."

"We can buy them houses for that."

The light changed, and Leya accelerated through the intersection.

Truscott pulled his cell phone from his pocket. Leya glanced at him but couldn't see what he was doing. His fingers bounced over the screen.

"Twenty-four million," he said.

They passed another homeless camp underneath the railroad bridge.

Truscott continued. "Four hundred forty residents." He glanced at her. "Is that the last number you heard?"

"It was as high as seven in the summer."

"But right now?"

"Four hundred forty," she said.

His fingers bounced a couple more times across the phone's screen. He grunted. "Okay, so that's about fifty-four hundred per person."

"So, not a house."

"No, but it's still twenty-four million. Doesn't that number boggle your mind?"

Evan Barkuloo's admonition came back to her then. *Who benefits from what's going on?* She shook it from her head. "It's money for shelter, food, and medical costs."

"Yeah. I guess so." He leaned his head back against the seat. "It's hard to think in terms of numbers like that."

A heavy silence fell over the car again, but Leya wasn't in a hurry to break it. She didn't want to find herself on the side of an anti-homeless argument and she didn't want to be on the side of supporting all those funds going to supposedly help, either. The teachings from her church often collided with her duties as a cop. The camp's existence pushed her feelings back and forth. She didn't know how she felt about the matter right now. Worse, she didn't know how she should feel about it.

Leya turned north on Ray Street. Interstate 90 loomed ahead.

Protesters assembled along Second Avenue. There must have been forty people in the group. A cluster of homeless men and women watched from the opening of Camp Faith.

She pulled the car to the side of the road and parked.

"This should be fun," Truscott said as he reached for his door handle.

Leya smirked. "That isn't how I would describe it."

***

Fred Zimmer stood on the corner in front of a large, spray-painted sign—*Honk for a cleaner Spokane!* He shouted into a bullhorn, "Our town! Hell no!" along with the rest of the protesters.

"Fred," Leya said as they approached.

He turned with the bullhorn. "Our to—" Zimmer's eyes widened, and he immediately stopped broadcasting, but the crowd finished the chant. "Homeless go!"

Cars and trunks blared their horns, and they drove by.

"I'm sorry," Zimmer said. "I didn't know it was you."

Leya nodded. "Do you remember us?"

"Detectives."

"We'd like a moment."

Zimmer's brow furrowed. "For?"

A semi hauling a load of cars rumbled by. Leya

flinched when it blasted its air horn in two long blasts.

She motioned him away from the protest. “Let’s talk over there.”

Zimmer nodded. “Of course.” He handed the bullhorn to a nearby woman.

Leya and Truscott walked toward their car, and Zimmer followed.

“What’s this about?” he asked from behind.

“We’d like you to come down to the station,” Leya said over her shoulder.

Zimmer stopped walking. “Why?”

“We’ve made some arrests in the burglaries.”

Zimmer hurried along now. “I haven’t heard anything about this.”

“That’s correct,” she said. “We don’t want this information getting out yet. Not until we know we have the right individuals.”

“But I was just elected the head of the neighborhood council.” Indignation crossed Zimmer’s face. “Surely, you’re not worried about me leaking information.”

Leya smiled. “Of course not.”

Truscott spoke now. “The department has taken a black eye on this whole matter. I’m sure you can understand.”

Zimmer’s eyes narrowed. “You’re not blaming me for that, are you?”

“No,” Truscott said, “but you can understand how bad it would be if we announced we caught those responsible and it turned out we were wrong.”

Zimmer looked around. “Yeah. I could see how that would play badly, but why do you need me to come to the station? I wasn’t at my business when it was broken into.”

“Totally understand.” Truscott motioned toward Leya. “However, we want to know if you’ve seen any of them lurking around before the break-in."

Zimmer's eyes widened. "Like maybe they were casing my business?"

"That's right," Truscott said. "Maybe you saw them, maybe you didn't, but we have to ask."

"So we're going to look at a line-up?"

"Sort of," Leya said. "We have some pictures to show you. We'll bring you back when we're done. Shouldn't take long."

Suspicion clouded Zimmer's eyes. "I don't know."

"There's nothing to be afraid of," Truscott said.

Zimmer took a half-step back. "I'm not afraid."

"Fred!" a woman called from the line of protesters.

He looked over his shoulder.

"What's going on?" she called.

Zimmer glanced at Truscott. "You promise it won't take long?"

"All you've got to do is point at some pictures. We'll bring you back when we're done."

"And if I say you've got the right people…?"

"You can tell whoever you want."

Zimmer smiled and turned back to the woman. "I'm going to help the detectives with something," he shouted. "I'll be back in a bit!"

Truscott lifted a hand. "We'll take good care of him."

***

Parker entered the small room. He nodded to Truscott, who stood in the corner before sitting at the interview table across from Fred Zimmer. He set a notepad, folder, and pen down before settling into the chair.

Zimmer had removed his coat and hung it over the back of his chair. His red polo shirt had a Lug Nutz logo over the left breast. His haircut appeared recent, and his skin was free of blemishes. A Rolex draped loosely around his left wrist. The man was likely worth a million or more. Zimmer might have been an impressive man in a different setting, but in a police interview room, he appeared small and out of his element.

"Thank you for coming in this morning, Fred. I'm Detective Parker. I work with Detective Truscott."

Zimmer looked at Truscott. "What happened to your partner?"

"She had a court hearing." He motioned to Parker. "They make us do this kind of stuff in pairs. Protocol."

"Ah." Zimmer nodded knowingly. "So you're the senior detective?"

Parker flicked a switch on the wall. "Just so you know, I'm recording our interview." He pointed above them. "That red light will let you know when the camera is rolling."

Zimmer's tongue darted across his lips. "Am I in trouble?"

"Why would you be in trouble, Mr. Zimmer?"

"No reason. I was just asking."

"All right," Parker said. "We're going to show you some photographs and ask a couple of questions. No big deal. If you were in trouble, we would read you your rights. Have you ever heard of them?"

"On TV, yeah."

"I can read them to you now if it'll make you feel better."

Zimmer shook his head. "It wouldn't."

Parker smiled. "Shall we start?"

"Please." Zimmer checked his watch.

"What you will see now are a series of photographic lineups. We're not supposed to point out the person we've arrested since the idea is for you to be objective. Do you understand? Just tell me if you see anyone you know."

Parker opened the folder. A Miranda Warning card was paper clipped to the inside cover. He removed a stack of photo arrays from the file Johnson had prepared. He laid the first on the table. Six scruffy white men looked up. Parker didn't know any of them. He could not have identified the man involved with the burglaries if his career depended on it. He spun the paper so Zimmer could see the pictures in their correct orientation.

The tire shop owner examined each picture for several seconds. Eventually, he looked up and shook his head.

"You're sure?" Parker asked.

"Positive."

The second and third arrays went much the same way. The pictures were of all white men and Parker didn't know the arrestees in them, either. Zimmer denied ever seeing anyone in those.

"It's a little frustrating," Zimmer said.

"I would imagine, especially since you had a security system." Parker held onto the fourth paper. "Security Solutions of Spokane, right?"

Zimmer cocked his head.

"I stopped by your building to check out the fire damage and saw the sticker on the door. Terrible what those burglars did to you."

"Yeah," Zimmer agreed.

"Did you ever get an account of what they stole?"

"There was no way to know. Not with the fire and all."

"Of course," Parker said.

He set the fourth paper on the table. This one was filled with white women. In the lower right corner was Jocelyn Webb. He spun it for Zimmer. "See anyone you know?"

Several moments passed. "Her." Zimmer pointed at

the woman in the middle position of the top row. “She’s been in the store before.”

“You’re sure?”

“Pretty sure.”

Parker handed his pen to Zimmer. “Circle your selection. Afterward, initial and date the paper.”

Zimmer circled a woman who was not Jocelyn Webb, then initialed and dated the page. He pushed the pen and paper back to Parker.

The next photo array had Trevor Crumbaker in the upper left position. Parker set it in front of Zimmer. “What about this one?”

It took less than two seconds for Zimmer to say, “Sorry, no.”

Parker swooped up the paper. “Only one more.”

This one contained a group of six men in their late forties. Parker watched Zimmer closely. Recognition flashed in his eyes and his body briefly tensed. However, when he looked up, he said, “No.”

“You’re sure?” Parker asked.

“Yes.”

Parker put the array into the folder.

“Is that it?” Zimmer asked. He set his hands on the interview table and prepared to stand.

“Hold on,” Parker said. “Tell me about Security Solutions of Spokane.”

“What about them?”

“Why’d you pick their system?” Parker asked.

“I don’t understand the question.”

Parker turned his palm upward. “Did they give you a deal? Did you want to support a local company? Was it owned by a friend?”

“I don’t see the point of this questioning.” He motioned toward the file. “I found someone who had been to the store. Are you going to follow up on that?”

"We'll get right on it." Parker slowly tapped the table. "So, going with Security Systems of Spokane didn't have anything to do with you being a partner in the company?"

Zimmer stared at him.

"We know," Parker said. "When did it happen?"

Fred Zimmer checked his watch. He rubbed a finger around its edge. Zimmer's tongue darted out between his lips like a lizard sensing danger. He fiddled with the watch for some time but Parker didn't push him to hurry along. It seemed as if the man was steeling himself for some revelation. Eventually, Zimmer said, "A year and a half ago." He looked up. "The company was struggling, and I saw an investment opportunity."

"Why were they struggling?"

"Management issues."

Parker jotted onto his notepad. "And what opportunity did you see?"

Irritation flashed across Zimmer's face and the man's voice rose. "Is this why I was brought down here? To pick through my businesses?"

Parker didn't let Zimmer's outburst bother him. The anger appeared contrived, the way a young stage actor portrays rage versus a veteran movie star.

"Humor me." Parker motioned to Truscott. "We're just a couple of dumb city cops. This business stuff is interesting. Tell us what opportunity you saw."

Zimmer crossed his arms and inhaled deeply. "Spokane might be beautifying, Detective, but an ugliness remains at its core."

"You're talking about the camp."

"That's only a manifestation of the problem." He pointed toward the door. "Look at the neighborhood out there; it's a festering wound. Pockets of rot litter this city and we ignore them at our peril."

"You sound like a politician."

He grinned. "What I am is a guy selling a security system."

"But you never publicly aligned yourself with the company." Parker gestured widely like a circus ringmaster might. "Why not tell the city you own a security business?"

"Had I done so, no one would have listened to me about the camp. So I kept my mouth shut and fanned the flames of fear. Maybe my company doesn't get all the calls, but a rising tide lifts all boats, as they say."

"You could have identified with the company prior to that, but you didn't."

Zimmer shrugged. "I'm what's known as an equity partner. My role isn't to promote or lead the company."

"Speaking of partners," Parker said. He opened the folder and pulled the last photo array from it. He laid it on the table and pointed to the picture in the middle of the bottom row—Grady Fitzgerald. "He's the majority owner of the security company. How could you not pick your own partner out of this lineup?"

Zimmer stood. "I don't know what you're trying to do here, but I'm leaving."

"That time has gone," Parker said. "Now, you're being detained."

Truscott moved to block the door.

"You can't do this," Zimmer said. "I have my rights."

"Yes, you do." Parker removed the white Miranda Warning card from inside the file. "You have the right to remain silent."

Zimmer dropped into his chair. "I'm not a bad guy," he muttered.

There was a light knock on the door, and Truscott opened it. He stepped out of the room.

Parker faced Zimmer and continued. "Anything you say can and will be used against you in a court of law."

***

Leya Navarro leaned forward and studied the monitor.

Captain Gary Ackerman sat next to her. Jessie Johnson and Lieutenant George Brand stood behind them.

"Do you know who he identified?" the lieutenant asked.

Leya shook her head.

The camera's angle covered the room, but it didn't provide details of documents. Maybe other department's had multiple lenses to get various views, but the Spokane Police Department only had a single camera per interview room.

Ackerman looked over his shoulder at Johnson. "Did you guys hear back from that arson investigator?"

"Nothing yet."

"What the hell is taking him so long?" Ackerman angrily shook his head. "Why would a guy like him burn his building?"

"Money," the lieutenant said.

"He's not losing it in a divorce, is he?" the captain looked at Leya.

"He's not married," she said.

The four fell silent for several moments as they watched Parker interview Zimmer.

Ackerman looked at Leya. "Do me a favor and check his property taxes."

She nodded but hesitated to leave. The captain watched her until she understood he wanted her to go right then.

Leya hurried back to her cubicle. Property tax status was provided by the Spokane County Assessor's Office. Leya found the website quickly and entered the address for Lug Nutz—she had it written in her notebook. The screen quickly populated with information such as parcel number, legal description, lot and building size, and annual assessed value. Near the bottom of the page was the annual property taxes. Fred Zimmer was behind two years on his property taxes.

She scrolled back to the top of the page and found the mailing address for his LLC. It listed his home address on the South Hill.

Next, Leya entered the new address into the search bar. When the screen populated with the new information, it showed a home registered to Fred Zimmer. She quickly scrolled to the bottom and found the most recent taxes had not been paid on this house.

Leya thought about her own home. She paid her loan monthly and the mortgage company handled the twice a year tax payments. If Zimmer had a loan, too, that meant the mortgage company failed to make his payment, which would only occur if he failed to pay his monthly fee.

She thought Zimmer owned other real estate but didn't know those addresses. Right now, she thought there was enough information. Leya copied both printouts and stopped by Interview Room 1. She lightly knocked and stepped back. Truscott stepped out.

"Not sure if you and Parker can use these," Leya said, "but Zimmer is behind on his property taxes." She handed him copies of both assessor's reports.

Truscott quickly scanned them. "Thank you."

"Thank Ackerman. It was his idea."

Leya returned to the observation room. She handed a copy of the printouts to Ackerman. "You were right. Behind on both his home and business."

The captain scanned the reports. "Lots of people get behind," he said. "Doesn't mean he did anything criminal." When he finished, he gave the papers to Brand.

"Let's see if Parker can do anything with it."

***

Parker tucked the signed Miranda Warning card into the file. Zimmer had stared at the card for several moments before declining an attorney and agreeing to answer questions. Parker was almost certain the guy was going to demand legal counsel, but he'd seen it many times—people often thought they could explain their way out of trouble. Or they wanted to learn what the police knew. They did so at their own peril.

Parker picked up his pen and held it over his notepad.

Truscott stepped back into the room with some rolled papers in his hand. He nodded an apology and took a position near the far wall. Hopefully, the interruptions were done for now.

Parker asked Zimmer, "How'd you and Grady meet?"

"High school. Lewis & Clark."

"You were friends?"

"Not really," Zimmer said. "We went through the years together but only really talked while in DECA."

"Which is?"

"A program to guide kids into marketing and finance careers, that sort of thing." Zimmer shrugged as wistfulness entered his voice. "It was an extracurricular program my father approved of. He didn't go for sports and, frankly, didn't support me doing any. The whole DECA experience was all right, I guess, if you wanted to be an employee."

"But not you?"

"Even in high school, I wanted to work for myself. A lot of kids in that program were checking a box for their college applications."

"What about Grady?"

Another shrug. "He had no idea what he was going to be. He was too busy trying to hump anything with a pulse. I don't mean that to sound bad. It's just we kept to our own circles. He was popular." Zimmer waggled his hand. "I worked at my dad's garage, so there was no time for any fun. That's why DECA was sort of cool. It allowed me something to do after school. I wish we'd had a Junior Achievement program. I would have loved that more."

Zimmer seemed almost happy talking about his high school years. Parker let him ramble about it as it didn't cost him anything. It also moved Zimmer further away from feeling suspicious and into a more relaxed state.

The man continued. "Most kids don't think critically about their futures. They barely think beyond the next weekend. I knew any business education I could get was going to help me." His words trailed off and his eyes grew distant.

Parker tapped his notepad with the tip of his pen. "Then you reconnected with Grady, and you bought a business together."

"It's not as simple as that."

"Simplify it."

Zimmer's thumb rubbed the edge of the table. "The former owner of Security Solutions was a mutual acquaintance."

"From high school?"

Zimmer frowned. "Spokane might be growing, but it's still a small town at heart. Grady and I were small business owners, and we ran in some of the same circles. We were bound to run into the same people."

"So this friend…"

"Acquaintance." Zimmer glanced at Truscott before continuing. "His business wasn't doing well. The concept was fine. Selling security systems isn't like selling tires.

People either buy an alarm system to prevent a break-in or they buy one after they've been victimized. The product isn't a necessity, and it essentially sells itself. It's not rocket science."

"What was the management problem the company had?"

"Our acquaintance had a prescription drug habit exacerbated by his wife's infidelity. She ran around because of his addiction." Zimmer spun his hand. "A vicious circle that almost ran their business into the ground. They sold their business to fund their divorce."

"How did Grady come into the picture?"

"This acquaintance offered to sell the business to both of us."

"A scam?"

"Not at all. He merely talked too much."

Parker cocked his head. "How did you find out about Grady?"

"He and I ended up in the security office on the same day."

"That was—" Parker was about to say lucky, but he chose another word. "Fortunate."

"Not really. We both wanted the business."

"You guys knew each other."

"Knowing each other from high school doesn't mean we remained friendly, especially since we both realized our acquaintance had undervalued his business."

"You said he almost ran the business in the ground."

"Almost, yes, but there were still contracted monitoring services that paid a residual he forgot to calculate."

"So what happened?" Parker asked.

Zimmer's face pinched. "Grady raised his offer by twenty-five thousand. I came over the top by the same. In a matter of minutes, we had pushed the offer up a hundred grand. I could see where this was going, even if Grady didn't."

"Which was?"

"My tire shop is a good business," Zimmer said. "I'm not as big as the regional players, but it puts food on the table. We do some minor repairs—oil changes, shocks, that stuff. We're a retail business, but we're fairly internet resistant. That's important today." Zimmer drove the tip of his finger into the table. "Even with my real estate holdings, I couldn't compete with a pawnshop. Grady did phenomenal business when the economy was bad, and he did solid business when it was good. He would have crushed me if the bidding war continued."

Parker looked up from his notepad. "What did you do?"

"I did what a dog does; I rolled over and exposed my belly." Zimmer waved his hand. "I suggested a partnership."

"If he could outbid you, why would he agree?"

"Because I would have run up the price, and he knew it. In the end, he agreed to a split that favored him—seventy-five/twenty-five—and I oversaw the financial operation."

Now Parker was confused. "Why would you accept a deal like that?"

"Twenty-five percent of something is better than a hundred percent of nothing. The contract was written that he could only sell to me and vice versa. If he ever wanted out, I'd be there to get the business from him."

"Why didn't you put your faces or names on the business?"

"It doesn't take much imagination, Detective." Zimmer looked toward Truscott. "It would look bad for someone involved in the pawn industry to proudly announce he also owned a security company. There's a perception people sell stolen goods to pawnshops."

Truscott muttered, "No shit."

Zimmer nodded toward him. "As for me, I didn't want brand confusion. My face is associated with Lug Nutz. I don't even let people know I own a coffee stand in Airway Heights. That way, my face and name stay true to Lug Nutz. It's what started my brand and I'm staying loyal to it. If my face popped up for security products, that would be weird. Had I bought a car stereo company, maybe it would make sense for me to put my face forward. But no, I needed to be in the background, just like Grady."

Parker crinkled his nose. "It certainly doesn't look good for the owner of a security company to have one of his businesses broken into."

"No," Zimmer said, "it certainly doesn't. I'd prefer if this doesn't make the news."

Truscott lifted the papers in his hand. "I'm assuming the security company saw an uptick in sales that correlated with the increase of crime along the East Sprague Corridor?"

Zimmer nodded. "You would be correct."

"Knowing that," Truscott said as he lowered his hand, "why would you want Camp Faith to leave?"

"I have another business to consider."

"How were the sales at Lug Nutz?"

"The camp wasn't helping."

Truscott eyed Parker before asking his next question. "How were they before the camp started?"

"What are you getting at?" Zimmer asked.

"You're behind on your property taxes for two years." Truscott opened the roll of papers. "Looks like you're behind on the taxes for your personal residence, too."

"Sales," Zimmer said, "might have taken a hit lately. I'm not sure what that proves."

"If you're behind on property taxes, the bank wouldn't want to lend on the purchase of the security business. Where'd the money come from?"

Zimmer stared at him. "I'm not a bad guy."

Truscott shrugged a single shoulder. "No one is saying you are."

"It sounds like you are."

"We're just trying to understand."

"I employ a lot of people." Zimmer crossed his arms. "Those folks can afford a place to sleep, food to eat, cars to drive because of my businesses. What I do helps stimulate the economy."

Parker expected Zimmer to say he helped pay for the police budget, but the man refrained.

"I'm sure your employees are happy for their jobs," Truscott said.

Zimmer nodded. "You bet they are."

"That still doesn't tell us where the money for the security company purchase came from." Truscott tapped the rolled papers into his hand. "With you being behind on your taxes, I'm sure a bank wouldn't look kindly upon that. So where'd the money come from?"

Zimmer squeezed himself tighter with his arms.

"Well?"

"I took a hard money loan."

Parker tilted his head. "Which is what?"

"A private lender," Zimmer said. "They charge higher interest with stiffer penalties for late payments."

Hard money sounded like fancy words for loan sharks, Parker thought. "Who loaned you the money?"

Zimmer looked down at his hands.

Parker ventured a guess. "Was it Grady?"

"I'm not stupid. If I borrowed the money from him, he would have defaulted on me and taken my share of the business as soon as he could."

"So you owe a hard money lender and have fallen behind on paying your taxes?"

"The county isn't going to take my property without proper warning. They're going to give me plenty of time to make good."

"Why are the tire shop sales off?" Parker asked.

Zimmer shifted in his seat. "Competition. The nationals and regionals opened new locations. They're squeezing me out."

"If sales were lagging due to increased competition, then that fire couldn't have come at a worse time."

"I don't think there is ever a good time for a fire, Detective."

"And the burglars got past a shoddily installed system."

Zimmer's face reddened. "I know how it looks, but I wouldn't put my business at risk by staging a break in."

"Relax," Parker said, "we're not arson investigators, and we believe you were burglarized."

"You do?"

Parker nodded. "It must have come as a shock when Councilwoman Hembree told you we suspected Grady Fitzgerald as being involved with the burglaries."

Zimmer's expression flattened. "I don't know what you're talking about."

"No? The chief told the mayor, who told the councilwoman. You two have been palling around on TV."

"Yeah," Truscott said, "you're on every channel."

Zimmer's gaze flicked to the other detective. "That doesn't mean she told me anything."

"She said she did," Parker said.

This was a bluff. Deception was often needed in interviews. It might come as an acceptance of the suspect's behavior. This approval often would bring an admission of wrongdoing by the suspect. Sometimes, a ruse came in the form of an outright lie, like Parker had just made about the councilwoman providing information on Zimmer's statements.

Lying to seek the truth was an approved tactic, but it was dangerous. If the suspect called the bluff, just like a poker player might, a detective could find himself holding a hand of garbage.

Parker didn't feel that would happen in this moment since the lie wasn't big or farfetched enough as to immediately dismiss. Besides, he imagined his statement would become true if he approached the councilwoman. He'd make it a point to do so immediately after this interview.

Those thoughts zipped through Parker's mind as he watched Zimmer blink several times. The tire shop owner lowered his gaze. That's when Parker knew his bluff had landed—the councilwoman *had* told Zimmer about the department's interest in Grady Fitzgerald.

Parker set his pen down and did his best to affect a look of caring. He softened his voice the way he did when dealing with one of his daughters. "What happened after she told you about Grady?"

Zimmer wiped a hand across the table.

"Did you go up to his house?"

Now, the man rubbed his fingers off the edge as if clearing dust away.

"Had you been there before to sign paperwork?" Parker asked. A thought came to him then. "Or maybe you saw his home address on some partnership documents. Was he surprised to see you?"

Zimmer's hand stopped moving and his lower lip trembled.

"You two sat at the dining table," Parker said, "to talk out your concerns."

He opened the folder and removed several photographs of Grady Fitzgerald's body. Parker lay them on the table. Zimmer's gaze briefly dropped to the pictures, but he didn't study them. His hand wiped the edge of the table once more.

"Grady must have tried to make the conversation cordial. He must have seen how upset you were."

Parker waited for Zimmer to agree, but the man remained silent as he dragged his fingers back and forth along the table's edge. Parker fired off a series of questions.

"Did he try to convince you he wasn't involved? Did he swear he had nothing to do with the burglaries? Did he beg for his life when you showed him your gun?"

Zimmer stopped rubbing the table. "I don't have a gun."

"What happened to it?"

He opened his mouth to speak, then closed it. He glanced at Truscott and back to Parker. Zimmer gnawed on his lower lip.

"Let me tell you something," Parker said. "I think you're a decent guy. I really do. You've had no trouble with the law." He looked at Truscott, who nodded in affirmation. "See? We both think you're a decent guy. The problem is decent guys don't know what they're doing when they commit murder."

Zimmer straightened, and his eyes narrowed.

"Hardened guys are no better," Parker said. "Those bastards have lived in the system since they were kids. They sit in that chair you're in and play the game. They don't think they're going to outsmart the system. Do you know what they think? They know they're going to lose. It's like they're at a craps table. You know that game? The one at the casino with the dice? Anyway, those hardened guys just keep rolling the dice until they're out of money. Even when they win, they can't stop. It's the game. They gotta start rolling again because they know they're eventually going to lose. Everyone eventually loses at craps."

Zimmer grabbed the underside of the table, only his thumbs were visible on top. He tried to keep his face impassive, but it wasn't working. A tic had developed at the edge of his left eye.

Parker collected the pictures of Grady Fitzgerald's body and put them back into the file. "Now," he said, "I asked you about your gun for a reason and you told me you didn't have one. You're lying again."

The tic worsened in Zimmer's eye and his jaw tightened.

"Do you know how I know that?" Parker leaned back in his chair.

Zimmer's hands relaxed. "Because I registered a gun."

"There you go." Parker spread his arms wide. "You also have a concealed carry permit. We get notified of that permit whenever we run your name. It's like a red flag warning—be careful around this guy." Parker blinked his hands three times. "So, let's try that again—what happened to the gun?"

Zimmer dropped his hands into his lap and looked down.

The clock on the wall ticked the seconds by. Truscott shifted slightly and the rolled papers in his hand crinkled. He raised his eyebrows in a questioning manner.

Parker nodded.

Truscott said, "Grady was never involved in the burglaries."

Zimmer lifted his head.

"My partner and I cleared him." Truscott pushed off the wall. "We arrested three of the people involved in the ring. A few others are still outstanding."

"But the chief—" Zimmer said weakly.

Truscott nodded. "We initially thought Grady was involved, but it turned out to be his nephew."

Tears welled in Zimmer's eyes. "But the chief—"

Parker leaned forward. "What happened to the gun, Fred?"

# EPILOGUE

## Chapter 20

"So it was Fred Zimmer?" Sergeant Ryan Yager asked. He glumly closed his red felt-tip pen and leaned back in his chair. "He confessed?"

"Yeah," Leya said. She smiled as she looked at Truscott, who stood next to her. "Took some time, but they got him there."

"Parker did the hard work," Truscott said. His brow furrowed as he studied the sergeant. "I mainly watched."

Leya waved a hand. "Don't let him fool you. He helped plenty."

"I'm sure you both did," Yager said.

She felt good about their recent success but couldn't understand why the sergeant wasn't in a better mood. "Is everything okay?" she asked.

The sergeant tossed the pen onto his desk. "The county's drug unit made a big bust today outside the WSDOT camp. The suspect had more than a thousand fentanyl pills, stolen credit cards, and a mini arsenal in his car. The guy was a one-man crime wave, and the sheriff is prepping for a press event now."

Leya and Truscott exchanged glances.

"Turns out the guy was staying in an RV at the camp." Yager shook his head. "The camp's director claimed she repeatedly asked for law enforcement help to clear him out."

Truscott grunted. "The sheriff's bust overshadows our burglary arrests. No one will hear most of the break-ins weren't associated with the camp."

Leya defiantly crossed her arms. "It won't overshadow Zimmer's arrest."

"You're right," Yager said, "but his arrest only distracts from the camp coverage. It doesn't change the narrative. Zimmer became a minor celebrity because he protested the camp. One news cycle and he'll be forgotten. What's worse, the burglaries you tied to Crumbaker and associates won't be reclassified as something else. They'll remain as burglaries in the Sprague Corridor. Those are undisputable facts."

Leya's arms slipped to her sides. "What's that mean?"

"It means the sheriff will claim his department is actively trying to break the camp while the mayor and the governor are working to keep it active. We continue to take the black eye."

"What do we do about it?" Leya asked.

Yager picked up his red pen. "You've got fresh cases to work, don't you?"

She nodded.

"There's your answer."

Truscott turned to her. "Find solace in the grind."

He patted her shoulder on the way out of the office.

***

Parker stood at the booking station counter. He'd already dropped Fred Zimmer off to the jail staff. He needed to complete the intake process, which involved him standing at a computer terminal and filling in the required fields.

The sliding glass door hissed open, and Captain Ackerman stepped inside. He turned to Parker. "There you are."

"Sir?"

Parker didn't remove his fingers from the keyboard. He continued to input information.

"I wanted to say you did nice work on the Zimmer arrest."

"Thank you."

"I just spoke with Johnson, and he confirmed Councilwoman Hembree had spoken to Zimmer about Fitzgerald's potential involvement in the burglary ring."

Johnson had texted Parker the same news a few minutes ago.

"When you get done here," Ackerman said, "swing by the chief's office."

Parker lifted his hands from the keyboard now.

"He and the PIO are working up a press release. They're trying to get some positive momentum in the whole WSDOT camp fiasco."

"Understood." Parker set his fingers back on the keyboard.

A jailer had told Parker about a suspect some deputies brought in right before Parker's arrival. The man was busted at Camp Faith with a large quantity of fentanyl and several assault weapons. The chief and the sheriff were about to have dueling press releases.

The captain nodded twice and said, "Okay, then." He turned to leave.

"Sir?"

Ackerman stopped.

Parker eyed the captain. "Why didn't you call?"

"Excuse me?"

"Or send the lieutenant. Delivering a message like this seems below your pay grade."

Ackerman's brow furrowed. "The message I came to deliver was nice work. That's never below my pay grade. Stop being an asshole, Parker."

Another swear word from the captain, Parker thought.

The captain stepped toward the door but paused again. "And remember. See the chief when you're done. It's that important."

"Yes, sir."

***

Ernie sidled up to the kitchen counter and sat on the stool. "Did you see the news?"

Leya looked up from the sink. She was cleaning up after their dinner of enchiladas. Ernie had outdone himself, so she sent him on his way.

The girls were in their room with the dog. She expected them to burst out soon, asking for a dessert. But for now, it was just the two of them.

"About the drug bust?"

Ernie nodded. "And the governor's response."

She scrubbed the pan the enchiladas had been in. "I heard about the arrest but haven't heard what the governor said."

"He said don't lump all the camp residents in with one bad egg."

Leya turned off the faucet.

"I get his gist," Ernie said, "but it wasn't very poetic."

"Not really."

"They didn't mention your arrests."

"That's how it goes."

"But you proved it wasn't the camp residents behind the burglaries."

Leya shrugged. “Some. There are plenty of other nuisance crimes linked to the camp—trespassing, shoplifting, graffiti, and littering. In the overall scheme, our arrest didn’t change much.”

“Don’t do that,” Ernie said. “What you did was important.”

Leya set the pan into the sink. “Proverbs again?”

“I don’t know what you’re thinking?”

“*The righteous care about justice for the poor.*”

Ernie nodded. “Proverbs 29:7. *But the wicked have no such concern.* You had concern.”

“I did my job.” She turned back to the pan. “If it wasn’t my job, I think I probably would have thought the worst of it all. I’m happy they’re staying down there and not in our neighborhood. Not near our girls. Is that bad?”

“No. It’s human.” He slid off the stool. “Thank you for cleaning up.”

She smiled and watched him leave the kitchen.

Leya returned to scrubbing the pan.

***

Brooke wrapped her arms around Parker’s waist. Her lips were close to his ear. Her breath tickled him as she spoke. “You know what you’re getting tonight?”

His arms tightened around her. He nibbled her ear. “Tell me.”

“Ew!” Hailey yelled.

Parker leaned back from his wife in time to see Willow flop to the carpet in dramatic fashion and splay her arms out.

Charlotte threw her hands in the air. “Gross!”

The three girls were in matching *Teen Titans Go!* pajama sets.

“Why aren’t you three brushing your teeth?” Brooke

asked.

"We're done," Hailey said.

Willow remained on the floor and made gagging noises

Brooke's brow pinched. "Really?"

"Yeah."

She looked at the middle child. "Charlotte."

"What?"

"Did you brush your teeth?"

Willow stuck out her tongue and kicked her feet. "Blech."

Charlotte glanced at Hailey before announcing, "Yes."

"Really?"

"Yes!" Charlotte slapped her hands against her legs.

Parker and Brooke had yet to break their embrace. She looked at their youngest.

"Willow?"

"What?"

"Look at me."

Willow sat up. Her face scrunched in horror. "You're not going to kiss again, are you?"

"Did you brush your teeth?"

She looked at Hailey.

"*Willow*."

The youngest's shoulders slumped. "No."

"Tattler!" Hailey and Charlotte yelled together.

"Upstairs," Brooke said. "Now."

The three girls clomped upstairs.

When they were alone, Brook tightened her grip on her husband. She pressed her hips into him. "Now, where were we?"

Parker smiled.

Then his phone rang. Reluctantly, he pulled it from his pocket. The screen read Dispatch.

Disappointment crossed Brooke's face. "Better get

that."

He answered. "Parker."

"Sorry to bother you, Detective," a male voice said, "but you're up on the rotation. Patrol is out with a body now."

Brooke slipped from his arms. "I'll go check on the girls."

Parker stood alone in his living room as the radio operator told him where he'd be spending the rest of his night.

# Did You Enjoy the Book?

Thank you for reading *The Path of Progress* and visiting the 509! I hope you enjoyed meeting some of the recurring characters. This is a continuing series with other characters occasionally stepping into the lead role. There are two parallel series to the 509 Crime Stories—the Flip-Flop Detective and the John Cutler mysteries. I hope you'll check them out.

I'm always grateful when a reader takes time out of their day to comment on one of my novels. If you do write a review, please email me, and let me know.

I'd love to say thanks!

# About the Author

Colin Conway is the creator of the 509 Crime Stories, a series of novels set in Eastern Washington with revolving lead characters. They are standalone tales and can be read in any order.

He also created the Cozy Up series which pushes the envelope of the cozy genre. Libby Klein, author of the Poppy McAllister series, says *Cozy Up to Death* is "Not your grandma's cozy."

Colin co-authored the Charlie-316 series. The first novel in the series, *Charlie-316*, is a political/crime thriller described as "riveting and compulsively readable," "the real deal," and "the ultimate ride-along."

He served in the U.S. Army and later was an officer of the Spokane Police Department. He has owned a laundromat, invested in a bar, and run a karate school. Besides writing crime fiction, he is a commercial real estate broker.

Colin lives with his beautiful girlfriend, three wonderful children, and a codependent Vizsla that rules their world.

Find out more at colinconway.com.

Made in United States
Troutdale, OR
04/18/2024

19265456R00192